THE ANGEL
OF
INCOMPLETENESS

A Time Travel Novel About Impressionist
Berthe Morisot

By

Dorothy M Parker

ISBN: 978-1-3999-6916-1

To all the women artists.

CONTENTS

"I do not think any man would ever treat a woman as his equal, and it is all I ask because I know my worth."

Berthe Morisot 1890

"... the distinction between past, present and future is only a stubbornly persistent illusion."

Albert Einstein 1955

CHAPTER 1

THE THIEF

Louise sat slouched on a log, staring into the bonfire, trying to ignore the babble of the party around her. She was concentrating on the flames, rummaging around in her brain to remember how fires work. Let's see … first the tree takes in sunlight and uses its energy to split carbon dioxide into carbon and oxygen. It stores the carbon as wood. When we put a log on the fire, the captured energy in the wood is released.

So, I'm really looking at sunlight being freed back out into the world, she thought. *It's magical.*

She watched the flames flickering, happy to be free. They would be great to paint – the reds, yellows and oranges – but so difficult. Impossible, probably.

The wind change direction and blew smoke into Louise's face. People near her moved away but she sat there, peering into the fire, blinking the sting from her eyes.

'Are you just going to sit there and take it?' Chloe asked, coming over to sit beside her.

Louise shrugged. Chloe wasn't talking about the smoke. She was talking about Paul, her tall handsome husband who was standing behind them at the barbeque, surrounded by a shimmer of bright young women. He was telling them – at great length – about his new documentary series, *Women Who Changed the World*.

'It's about Marie Curie, Jane Austen, Florence Nightingale, Emmeline Pankhurst and Mother Teresa,' he said. 'I'll dramatise sections using famous actors: Florence Pugh as Florence Nightingale,

Emma Mackey as Emmeline Pankhurst ...'

Paul's boss put an arm around his shoulder.

'It's a great commission, Paul. The channel loves it. You've really captured the zeitgeist.'

Paul glowed in the admiration of his boss and the young researchers.

'You're such a good feminist,' one said.

Louise dragged in a long breath and sighed. *Paul, a feminist?*

'Honestly, I can't believe he's doing this,' she said to Chloe. 'I have tried to talk to him ...'

'Well, it's not right and it's so unfair,' Chloe said.

'I know. It's ridiculous.'

Louise spotted Paul heading for the bathroom.

'I'll go and talk to him, again ...'

She got up to catch him.

'Paul, stop. I want to talk to you. Did you tell your boss that it was my idea? Did you even mention it to him?'

'Look,' Paul said, 'we've been through this. It's good for both of us if I produce it. You know that. Anyway, you can't do it.'

She looked into his dark brown eyes; those eyes had loved her. Where had he gone?

'But it's my idea! I did all the research ...'

'Louise, this is a work do. I've got to get back. We'll talk later.'

He walked off. She stared at his back, gritted her teeth, and went back to sit beside Chloe.

'How did that go?' Chloe said.

'Not well.'

'Oh dear. How did he even get hold of your idea in the first place?'

'A few weeks ago, I was going to pitch to a production company, you know, when I was trying to get that producer job. I showed it to

Paul, the proposal. He wasn't impressed. He said the format was too straightforward, needed a better angle, a lot more work, before I could present it to anyone.'

'That's pretty brutal.'

'Yes. I was crushed. He sliced a huge sliver off my confidence. I didn't get the job, and then a week later he came home and said his boss was interested in producing it. He'd shown my proposal to him, just to help me out of course. They'd made lots of changes, it wasn't really my proposal anymore, blah blah blah ...'

'And was it? Different, I mean?'

'I looked at it – his "new" version. It was mine, exactly as I'd written it.'

'God, you must be furious!'

Louise took a deep breath.

'I don't even think he told his boss it was my work. He just stole it, and after he'd made me feel so stupid.' She sighed and rubbed her eyes. 'I don't know what to do. Maybe it doesn't matter, I don't know. I just feel sort of ... numb all the time.'

'Numb?'

'Yes, since, since, you know, since Mum died ...'

'Oh, I know, I'm sorry.' Choe gave her a hug and held her for a few minutes. She got up. 'I'll go and get us some beers.'

Louise threw a log onto the fire and sparks spiralled upwards. She gazed into the crackling flames. The smoke and the smell of burnt sausages swirled around her, like the betrayal.

CHAPTER 2

QUANTUM FAMILY

Louise left the barbeque early. Paul wouldn't be home for hours. She dragged herself along the leafy streets of Chiswick to the underground station and went down on the escalator, away from the bustle of the bars and the traffic. Down, down into the earth, past the water and sewage pipes, the broadband and electricity cables which connected the lives up above. The children, the mothers and fathers, the nuclear families of the suburbs, all carefully linked together.

Her family had been a quantum family. Her father left when she was five. She and her mum had lived in their tiny sixth-floor flat in Glasgow, just two particles bound together, spinning tightly in orbit around each other.

Louise waited on the platform. Two minutes, the sign said. A train rattled in on the other side and disappeared again, pushing and pulling the air around her. She took a deep breath. She kind of liked the stale smell of the wind in the London underground.

She could remember her father throwing her up in the air, pushing her on the swings on a sunny day in the park, playing horses in the living room. Then he vanished; she didn't know why. For years she'd gazed out of the window, down at the little figures below, fantasising that she'd see him saunter up the path and come home to make their family complete. But he'd never even come to visit. He lived in some other part of Glasgow with a new wife.

Her train trundled into the station. She sat in the near empty carriage. Only a mother and little boy sat opposite. The mum held some bags from London Zoo. The boy was clutching his new giraffe, fast asleep on his mother's lap.

Foxy, an arctic fox – that had been her best friend. When Louise heard her mother yelling down the phone, she would sit on her bed hugging Foxy. When her mum stopped shouting and started sobbing, little Louise went into her bedroom, climbed on her lap and hugged her, as if she and Foxy and could make everything better.

The train screeched through the dark tunnels. Louise looked up at the adverts above the windows. "Out of the Box – an Exhibition of Contemporary Art inspired by Science". If she had been in that exhibition, she would have drawn a nuclear family, a nucleus with the mum as the proton and the father as the neutron. Around them two electron children would whizz in their happy little orbits. For her quantum family she would draw just two particles revolving in a tight figure of eight around each other.

She'd been good at art; maybe, in another life, she could have got into that exhibition.

'She'll easily get into art school,' her art teacher had said to her mother, but Mum told Louise that she needed a "proper job", a good career, to support herself so she would never have to rely on a man. Art would be a hobby, on that point her mum had been adamant.

Perhaps it had been the right decision. She'd enjoyed studying French and journalism at university. She'd lived in a huge flat with her friends and they had a wild time, endless clubbing and parties. She found she could stay up all night dancing – dance, dance, dance herself transparent – and still pass her exams the next day. She tried a few drugs, had more than a few boyfriends. One lovely summer she worked in a café in Paris, and explored the city, lying in parks and gardens with a beautiful waiter called Antoine. She got a first-class degree, and a position as a graduate trainee at the BBC. Her mother was delighted.

'My work is done! You are an independent woman,' she'd said.

Louise got off the train and walked through the over-lit tunnels to the Northern Line. Probably just as well she hadn't done art. She really liked working in TV. Making documentaries was fascinating, learning about different subjects, interviewing interesting people. She'd done really well in Scotland, won several big TV awards. But then Paul got this job in London.

On the train and off again at her station, Clapham Common. It was midsummer's eve and there was still a little light in the sky as she trudged along the street of identical houses to number 135. She opened the door to their tiny ground floor apartment, so small it would have fitted into the kitchen of her old Glasgow tenement flat. When would Paul be home? Not for hours probably.

She dumped her bag and went into the miniature kitchen. Laptops, a Nespresso machine, and an Alexa she secretly hated sat on the shiny black worktops. And, ah, a bottle of red wine. She poured herself a glass, kicked off her shoes and sat on the cream sofa in the living room. Their wedding photo on the sideboard stared back at her. Black and white in a black frame. She and Paul, such a good-looking young couple, people said, so happy.

The first time she'd caught sight of him she had melted. Her first job in television, and he was the tall, dark, talented producer/director. She was "his" researcher. He was exciting, wild, full of brilliant ideas and brimming with confidence. They fell in love and got married two years later. She couldn't believe he wanted her.

They'd been in London for four months now. Paul had said it would be much better for their careers if they moved from Glasgow. So far it had only been better for his. Why had she come? She'd left her flat and her friends. Chloe was the only person she knew here. And she'd left her mother in her cottage on the Isle of Harris, the cottage they'd gone to every summer holiday for years when Louise was growing up. Her mum had finally got the money to buy it, but she'd only lived there for six months before she died. Louise had managed to visit just a few times. Paul had never come with her; he liked being at the centre of things and the Outer Hebrides were the end of the universe to him. Her mother had told Louise not to worry if she didn't have time. She was happy now she had the freedom to paint in her little cottage near the beach.

Louise looked around her. *This flat is like a sterile laboratory.* Paul and his minimalism, no mess. The only bit of colour was her mother's exuberant painting of the beach in Harris, which Paul said it was "a bit much".

It was only three months ago that she'd spoken to her mother for the last time. Her mum had asked her to come and visit. No particular reason, she said, she'd just like to see her. It was so unusual for her to ask, but Louise hadn't gone. Paul had a rare weekend off and she wanted them to go away to a country hotel, spend time together, recapture the magic, talk about having a baby – again. A waste of time. Paul had been non-committal. He'd struggled to talk to her at all. They sat at the hotel dining room table in silence. Louise was embarrassed, sure the waitress and other guests noticed. How could a couple get to the stage that they had nothing to say to each other over dinner? She had looked at Paul across the table in the restaurant. He seemed to be on another planet, in another universe, a cold remote place. By the time her dessert arrived, she was holding back tears. She hardly had the strength to crack her creme brulé. Meanwhile, her mother was lying dead on the beach in the painting. She'd had a heart attack. On *that* beach in *that* painting.

Louise gulped down the rest of the wine, put her glass in the mini dishwasher, undressed and climbed into the cold, empty bed. It was midnight. She lay alone in the dark, listening for the sound of Paul's key in the lock.

CHAPTER 3

THE QUESTION

Louise was getting ready for work. It was two weeks after the barbeque and she'd finally got a job as a researcher, two grades below the producer grade she had been in Glasgow. *You have to take what you can get*, she told herself. *No, you get what you settle for.*

She had her head upside down, drying her long blonde hair, when she stopped, turned off the hairdryer and walked into the kitchen.

Paul was sitting at the table with his coffee, looking at his phone.

'What's going on, Paul?'

He kept looking at his phone. He was getting a bit jowly, double chinned. She hadn't noticed that before.

'You're never here, you come in at all hours ...'

Paul kept staring at his phone.

'Paul, for God's sake! I'm talking to you!' she said.

'What?' He turned to look at her.

'What's going on?'

He turned back to his phone.

'Are you having an affair?' Her voice was raised now.

No answer.

'Well – *are you*?' she shouted.

Silence, and then ...

'Yes.'

'What?' She gasped and fell back against the wall. She hadn't expected that. She hadn't even really thought he was having an affair. She'd only wanted to goad him into noticing her.

'Who?'

'It doesn't matter.'

'It *does* matter! Who is it?'

'Someone at work.'

'Someone at work.' Her mind seemed to be frozen — an affair, someone at work ... 'How long?'

'It doesn't matter.'

'How long?'

'A month.'

'A month.'

That probably meant months, several months, many months. She went back into the bedroom and stared out the window. A few moments later he came in.

'I'm sorry, Louise. It doesn't mean anything. I still love you. I do.'

He touched her arm. She brushed him off and stepped away.

'Don't touch me. Do you love her?'

Silence.

'Well, do you?' She turned to him, her heart pounding.

'Maybe. I don't know. You can love two people at once.' He reached for her hand. 'I know I still love you.'

She pushed him away.

'I don't want us to split up,' he said.

'Are you going to give her up?'

Silence.

'Well, are you?'

'I'm so confused,' he said, pushing his floppy hair back.

'Oh, poor you.'

'I didn't mean for it to happen,' he said. 'It just did.'

Just did, like tripping up, breaking a glass – breaking my heart.

'Look, I have to go to work now. I've got a haircut first. I'm late,' he said. 'We can talk about it tonight when I get back.'

And he just left – to get his hair cut – as if nothing had happened. She watched him walk down the street to the underground station as if it were any other morning. How could he just leave like that?

Something cold grew inside her; it spread through her veins. She went to the wardrobe and pulled out a bag. She started packing. Some warm fleeces. Boots. A waterproof. Waterproof trousers. A few – several – changes of clothes.

In the taxi on the way to the airport, she called her boss. She was going to work from home on the new proposal. He didn't need to know that she was going to Harris in the Outer Hebrides. She was surprised that her new boss agreed, but he was up to his eyes in another project. He didn't have time to think about her. Fine.

She flew to Inverness, hired a car and drove. She didn't see the beautiful scenery on the way to Ullapool or on the lovely drive down to Loch Broom.

On the ferry to Stornoway, she stood alone out on the empty deck. Everyone else was huddled inside in the bar drinking Tennants and eating fish and chips. The boat ploughed across the long miles of the Minch, lurching up and down through the waves. She watched the raging inky black sea and the low scudding grey clouds. *Can you love two people?* She loved Paul. She couldn't imagine being with someone else, having sex with anyone else. Maybe men were different. Maybe it was all about the sex. The sex must be better with *her*, the other woman. It must be Amy, his new researcher. Or maybe the presenter of the series he's working on, Sue someone. She didn't care … she *did*.

She paced around the deck. How could he do this to her? And now, when her mother had just died? That's why he'd been so remote that weekend at the country hotel, the weekend she should have been with her mother.

She'd have to move out. Or he could move out. *He can move in with her.* She couldn't stay with him even if he did give her up.

It's all ruined now.

The boat swayed through the swell and Louise held onto the railings, struggling to keep her feet. A strong wind buffeted her with rain and whipped the breath from her lungs. She clenched her hands on the bars and stared into the churning dark waters. She had wanted to have a baby. Now she would have to meet someone else.

I'm nearly thirty. There won't be time, now; no time to have a baby.

All those years with Paul. Lost time, so much lost time. Married for six linear years; together for eight. *Now we aren't. We've hit the buffers. End of the line. Time's up.*

Cold water dripped down her neck.

CHAPTER 4

LUSKETYRE

It was evening when Louise got to her mother's cottage. She dumped her bags in the tiny spare bedroom in the attic and went straight to bed.

She woke to the gentle sound of distant waves. For a moment she expected to hear her mum clattering about in the kitchen below but of course her mother wasn't there.

She squeezed down the tiny staircase into the dark musty living room. It was crammed with her mother's things: paintings, art stuff, shells and feathers, and loads of books. She ran her fingers along one of the dusty rows in one of the old bookcases. Beautiful art books with their strong spines erect. Inside, glowing wonders, just waiting for someone to open the pages and release the wondrous images to a delighted eye. The books weren't arranged in any kind of order: Picasso came before the Pre-Raphaelites, Titian after Turner. It was art history disassembled.

She pulled out two randomly placed books. *I'll organise them. It will be a tiny effort against everything spinning out of control, a finger in the dyke.*

She stopped, the books weighing heavily in her hands. But you can't stop entropy. It's the law, the second law of thermodynamics: everything tends to disorder. Books, my life, myself. *I can't even keep my thoughts in order. They keep scattering to the sky like a startled flock of crazy seagulls.*

Louise put the books back where they had come from. Her hands hung heavily, uselessly, at her side.

Maybe she could come and live here, like her mum, get a dog, walk on the beach. But she didn't have the money. She and Paul would split up now, surely. He'd want to move in with his new girlfriend – whoever she was. They'd get divorced, sell the flat. She couldn't afford to keep it on her own. She couldn't leave London, give up her job, not now.

'What am I going to do?' she whispered to the room. 'My mother is dead; my husband is having an affair.' She said it louder. 'My mother is dead; my husband is having an affair.' She shouted then. 'MY MOTHER IS DEAD; MY HUSBAND IS HAVING AN AFFAIR!'

A heavy grey blanket of silence stifled her words. The gloomy living room didn't care. She dragged in a deep breath and looked around.

I have to get out of here.

She grabbed her mother's art bag, an easel and a canvas and headed for the beach.

*

The sunlight glimmered and shimmered across the sea. Louise stood at her easel, gazing out at the water, then back at her painting. How could she capture that sparkling light? If she had some glitter she could just throw it over the water on her canvas, but that would probably be cheating.

She picked up a dry brush, dipped it in a little white paint, and gently drew it across the water in her painting. She turned, walked a few steps, and looked back quickly, as if to catch her painting by surprise.

It stared back at her glumly, unimpressed.

Well, the white doesn't work, she thought. And the colours aren't nearly strong enough for the silver sand of the beach, the clear turquoise of the sea, the purply-blue of the sky. That wonderful intensity of the Outer Hebrides, far on the northwest edge of Scotland, but with the bright colours of the Caribbean. It was so beautiful it hurt her eyes. Her painting was dull and flat in comparison. Like the muffled sound of a neighbour's music, it was lacking in brilliance.

She put down her brush, wiped her brow and sighed. She couldn't think of anything else to do to it. Her inspiration had flown off in the breeze. There it went, away down the beach. It would land on that dog walker in the distance. He'll strike his forehead and say, 'Of course!'

The sun shone brightly, the waves lapped quietly, oystercatchers peeped. A light breeze wafted the sweet salty air over her. It was a perfect day. She knew she should feel alive, exhilarated, blissful, blessed to be in this perfect place. The sun warmed her skin but it failed to penetrate. Inside, she was cold, numb, as if all her nerve endings had been cut. She looked out from behind a thick pane of glass.

She checked her watch. One o'clock. She'd been here for hours. Painting was so frustrating, but completely absorbing. You got lost in time. They call it *flow*, but really, it's more like *pause,* stopping time, she thought.

She abandoned her painting and wandered down to the rocks by the sea. She leant over a rock pool to look at the little anemones waving.

'Hi,' she whispered. A breeze rippled the water, disintegrating her face and lifting strands of hair from her loosely reined ponytail. Suddenly she was a girl, here on this same beach twenty years ago, on a very different day, with the wind whipping the spray from the waves. She remembered running around the beach like an excited puppy, exhilarated in all the wildness.

Her mother had thrown a stick into the water.

'Fetch!' she'd shouted over the roar.

Louise had run in with all her clothes on, jumping through the waves to bring it back, being her best puppy. Her mother watched and laughed.

Something behind Louise's eyes cracked and burned. A bubble of pain erupted from deep inside her and burst out in a gasping sob. She sank to her knees in the soft sand, felled by grief. Why had she not been here? Why had she not come that weekend, instead of trying to save her doomed marriage? Her mother had died here, somewhere on this beach, alone.

Paul. How could he do this to her now? He'd just admitted it, confessed he was having an affair. So matter of fact! Her loving husband. He knew she was distraught from her mum's death. Apparently, that didn't matter.

It's just too much. I can't cope with this, any of it.

Louise put her hands over her face and pushed her head into the sand. Could she stick her head in it? Bury herself in it? Disappear? She pushed her head down hard and screamed. It came out as a mangled, strangled sound. Sand got in her mouth.

The cold wet seeped through to her knees. She hauled herself up and gathered her art things. She folded up the easel and stuffed the oil paints, brushes and rags into the bag, and grabbed her tragic painting. She struggled up the beach, trying not to get paint on her mother's dungarees.

She reached the little car park and a grey-haired woman with a bright bandana leant out of her tiny camper van window.

'Have you been painting?' she said. 'May I see?'

Louise shuffled around to show her the painting.

'That's wonderful. Did you just do it?'

'Yes. Thank you. Would you like to buy it?' Louise was only half joking.

'Sorry, no room,' she indicated round her little van, 'but it is lovely.'

Louise trudged on.

Maybe I could buy a camper van and live in it. Get a bandana. Travel around Scotland, sleep in lay-bys.

Lay-by my life.

Along the single-track road to her mother's little white cottage, past the lonely windswept tree, the demented border collie, in through the wooden door, blue paint flaking. No need to lock it. The red wooden parrot on its perch in the hall as always. The flickers of yellow and green on its wings and tail and the orange on its beak were faded now but it still balanced perfectly on its perch. Its tail was slightly weighted. When she was little on holiday here, the first thing she did was run in and give it a push. It would happily rock back and forth and make a faint wooden wobbly sound. How hard could she push it before it fell? She'd got it down to a fine art.

She dumped the painting stuff in a heap on the hall floor. She should sort it out, clean it up, break up the painting and use it to light the fire. She gave the parrot a push as she passed. It wobbled and fell onto the carpet at her feet. She stared at it, lying there. It never did that.

*

The funeral had been two months ago. She'd meant to come back and sort out the cottage, clear it out, put it up for sale, but she hadn't been able to face it. Well, she could make a start now, and box things up.

In the living room, her mother's treasured possessions cluttered around her. A clump of oily sheep's wool sat on a shelf. Louise picked it up and rubbed the oily fibres through her fingers. Why had her mum wanted it? Her fingers had touched it only a few weeks ago.

Louise gulped. She turned away too quickly and stumbled, falling hard against the bookcase. A photo frame fell, and the glass smashed on the floor. She stared down at it: it was a sunny photo of her and her mother outside the National Gallery in Edinburgh. An Italian man had taken it. She'd been nine. Little Louise and her mum looked up at her from the floor, laughing together amongst the shards of glass.

'Two beauties on a beautiful day!' the Italian had said.

Inside, the National Gallery was a treasure trove. In one of the rooms was a seascape by Turner. Louise loved it, it was mesmerising, but her mother had dragged her into the next room. When her mum was distracted talking to a friend, Louise snuck back to look at the

Turner. She sat alone on the long shiny wooden bench with her little legs straight out, gazing at it. It was a very windy day in the painting. The waves were thrashing onto the beach, the sea and the clouds were all mixed up, merging into each other, everything confused. Louise stared deeply into it. The waves crashed around her. The wind and the spray fell on her face, and she tasted the salt on her lips. She breathed in the wet sea air, and felt herself dissolve into the painting.

Her mother had grabbed her arm and pulled her off the bench.

'I was looking all over for you.' Louise struggled not to fall in the wet sand.

*

A shaft of sunlight struck the broken glass on the floor, shattering light into Louise's eyes. Her mother's voice reached her over twenty years like an echo. *I was looking all over for you.*

Louise knelt down on the floor and put her hand down to touch her mother's face in the photo. Her finger stabbed hard into a thin sliver of glass. She looked blankly at her finger with the glass sticking out it and watched a drop of blood slide down. The blood dripped onto the grey carpet. A piece of glass on the floor glinted in the sun, winking up at her. An enticing evil spirit said 'Pick me up, go on, you know you want to.'

She picked it up. And held it to her wrist. She could slice here and end it all. Her bright red life would empty out all over the floor. She would bleed slowly to death. It would probably ruin her mum's carpet. How long would it be until she was found? Who would come looking? A neighbour? The postman? It wouldn't be Paul. No. Not him, the person she was closest to in all the world. He didn't even know where she was. She would lie here and decay. The mice would eat her.

It's easy. I'll do it. Now.

She sat staring at the glass.

Oh, for God's sake.

She stood up suddenly, her legs numb, and staggered into the kitchen. She pulled the glass out of her finger and put on a plaster to hold the cut together. *Better pull myself together, stop thinking like this or I'll go crazy.*

She'd do some work – that would force herself to think about something else. She'd do some research for her proposal on quantum physics.

She made a cup of tea, sat down at the kitchen table, fired up her laptop and stared out the window at the waves. The laptop struggled into life. Maybe it didn't matter; Paul could have his affair. As long as she could have a baby. She wanted a baby.

The calendar on the wall caught her eye. There was a circle round today's date. Today was her wedding anniversary.

'Huh,' she said.

She put in her password. She was a TV researcher (*not* a producer, she reminded herself, but if she did a decent job ...), writing a proposal for a series about quantum physics. It was her first chance to impress her new boss.

It was quite a challenge. Quantum physics was so difficult to understand – she'd studied French and journalism, not science, but it was intriguing. It revealed such a weird world, an alternate reality, like when Alice fell down the rabbit hole and discovered a place with totally different rules. To fall into another world – how appealing!

She worked on a chronology of theories – so many theories – until she was up to date. The latest scientific paper on quantum theory proclaimed that everything we think of as a solid thing is not really solid at all. Ever thing is just a passing moment in time. Even a hard object like a rock is a process. It's temporary, constantly changing in time.

'Really?' she said out loud to the empty kitchen.

Her phone rang, juddering on the table beside her. She jumped.

'Hello?'

'I'm outside the café. Where are you? We're supposed to meet for lunch.'

'Oh, Chloe, I completely forgot, I'm sorry. I'm in the Outer Hebrides.'

'The Outer Hebrides?'

'In Harris, at my mum's.'

'Oh, you didn't say you were going. You're clearing out the house?'

'Yes, it's not going very well.' Louise looked around the cluttered kitchen.

'It must be really hard for you,' Chloe said. 'Are you okay? You sound a bit weird.'

Louise hesitated. She couldn't bear to tell Chloe about Paul, not yet. It was too raw.

'Yes, fine. I'm doing some work, researching quantum physics.'

'Quantum physics? What on earth for?'

'For a TV proposal, you know, for my new job. It's so weird. Did you know that things don't really exist? Every single thing is just a temporary process. Even people, us.'

'That's strange. I can't imagine that.'

'Yes, you, me, everything. We're just processes in time.'

'Really?'

'Yes, hard to get your head around. How are you?'

'Oh, busy, you know. Actually, I've got to go and grab some lunch, I've got a meeting. When are you coming back?'

'I don't know.'

'Well, let me know. Look after yourself. It must be really difficult for you.'

'Yes, thanks. Sorry about today. Bye.'

As Louise rang off, she saw she had a series of messages from Paul. She put her phone down. She gazed out at the sea. If she was a process, she was like a wave cresting and breaking, rising and falling, appearing, disappearing, coming together for a brief time then dissolving back into the churning ocean. Swelling, breaking, vanishing. That would be lovely, to dissolve into the sea.

She forced her attention back to her laptop and read on. Apparently she was not made of the same atoms as when she was born. She was constantly changing; she was a happening, an "event".

She liked the idea of being an event. An event was exciting, something to look forward to.

And events were not organised from the past to the present to the future as you might think. They didn't follow on from each other, one after the other. They jumped around randomly like rambunctious rabbits. Time was not a line but a bunch of dots, like a Seurat painting.

Time was not linear! Events bounced around in time! They were like the art books on her mum's bookshelf which were randomly placed; they had lost their chronology.

If I'm an event, maybe I could bounce around in time. Bounce back and see Mum. Take her to the doctor, get her heart checked, save her. I failed her. So completely.

Louise slammed her laptop shut. She couldn't make a TV programme about quantum physics. She couldn't concentrate on this. Or anything.

She went into the living room and slumped onto the tatty old sofa. She sat there for some time, staring into space. Slowly, she focused on the bookcase opposite her.

Looking at art usually made her feel better.

CHAPTER 5

INTO THE LIGHT

Louise reached over and pulled out a book called *Impressionism*. She flicked through the pages: Monet, Manet, Degas, Pissarro, Renoir – such beautiful paintings. That had been such an amazingly creative time, when all those painters had been together in Paris, one of those exciting, magical times in history when everything was changing. It must have been a great time to be alive.

And here, a painting of a young woman stared out at her, by a painter she'd never heard of. 'Berthe Morisot,' Louise said to the kitchen. 'I didn't know there were women Impressionists.' She flipped through more pages – descriptions, quotes, and a letter signed *Berthe Manet*. She must have married the famous Manet.

Louise went back to the painting of the young woman – she was intriguing. Berthe Morisot saw the woman not as a man might, as an object of attraction to be judged, assessed, valued for her beauty, but as a real person, a bright being with hopes and dreams. The woman was looking back at her from over more than a hundred years ago. She looked about the same age as her; she had the same hair. What was *her* life like then? Did she have a lover who betrayed her? What was she feeling at the moment the painter captured her on canvas? She looked so alive, so present in that moment of being painted, like a snatched photograph but more real somehow because she was broken by light, as you might glimpse someone just before they moved away.

And what a lightness of touch the painter had! The fluttering, flickering effect – like a butterfly had dipped its feet in her palette and flitted across the canvas. The light in the painting was so beautiful – evanescent, ephemeral – that the woman seemed to shimmer and glimmer. She was a presence made of light.

How had she never heard of Berthe Morisot? It was like she knew about light, about photons, about light being both a wave and a particle. But could she have? Louise looked up the chronology on quantum physics she'd just completed. No, Einstein first talked about that in 1905 and this was painted in the 1870s.

She flicked through the book and found other paintings by Berthe Morisot: *Young Girl with Greyhound*. There was a chair and a sofa, hardly there, disappearing. And another one, *Summer's Day*. Two women on a boat caught in a moment; they were not even fully on the canvas. And a woman on a bench in a garden – you could almost see right through her. She looked like she was dematerialising, disintegrating. It was so unusual, as if this painter understood something about quantum physics – that we are not really here, we are constantly changing.

But that would be impossible.

Louise turned back to the first painting of the young woman. It was such a compelling image. She'd try to copy it.

She got her art stuff from the hall, set it on the kitchen table, propped the book up, and started. It was difficult. The painter had worked so freely, quickly, easily. How could Louise get her mind into that loose, light state? She struggled to escape from the weight of her worries and just be, just paint.

The woman was sitting at a window in a white dress with her hair tied back in a ponytail. She had a blue, black, grey ribbon round her neck. Behind her was a garden which seemed to be fully alive – loose broad strokes of light and dark greens roughly dabbed in, blues for shadows, pink and white for flowers; were they roses?

Louise covered a fresh canvas quickly with white. It seemed like the best base colour for the lightness of the painting. She mixed some greens and yellows and dabbed them on for the background. She roughed in some flesh tones for the face, light browns for the hair, but it was difficult to pin the woman down amongst all the colours.

She stared closely into Berthe Morisot's painting. The woman seemed to quiver amongst streaks of whites and blues, greens and browns, lavenders and greys. She had a slightly surprised look on her face as if she was about to stand up and say, "I don't want to be painted."

There were highlights of the white ruffles of the dress, and, lower, rough broad verticals of browns for shadows. On her lap, two wide horizontal strokes of blue. Was that a parasol? Her arms fell into a few white strokes for the sleeves and then … where were her hands?

Louise peered closer. The light in the painting flickered and fluttered through the colours, popped into her eyes, and crackled around her brain. Where were the woman's hands? She didn't seem to have any hands. She peered closer – she must have hands.

Louise struggled to keep painting, but it wasn't working. She couldn't pin anything down. Her skin was cold, clammy. She wiped her brow with her sleeve. Her fingers started tingling, trembling, shaking. The brush fell from her hand. She looked at her fingers. They seemed to be turning white; now they were fading away, disappearing. What was happening? Where were her hands? Her heart started racing. She tensed and gasped for air. Panic swept through her. Was she having a heart attack? A stroke? She watched her arms getting brighter, turning whiter and whiter. Her vision blurred. She couldn't see. She sat down abruptly, dizzy, and closed her eyes.

*

Louise lifted her head. She was looking at a young woman. A tall, dark, beautiful woman, standing at an easel, painting. She pushed her long black hair back behind her ears. Her dark brown eyes screwed up as she peered into Louise. She was staring intently at her, concentrating furiously. *She's looking straight through me*, thought Louise. *Am I invisible?*

Louise looked around in a daze. She was sitting in front of an open window. There was a garden behind her. The room was richly decorated with antique furniture: ornate gold mirrors, an elaborate clock ticking on the mantelpiece, a four-poster bed covered with an ornate red and gold blanket, a chaise longue patterned with shades of blues. Paintings everywhere, either hung on the walls as high as the ceiling or stacked the floor. A glowing walnut dressing table held not make-up and hairbrushes but jars full of paintbrushes, piles of paints, rags and bottles. Sunlight flooded in from the open window. A glass chandelier scattered broken light around the room.

Several minutes passed with the woman painting and Louise staring back at her, frozen in place. Then the woman stepped back from her easel to get a better view of the painting.

'Yes,' she said.

'Are you … are you painting me?' Louise said.

The woman lifted her eyes from the painting, looked at Louise and saw her as if for the first time.

'What? Who – but who are you? I was painting the garden …' She slammed her brush down. 'Who are you? What are you doing here? You are an intruder!'

She moved away from her easel. She was going towards a bell on a table. Beside it was a strange ornate old-fashioned pen and ink pot – that was weird, Louise thought. But if the woman rang for help, what would happen? Would the police come? Maybe Louise would be charged with breaking and entering, be arrested.

'No, no. Wait! Please, please don't. I don't mean any harm. Please, please don't!' Louise said.

The woman looked at Louise.

'But who are you? You cannot just come in here, break in. I shall call the servants.'

Servants?

The woman picked up the bell again.

'No, please, I beg you,' Louise said.

The woman looked at Louise's pleading face and hesitated. She put the bell down.

'But how did you get in here? Who are you?'

She returned to look at her painting, at Louise, at the painting again.

'I was painting the garden, and then the light began to change, and the colours, and then it seems I was painting you, your hair, your face. You, you emerged somehow. How did you do that?'

'I don't know.'

'But where did you come from?'

'I don't know!' Louise said, louder. 'I was painting too. I got dizzy. I sat down. When I opened my eyes, I was here.' She looked around wildly. 'I have no idea what happened.'

The two young women stared at each other. There was a long moment of silence. A woodpecker hammered in the garden.

'May I see?' asked Louise, indicating the painting.

'It's just started but yes, you can.'

Louise got up and stumbled over the long white dress she seemed to be wearing. She went over to the easel and looked at the painting. It was the one from the book, the one she'd been copying.

'My God,' she said.

'Is it that bad?' the woman said, frowning at it.

'No, it's ...' Louise had no words. After a long pause, she said, 'Where are we?'

'In my home. In Paris, of course.'

Louise looked out the window. Paris, yes. It was familiar. There was a great view of the city from here, she could see for miles. But there was no Sacré-Cœur on Montmartre, and no Eiffel Tower across the river. And it was so quiet. Why was it so quiet? There was no sound of traffic. Nothing. *When* are we, she wondered.

'What's the date?' Louise asked tentatively.

'It is 12th August.'

'And, erm, the year?'

'Hah! It is 1871 still, I believe.'

Louise struggled to breathe.

'And ... who ... who are you?'

'I am Berthe. Berthe Morisot.'

Louise stared at Berthe Morisot. She'd been painting Berthe's painting and Berthe was painting her. She, Louise, was the woman in the painting in the book. That was why she had felt such a connection with her.

She seemed to have travelled through the painting. It was unbelievable, impossible, and yet here she was – with this amazing artist. She looked at Berthe: her dark eyes were boring into Louise again.

'I do not understand how you got here,' Berthe said. 'Who are you?'

Berthe was speaking in French. They had been the whole time. Louise was fluent in French, and her brain must have automatically switched into it. But Berthe's accent was different, rather strange, formal.

'I found this painting, your painting, in a book,' Louise said. 'I tried to copy it, paint it. Then I, I appeared here. I know. It sounds crazy.' Louise voice cracked. She looked around in desperation.

Berthe stared at her.

'You're painting me,' Louise said. 'Your painting, this painting, it's in a book, in the future. I seem to have travelled through it, through time –'

'What do you mean, a book in the future?'

'Well, you're Berthe Morisot. You're a famous painter.'

'Hah, that is most definitely a joke,' Berthe said.

'I don't know. Are you sure this is 1871?' Louise said.

'Yes,' Berthe snapped.

'Sorry. I feel a bit weird,' Louise sat down again. 'How will I get back?'

'Back where?'

'To my time.'

'Your time? When is that?'

'2024.'

'2024! That is, hmm, one hundred and fifty years in the future! Do not be ridiculous! Are you insane?' Berthe looked her up and down and then at her painting. 'My paintings are in a *book*?'

'Yes. You are a wonderful artist.'

'You cannot be from the future, that is most definitely ridiculous. I should contact the police. You are an intruder.'

But she didn't move and eventually said, 'You like to paint too?'

'Yes, but I'm nowhere near as good as you are,' Louise said. 'But sometimes I feel I just *need* to paint.'

'Yes, it is as if you have no choice. It is the only thing that makes me feel at all sane.'

There was a long pause and Louise said, 'I like your dress.'

'Thank you. This is just for painting.'

'How am I wearing this?' Louise gestured to her white dress.

'I do not know. It is a tea dress.'

'What's that?'

'Well, you wear it at home, not for going out.'

Not for going out ... what? Louise's heart started racing. Tea dresses, Berthe Morisot ... This is crazy! *Travelling through a painting? I must be having some kind of breakdown. I need some air. I've got to get out of here.*

Louise jumped up and ran to the door. She found herself in a large hallway at the top of a long staircase. She ran down the steps, opened a heavy wooden door and stepped out onto a street. She froze. There were horses and carriages, people wearing old-fashioned clothes, women in long dresses with parasols. Men in top hats. She rubbed her eyes; what was all this? The street tilted in front of her.

She struggled to breathe and put her hand to her chest. Her hands shook, her heart pounded.

No, no ... it can't be.

She broke into a sweat, slid down the wall onto the pavement and passed out.

CHAPTER 6

BERTHE

Louise woke to the sound of birdsong. The birds sounded strange this morning. Sleepily, she reached for the bedside light. It wasn't there. Must have fallen off the table. She opened her eyes. The sun was just beginning to penetrate the heavy brocade curtains. She could just make out ornate wooden furniture, gilt mirrors, walls covered in paintings. She closed her eyes. Where was her mother's musty cottage with its Ikea furniture and shell collections? Surely that had been a dream, an elaborate dream, that thing with Berthe Morisot? It must have been the trauma of her mum's death and Paul's affair – she had had some kind of breakdown. She couldn't be in Paris. Tentatively, she touched the sheets. They felt hard, starched, definitely real. But she couldn't be in 1871.

If she tried hard enough, maybe she could get back to the cottage. She imagined herself into the bed in the tiny upstairs room, the soft lightness of the cotton flannel duvet around her, the damp musty smell, the waves lapping on the beach. She willed herself back into that little attic bedroom.

She opened her eyes. No, she was in a large nineteenth century bedroom in Paris, lying in a four-poster bed with starched white sheets and heavy blankets. This was Berthe Morisot's home. Impossible. *Not possible.* But here she was.

Climbing out of bed, she floated around the room in a long lacy nightgown – where had that come from? She touched the curtains and furniture, testing their solidity. She was like a ghost, re-materialised in a new old world.

The door opened and Berthe came in.

'Ah, you're awake.'

Louise stared at her.

Berthe seemed to be checking around the room. Was she looking to see if she'd stolen anything?

'Would you like some tea?' she said. 'I will get us some tea.'

Berthe rang the bell. There were bells everywhere it seemed. Moments later, a maid appeared. Her blond hair was tightly packed into a bun, her flighty hands smoothed down a long stiff white starched apron on top of a black uniform. She was young, alert, and as nervous as a gazelle ready to spring into action. Her eyes darted around the room.

'Yes, Mademoiselle Morisot?'

'Giselle, I know it is early. But could you get us tea, and do we have any madeleines left? Some of those as well. This is …'

Berthe turned to Louise and whispered: 'What's your name?'

'Louise.'

'This is Louise,' Berthe said to Giselle.

Giselle rushed off to get the tea, looking bewildered.

'You have a maid?' Louise said, rubbing her eyes.

'She is new, only sixteen. This is her first position. She has only been here for two weeks. I do not know if she will be any good.'

Louise sat up.

'Where am I?'

Berthe sighed. 'You collapsed on the door step. Father insisted on bringing you in and putting you to bed. How you got here before that I do not know.'

'No …' Louise rubbed her chin. She had been painting …

'Who are you?' Berthe said standing over her.

'Louise.'

'Yes, you said. Where are you from?'

'I was painting …' Louise shook her head. She must be ill, hallucinating, or had a head injury maybe.

'You said my paintings were in a book. What book?' Berthe said.

Louise opened her mouth, but nothing came out. She stared at Berthe.

'What kind of book?' Berthe said.

'Impressionists, famous artists –'

'Who? Famous artists?'

'Is this really 1871?' Louise said.

'A book in the future? But how can that be?'

'I don't know.' Louise blinked rapidly and gazed around.

'So, what are you going to do now?' Berthe said.

'What am I going to do? I have no idea. Thank you for not calling the police.' What would she do if Berthe called the police? 'I don't know how to get back. I don't have anywhere to go. I don't know anyone, here, now. I don't have any money. Nothing.'

Her heart thudded. She put her head in her hands. She was stuck, totally dependent on this woman, believing her, trusting her.

Berthe stood and looked at her in silence.

'Well what am I supposed to do with you?'

'Maybe I'll disappear in a minute. I don't know how long this lasts.'

'What lasts?'

'This travelling through –'

'You do not really expect me to believe you travelled through my painting.'

'No. I don't know.'

'That is all you can say: "I don't know".'

'Well, I don't!'

Giselle brought in the tea and madeleines, light, gold, fluffy madeleines. Berthe sat down on a chair beside the bed, and they ate in silence.

Louise struggled to swallow. What will I do if she turns me out onto the street? Where will I go?

'I really don't have anywhere to go,' she said. 'Could I stay here – just for a bit. Please? I would be so grateful.'

'For how long?'

'I don't know. Until I feel a bit better?'

'Hmm, I suppose Father will insist. He seems to think you are a friend of Edma's from Brittany coming to visit us anyway. I do not know why.'

'Really? Does he? Oh, thank you so much. That would be great. Maybe I'll be gone soon.'

'I suppose Mother will be pleased. She misses Edma, my sister. You will not steal anything, will you?'

'No, no, of course not. Thank you so much. You're so kind.'

Berthe grunted.

'You will meet Mother at breakfast. I expect Father has already gone to work. Do not take too long.' She left the bedroom.

Louise took a bite of the delicious madeleine and looked out the window at the arrival of the Paris dawn.

Paris 1871? *Really?*

*

Giselle knocked and came in with a jug of hot water. She poured it into a delicate, blue-patterned porcelain basin.

'Good morning, Mademoiselle Louise. Mademoiselle Berthe and Madame Morisot will see you at breakfast.'

'Yes. Thank you.'

'You will need these,' Giselle said.

'What?'

'Em, underwear, mademoiselle. For under the dress.' Giselle pointed to the dress, the "tea dress" that Louise had been wearing yesterday.

Had she come without any underwear? She felt under her nightie; she didn't seem to have any on.

Giselle left Louise to wash in the basin with a small slab of dry soap. Louise tried not to think about showers. She found a silver hairbrush to drag through her mussy hair and fumbled with the camisole and the huge pants Giselle had left.

She had to get home. This was crazy. She couldn't stay here with these people. How long would she be here? How would she get back? Maybe there's a time limit, and she'd just go back when the paint dried on the painting or something. Her hands would start to tingle – that would be the sign. She looked at her hands. Nothing.

She'd have to go through with this. What else could she do? Maybe they'd put her in prison, an insane asylum? This was so weird, so scary.

Louise put on the dress she'd been wearing the day before, the white tea dress from the painting, and some white slippers. Was this the right thing to wear? She left the bedroom and went into the hall. There were lots of beautiful wooden doors. She listened at one but heard nothing. She opened it – maybe there was a bathroom, a power shower? No, just a room full of more antiques. She peeked through another half-open door; it was an old bedroom. She stood and looked around. There were no signs of modern life – no lights or electricity sockets. She drifted down the long extravagant staircase with its red carpet and carved wooden banister, feeling uncomfortably like she was on a movie set, but without a script.

The heavy ornate wooden door to the dining room was open. She went in and sat beside Berthe at a long breakfast table. It was covered with a beige lacy tablecloth with silver cutlery and candlesticks, and pretty, patterned porcelain dishes brimming with fruit and croissants. An older woman sat opposite. She must be Berthe's mother, she thought.

'Good morning, Louise,' she said. 'Are you feeling better? I heard you had a funny turn.'

'Good morning, Madame Morisot. Yes, thank you.'

'Call me Cornélie, please.'

Louise looked at Cornélie. She was a short woman with small sharp features. Very pretty, tidy, immaculately dressed. Her black velvet dress had a crisp, very white starched collar and white cuffs. No nonsense. Sharp eyes, like an intelligent crow. Cornélie stirred her coffee and precisely sliced up some pineapple.

'Did you sleep well?' she said.

'Yes, Madame, sorry, Cornélie, thank you.'

'You're a friend of Edma's from Brittany?'

'Er, yes.'

'Welcome,' she said and gave Louise a tight smile. 'Do have some coffee and croissants. And look – have you tried this? Pineapple, it's called.' She pushed a plate of pineapple towards Louise.

'Yes, I have, thank you.'

'Really! You have? I didn't think it would have reached Brittany yet.' Cornélie seemed disappointed.

Berthe interrupted with a glance at Louise. 'I gave her some last night.'

'Aah. I see,' Cornélie said.

That was a mistake – the pineapple. She'd have to be careful. But this was ridiculous. She must be dreaming. She looked at a small knife by her plate on the table, engraved silver with a bone or ivory handle – beautiful. She picked it up and held it under her napkin beneath the tablecloth. She stabbed it hard into her hand. Ouch. But nothing happened. She was still here.

'Well, it's nice to have you, Louise. And it's good for you to have a companion, Berthe,' Cornélie said.

She turned to Louise. 'Yves, our oldest daughter, has married, and our son is away getting a good education; at least I hope so. Now Edma has left as well, Berthe has been quite lonely and morose. All she has is Erwin.'

Cornélie indicated the pretty ginger cat asleep on a beautiful tapestry chair by the window.

'Edma married a dashing naval officer, Adolphe. He's lost an arm, but he's still very handsome. They're living in Lorient now, Brittany. But, how silly of me, you know of course. You are her friend, are you not?'

'Er, yes,' said Louise.

'Strange she hasn't mentioned you to me. Or your visit. The letter must have been lost. Not surprising given the times we live in. How is she? I think she misses the excitement of Paris. Brittany can be quite dull. But she has children now. She's a wife and mother, she'll just have to put up with it.'

Berthe sighed and sullenly looked at her plate. Cornélie snapped a stern glance at Berthe, who pretended not to see.

Cornélie didn't seem to expect a reply, or any contribution from Louise or Berthe. She talked on. Berthe said little and Louise less. Berthe endured her mother's monologue, her face closed, her mind elsewhere. She picked at her food, pushing it around the plate, eating next to nothing.

'Berthe, what will you do today?' Cornélie said.

Berthe's attention snapped back.

'Why not show our visitor around?' Cornélie said. 'I have some errands to do, and I must pop in and visit Madame Ingres. She's been poorly. I don't know what's wrong with her.'

Cornélie put down her coffee cup and got up.

'Well, I must be going. Have a lovely time, and don't forget we have guests this evening. That will be interesting for you, Louise.'

Cornélie left the room and Berthe sighed.

'You are still here,' she said to Louise.

'Yes,' Louise shrugged. 'Sorry.'

'It seems that I am stuck with you. But what am I supposed to do with you?'

'I don't know. I'm as frustrated as you are.' Louise stood up and walked over to the window. Her insides were knotted up. 'I don't know what to do either. Please help me. You're the only one who can.'

She looked at Berthe's closed face.

'I should report you,' Berthe said.

'Please just let me stay here until I figure something out. Your mother doesn't seem to mind. I can be Edma's friend from Brittany.'

Berthe frowned. Louise looked down at her hands. *Please let me disappear now.* Nothing happened. She waited for Berthe's answer.

Berthe got up.

'I suppose I could take you out, show you some of Paris. Until we, I mean *I*, decide what to do with you.'

'See Paris?' said Louise. 'That would be wonderful. Can we walk from here? It doesn't look too far.'

'Walk! No, of course not. I will have Gervais bring the carriage round. We will have to get dressed first.'

Louise looked down at the white dress.

'What's wrong with this?'

'That is a tea dress. You cannot go out in that. You must get *properly* dressed. We will see if we can find something of mine, or Edma's, that will fit you.'

CHAPTER 7

THE CITY OF LIGHT

Berthe called Giselle and they went up to Edma's old bedroom. Berthe pulled out dresses, jackets and underskirts from a beautiful old wardrobe while Louise watched, fascinated. It was like playing dressing up. She felt nine years old again.

'First these.' Berthe handed her some enormous cotton thing with embroidery, ribbons and bows.

'What on earth is this?'

'Pantaloons – underwear.'

'But I have some. Giselle gave me –'

'No, not those. These.'

Louise stepped into two voluminous legs and Giselle tied them at her waist.

'But there's a gap between the legs. What's that for?'

'So you can go to toilet, of course,' Berthe said. Giselle blushed.

'Ah, so this is how you pee under those enormous dresses.' Louise looked at Berthe, but she'd turned away.

Giselle gave her a thin undershirt with lace patterned edges and an impressive satin corset, heavily boned. Louise didn't know how to put it on, which way was up. Giselle helped her, laced it and pulled it tight.

Louise gasped.

'Oh God, I can't breathe. Does it have to be so tight? This is like torture. How can you go anywhere in this?'

'You get used to it,' Berthe said.

'Haven't you worn a corset before, mademoiselle?' Giselle said. 'Don't they have them in the countryside?'

'Not where I'm from.'

They helped her pull on several petticoats and then the overskirt, a beautiful heavy blue silk patterned with tiny embroidered yellow flowers. It had a matching jacket, tightly nipped in at the waist. Louise was swathed in frills and ruffles, layered like a filo pastry, but nowhere near as light.

'I feel like I'm wearing curtains,' she said and looked in the mirror. 'Wow, I can't breathe but I look great!' She twirled around. What would Paul think of her like this? Paul, her unfaithful husband. She stopped twirling and looked down at her immense skirt. 'But I can't go to the toilet with all this on.'

'Of course you can,' Berthe said.

'How?' Louise tried to lift the heavy skirts.

Berthe sighed with frustration and grabbed a chamber pot from under the bed.

'Look, like this.'

She put the pot on a chair. She didn't turn round to sit on the chair but stood over it, facing the back of it. She lifted her skirts a little and squatted. 'It is easy, or you can just do this.' Berthe took the pot off the chair and put it under her skirt. 'You just pull the pantaloons out of the way.'

'Ah.'

By now Giselle couldn't contain her giggles – Mademoiselle Morisot demonstrating going to the toilet! Louise burst out laughing too.

'Oh, for goodness' sake,' Berthe said. She didn't even smile. She gave Louise a perfectly matching blue hat, gloves and parasol. 'Come on.'

'Do I really need to take all this?' Louise said.

'Yes, of course.'

They went downstairs, Louise with some difficulty, trying to keep up with Berthe. Outside, the carriage waited for them, a beautiful shiny black open affair, its wheels trimmed with yellow and sporting red spokes. Two perfectly groomed bay horses with bright brasses shook their silky manes and pawed the ground. An old driver with long grey whiskers dressed in a black coat and top hat helped Louise climb up.

Wow. I feel like I'm in a costume drama, like Bridgerton!

Louise wiped her forehead with a beautiful blue glove. Maybe this was some huge practical joke. Maybe someone had set all this up to confuse her. But it was a very elaborate set.

*

The horses clopped along a leafy suburban street into the city, the warm smell of horse manure mixed with the scent of flowers. It was summer in Paris and the sun was shining. Louise looked up to the hill of Montmartre.

'Oh, look at all the windmills!' she said. 'There must be at least thirty! In my time, there's only a couple left on Montmartre and there's a huge white church on the top – the Sacré-Cœur.'

Berthe made no response. She was looking out of the carriage in the other direction, frowning. *She doesn't seem the chatty type*, Louise thought. She rubbed her forehead. She was embarrassed about her excitement in getting dressed. Berthe didn't seem impressed by frivolity; she would probably prefer to be painting than playing the tour guide. Louise would keep quiet and try not to annoy her. She had to keep Berthe happy. If Berthe got fed up with her, she might turn her out – or worse, turn her in.

Louise gazed at her hands. Were they tingling? Could she make them tingle so she could go back home? She concentrated hard on making one hand tingle, just one finger, just the tip, but no. She was stuck. It was insane, impossible, to be here, stranded in the wrong century.

They emerged onto a bright new boulevard, a broad cobbled street with wide pavements, and fresh terraces of five-storey apartments, each with its own ornate iron balcony. The warm polished limestone, freshly hewn from the hills, shone in the sunlight. The new pavements were dotted with benches, flowers, kiosks and trees.

'The new boulevards …' Louise said. Her hand reached for her phone in her back pocket to take a photo. But, of course, she didn't have a phone – or a pocket.

'Oh, those trees were not here last week,' Berthe said, pointing to the plane trees lining the street.

'But they're fully grown,' Louise said.

'Yes, they bring them and plant them at night.'

'What, at night? Really?'

Louise looked at Berthe, but she turned away again. Louise's excitement ebbed away. The carriage rocked along and she sat in uncomfortable silence.

'I'm sorry if you had other plans today, Berthe,' Louise said. 'I don't want to be a burden to you. You'd probably prefer to be painting.'

Silence.

Then Berthe turned to her. 'You cannot travel through a painting. You *do* know that, don't you?'

'Yes … no. I don't know.'

'Have you escaped from an asylum for the insane?'

'No.'

'Well, I do not understand,' Berthe said. 'You say that you are from the future, so tell me about it then. What is it like?'

She's challenging me, Louise thought. She looked around her, at the passing carriages, 'Well, there are cars. This street would be full of cars, not horses and carriages. Cars are machines you sit in and drive.'

'Machines? Like steam engines? Impossible. You are making this up.'

'No. Cars *are* sort of like steam engines I suppose but smaller, a lot smaller. Most people have one. They drive themselves. It would be a lot noisier than this with the engines.'

Berthe snorted.

Louise looked up. 'And there are planes.' She pointed to the sky.

'Planes?'

'There are lots of planes flying overhead. They're machines, too. You can fly around the world in them.'

'What! That is ridiculous,' Berthe said.

There was a faint glimmer of a half-moon in the sky.

'And rockets. We've been to the moon. Men have walked on the moon, up there ...'

'The moon! What a story. You *are* crazy.'

Louise froze and put her hand over her mouth. If this was time travel, the first rule was not to interfere; all the movies said that. She must not interfere, say or do anything that might change the future while she was here. Had she already said too much?

She looked at Berthe. *She doesn't believe me, anyway.*

They passed a young woman in rags hunched in a doorway, her hand out, begging.

I'll end up like her if Berthe throws me out. Louise gulped. *I have to make her like me, let me stay.*

'It's so good of you to look after me,' she said. 'I don't know what I would have done if you had thrown me out.' She *did* know, however; she'd be on these streets with no money, nothing.

'I do not understand where you came from,' Berthe said. 'Tell me how you broke in.'

'I didn't break in, honestly. Like I said, I'm from the future, through the painting. I know, it's—'

'Mad,' Berthe said. 'So, you think people could actually do that in the future, travel through time?'

'Well, I don't know. I'd only heard about it in stories but now it seems to have happened to me.'

'So, how did you do it, then? Do you have a special "machine"?' Berthe said. Louise looked at her; she was being sarcastic.

'I don't know how it happened,' Louise said. 'I told you. I was painting *your* painting, trying to copy it, or myself, as it turned out.' She took a deep breath. 'I don't know! I really don't know what happened, or how to get back!' She clutched her parasol hard; her eyes began to burn with tears.

Berthe stared at her and looked away again. Louise tried to stop herself panicking. She watched Berthe's impassive face and took some deep breaths. The carriage rumbled over the cobblestones and Louise held on tightly.

Eventually, Berthe turned to her. 'Well, you seem harmless enough, even if you are mad. And actually, you could be of use to me.'

'Yes. Anything. Please! I'll do anything.'

'Since Edma left, I cannot go anywhere. Mother will not let me go out on my own. It is not respectable, apparently. And now I have no one to go out with. I cannot go *anywhere*, except with mother. You could be my chaperone.'

'Yes, of course I can do that!'

'You just come out with me, like we are doing today, now. We will tell Mother and she will be happy with the arrangement. You do not tell anyone if I have to, er, go off by myself sometimes.'

'Yes, yes. Of course! I might disappear, back to my time, at any moment. But yes, I can do that.'

'Can I trust you? You will not tell Mother about anything I do?'

'Of course not. You're saving me.'

'You promise?'

'Yes,' Louise said. If she could help Berthe, be useful to her, that would do for now. Until she figured something out, or something happened.

Under her breath Berthe said, 'And I can finally escape my mother.'

Berthe turned and smiled at her. Something had shifted in her.

'Good, that is settled. You are my chaperone. And in exchange, you can stay for a bit, a few days anyway, earn your keep. And I will be able to go out.' She rubbed her gloved hands together in excitement.

'Oh, thank you so much. I promise you can trust me,' Louise said and relaxed a little.

'Mother was right,' Berthe said. 'Although I hate to admit it, since Edma left I *have* been quite lonely. It is a beautiful day today. It is so wonderful to be out of the house. I feel like I have been stuck inside forever. So, let me show you Paris. It is an exciting time.' She looked around. 'It used to be so filthy, smelly and crowded, but look how clean and fresh it is now. Do you know what is happening?'

'No.'

'Napoléon appointed George-Eugène Haussmann twenty years ago, to create a new city. He has demolished whole sections to create these wonderful new boulevards and garden squares. And you can see the river now. Look at the light sparkling on the water.'

Louise looked at the fetid brown sludge of the Seine. The light struggled to muster up a glimmer. That was an improvement?

'It's a bit smelly,' she said. 'Sorry.'

'Smelly? I do not smell anything. Look, the light has flooded in. They are calling Paris "The City of Light" now.' Berthe gazed around her. 'Some people say Haussmann is destroying the character of the city, but I think it is much nicer like this, much better than those twisted, dark lanes.'

They passed along the elegant Champs-Elysées towards Notre Dame Cathedral. It looked the same, yet different. It was like déjà vu – just as she remembered, but fresher and brighter.

Is it still déjà vu if I've seen it before, but in the future?

'The Île de la Cité was a rabble of shacks, damp, dilapidated filthy streets running with sewage, full of thieves, infested with disease,' Berthe said. 'Now look. It is bright and open. Is it not wonderful?'

'Yes, it is beautiful,' Louise said. And it was. Paris without the traffic, the noise, and the air pollution. 'Can we get down and walk a bit now?'

'Yes, it is possible here. Look – do you see the new bridges over the Seine?'

'Yes, they're new, aren't they?'

'Yes, let us go over to Notre Dame. You must see it.'

They crossed over one of the bridges and walked towards the cathedral.

'You can see the front of it now,' Berthe said. 'They have cleared away the shambles and shacks. It was restored ten years ago, thanks to Victor Hugo. His story about the hunchback made everyone realise how they had neglected it. They have added a new spire, look.' She pointed. 'And do you see the lovely stained-glass windows?'

Louise gazed up at the magnificent Gothic cathedral, its three arched doorways, the rose window and the spire, standing tall and proud, piercing the bright blue sky. This wonderful building had stood for hundreds of years and in *her* time it had almost been destroyed. The fantastic grotesque gargoyles looked down, snarling at her, designed to keep evil spirits away from the church. *She* was the evil spirit here, from the future which would fail them so badly. A lump grew in her throat. She couldn't bear to tell Berthe what would happen to her beautiful cathedral.

She turned away towards the cafés with awnings spilled over the streets, men drinking coffee and reading newspapers. The smells of fruit, oysters and fresh bread wafted over from the jumble of stalls. Women in shawls sold fresh fruit and vegetables from baskets on carts. Sellers shouted, horses neighed, children played.

'After the siege, everyone is desperately trying to get back to normal,' Berthe said. 'At least there is food now.'

'Siege. What siege?' Louise said, looking around.

'You do not know?' Berthe stopped and stared at Louise.

'Sorry, I was never very good at history.'

'History?' Berthe stared at her. 'You know about the war with the Prussians?'

Louise shook her head.

'We were at war with the Prussians, who besieged Paris,' Berthe said as if talking to a child. 'They were determined to starve the city into submission.'

'What? *Paris?*

'We were lucky. Our family was able to escape to the country before it got too bad, but here there was no food. Butchers were selling cats, dogs, rats. Nearly every animal in the zoo was eaten.'

'Really?'

'People starved. Smallpox killed hundreds, many children. Paris had no option but to surrender. And then there was the disaster of the Commune ... But oh, let us not dwell on that. Look out!'

A box fell off a cart and apples tumbled around their feet. Louise jumped out of the way, trying not to stand on any of them.

'Be careful,' Berthe said to the driver.

'Sorry, mademoiselles,' he said and cuffed his boy on the head.

Louise leant down to help pick up the apples, but she couldn't bend very far in her corset.

'What are you doing? Leave them,' Berthe said and pulled her away.

They walked on for a while. Louise was struggling to walk in her long heavy skirts. She had to take tiny steps.

'Can we go to that café?' Louise said, exhausted already, her head reeling with the awful history. How had she never heard about any of this?

'Oh no, respectable women do not do that. That is another rule. You cannot go into cafés. They will think you are a prostitute. You cannot go there, do this, do that. So many rules for women.'

'I don't know how you can do anything at all in all these clothes,' Louise, tugging at her tight corset.

'Yes, they are uncomfortable, are they not? Men keep us trussed up like chickens so we cannot spread our wings.' She indicated a group of young men in black suits walking casually past. 'Look at them striding around as if they own the city. Well, they do, it is true.'

'Do you know that in China they used to bind women's feet, to make them small and pretty? They could hardly walk at all. They must do that now, I mean, in 1871, in China.'

'Is that true? How did they do that?'

'I don't know. With cloth, I suppose.'

'So, if you really do come from the future, what do you wear in *your* time?' Berthe said.

'Trousers, jeans, leggings. Much more casual, comfortable clothes. So, it *does* get better. In my time, women are equal, mostly, well, nearly, although some women still wear high heels for some reason. But we have a fabric called Lycra, and shoes called trainers.'

'What are ... *trainers?*'

'They're, er, special bouncy shoes for going running.'

'Bouncy? Why do you have to run?'

'To keep fit.'

'Keep fit? What is that?'

It would be impossible to explain fitness to Berthe so Louise said, 'Don't you ever feel like just running down this street as fast as you can?'

'Yes, I do, I often feel like running – running away,' Berthe said. She stared down the boulevard. 'All these rules about clothes, how we behave, everything. It is all so very tiring. Running away would be a pleasure.'

'You can't wear this, you can't show that – an ankle, a knee, a shoulder,' Louise said. 'Through history, different cultures, it goes on and on. You know, I think men control women because they can't control themselves.'

'Yes,' Berthe said, turning to Louise. 'You are absolutely right.'

They continued walking.

'You do say the most extraordinary things, Louise,' Berthe said, 'but I cannot believe you are from the future. How can you prove it to me?'

Louise could tell Berthe more about the future but that wouldn't prove anything. She didn't have her phone, which would have been good. But it wouldn't work anyway – there wouldn't be a signal. What did she have? Only her body. She had her ears pierced, but anyone could do that.

'I know. Look at my fillings.' She opened her mouth and pointed to the fillings in her molars.

'I do not see anything. What are fillings?'

'They fix your teeth. But they're white fillings, of course, so you can't see them. Oh well, I don't know how to prove it to you. You'll just have to believe me.'

'Or believe that you are crazy,' Berthe said. 'I cannot believe these stories you tell me. No one can travel from the future to the past.' And, after a pause, 'Your teeth are very good, though, and you have an exceptionally good imagination.'

Berthe took Louise by the arm and they walked on along the newly built embankments by the side of the Seine.

Louise relaxed a little. Maybe Berthe was warming to her, even if she didn't believe her. But she should stop telling her about the future in case it was "interfering" with history, although surely describing clothes couldn't do any harm?

'It is so lovely being able to walk by the river now,' Berthe said.

She pointed out the huge barges which held large lumps of sandstone waiting to be turned into the next boulevard. There was a loud crash in the distance ahead of them and an enormous plume of dust billowed up. Labourers hitched to ropes were pulling down the walls of houses, rows of houses fell, creating huge piles of rubble. Dust blew everywhere, carts, horses and men turned white. Tools cutting stone screeched and droned as workers shouted and swore.

Louise put her hand over her nose, trying not to breathe in the dust and musty smells of the demolition.

'There was a lot of damage during the bombardment of the city,' Berthe said. 'Some of the buildings in danger of collapse are being pulled down. Others are being demolished for more new boulevards. Over there you can still find parts of the old city.'

'What about the people who lived there? Where will they go?'

'Haussmann has built new houses outside the city for them, wonderful clean houses. Much better.'

That seemed doubtful, but Louise didn't say anything. She didn't want to annoy Berthe, just as it seemed she was beginning to be accepted by her.

And it wasn't her place, or her time, after all.

CHAPTER 8

THE SOIRÉE

The house was in uproar when they got back. Cornélie was issuing instructions to the servants who were rushing around, piling fruit onto silver plates, polishing crystal glasses and arranging embroidered napkins. It was only mid-afternoon, but Cornélie told Berthe and Louise to go and get ready.

It turned out that dressing for the soirée was even more elaborate than the morning's palaver. Berthe found an embroidered silk dress decorated with pearls for Louise. Giselle put her hair up into an elaborate coiffure, powdered her arms and pushed silk Cuban-heeled slippers onto her feet. Louise wasn't giggling now. She felt ridiculous, dressed up like a doll. She adjusted her hair, wiggled around in her even tighter corset and tugged at her dress, trying to get comfortable. She looked at herself in the mirror. If only she had her phone with her, she could take a selfie and send it to Chloe and say: "Guess where I am?" Paul would have told her she looked ridiculous.

She turned away from her reflection. This was absurd. Why hadn't she gone back yet? How was she supposed to get through this evening? Her French was probably good enough, although it was different from the more formal version the people she had met so far were speaking. But how was she to behave? She didn't know the rules and etiquette of this time. Would they accept her? Maybe she could pretend to be ill and stay in her room, but she didn't want to annoy them. She would have to try to fit in.

Draped and decorated, adorned and ornamented, she took a deep breath and carefully went down the stairs, holding onto the banister. Berthe's father, Edme-Tiburce was standing at the bottom. He introduced himself.

'Just call me Tiburce.'

Berthe had told Louise that he was a local prefect, a high government official. He looked a bit severe, tall with white hair and long white whiskers, but he had kind eyes and welcomed Louise warmly. She relaxed a little.

'Are you feeling better?' he asked.

'Yes, thank you,' she said.

The carriages started arriving, and Berthe came down the stairs, stunningly elegant in a close-fitting black gown with a black choker necklace and silver earrings. Everything about her was tightly controlled: her hair, posture, expression. In the hall, Louise stood just behind her, trying to keep her own costume, and her mind, in place. She had no idea how she was supposed to greet people when they arrived.

A carriage rumbled up, and the first guest to enter was Édouard, a tall, handsome, sophisticated man in his forties. He had a bushy beard, long curly fair hair, and sharp, intense eyes. Broad shouldered with a slim waist, he was very elegantly dressed in black top hat and coat, red silk cravat with white spots, lemon suede gloves, shiny black shoes and a silver-topped cane.

Wow!

Louise was introduced as a family friend from Brittany.

'It is a delight to meet you, Louise,' he said, taking her hand, kissing it and giving her a piercing look. A tingle jingled up her spine.

Then came his wife, Suzanne. She was surprisingly different, plump, pretty and placid, a blue-eyed blond smothered in a huge, frilly white dress with a velvet lilac choker, a bit older than her husband.

Next, Eugénie-Désirée, Édouard's mother, tiny and graceful, dressed in black. She had a small tight face with sharp features, arched eyebrows, a thin mouth, and small alert eyes. No nonsense, a bit like Cornélie.

Eugène, Édouard's brother, was tall and handsome with a bushy beard. Another beard – they must be in fashion, Louise thought. He had a twinkle in his bright blue eyes which he aimed at Louise.

Who knew that men in the past were so attractive?

As more people arrived, there was a confusion of names amongst the gleaming top hats, canes, scarves, shawls, and huge, sumptuous dresses. Giselle and the butler circled with crystal glasses of champagne on shiny silver trays. Louise lost track of all the people she was introduced to. The chandeliers sparkled in the candlelight, as did the conversation around her. She kept in the background, listening, and watching how the other women stood and held their glasses. She copied their postures and expressions and tried to smile at anyone who looked at her.

This was the first of the Tuesday soirées to be held at the Morisots' home since they had returned to Paris after the war and everyone was catching up with each other. Édouard's wife and his mother had been in the Pyrenees during the siege, but he had stayed in Paris with Eugène to defend the city from the Prussians.

'Paris has been so sad,' Édouard said. 'Thousands died during the siege from illness and starvation. Then, unbelievably, it got worse.'

'What happened?' Louise said. She couldn't contain her curiosity, but no one seemed surprised that she didn't know anything. She was from Brittany, after all.

Édouard explained that after the war and the siege, the working class felt the government had failed them. So, they established the Commune of Paris, a communist society, a republic. They raised the red flag over the Hôtel de Ville and proclaimed a new France, a society of justice and liberty.

'But of course, it all ended in tragedy,' Édouard said to the group gathered around him. He was used to holding an audience. 'You know my friend, Émile Zola? He was at the heart of it all.'

'Émile Zola, the writer?' Louise whispered to Eugène, who was standing next to her.

'Yes. You've heard of him?' Eugène said. 'How do you –?

'Shhh!'

'The government sent troops out against the Commune,' Édouard continued. 'There were fires across the city for days, and then a massacre, a bloodbath, for a whole week.'

'Twenty-, maybe thirty-thousand were killed,' Eugène said.

Louise's mouth fell open. Thirty thousand people? She'd been to Paris so many times. Why did she not know about this horrific history?

Édouard sighed. 'Neighbours fought on different sides, soldiers against rebels. They killed each other. It's heart-breaking. I do not know how we can ever move forward from this.'

He bowed his head in despair. The others fell into a long awkward silence.

'Today I heard that they're going to build a large church on the top of Montmartre, to recognise those who died during the war,' Tiburce said.

'A church on Montmartre!' Berthe said. She turned to Louise in astonishment. Louise smiled. So Berthe *had* been listening to what she'd said in the carriage. Would she believe she was from the future now?

'The bishop says that the defeat of Paris in the siege was divine punishment for our sins,' Tiburce said. 'He thinks that after the Revolution, the city sunk into such total decadence that we brought it on ourselves. The church will be called the Sacré-Cœur.'

'The Sacré-Cœur?' Berthe whispered.

'It will sit astride Montmartre,' Édouard said, 'and the authority of the government will crush the spirit out of the rebels.'

Berthe came over to Louise's side. 'It is true then? The church on Montmartre?'

'Yes, I told you, the Sacré-Cœur.'

Berthe reached out and touched Louise's arm, 'Are you really from the future?'

'Yes.'

Berthe gazed at her in astonishment. Louise shrugged.

'Well, let us not get too morose about it all,' Cornélie was saying. The discussion on the war had gone on long enough; her soirée was becoming depressing. 'I am sure now the fighting is over we can all get back to normal. And Suzanne, you must be glad to be back with Édouard?'

Suzanne agreed and talked about her stay in the Pyrenees, the fabulous cheeses and the recipes she'd found.

Cornélie turned to Louise and Berthe and whispered, 'I think she was eating the whole time she was there. Édouard must have been shocked to see her, the way her figure had bloomed when he saw her again!'

Louise spluttered into her champagne and Berthe laughed.

'I hope things don't return to exactly as they were before the war,' Édouard's mother said. 'Remember last year, Édouard, you got into that duel with Louis Duranty? You were nearly killed!'

'I know, it was quite ridiculous,' Édouard said. 'First I slapped him over his review of one of my paintings and we ended up in a sword fight! How could we have gone to such absurd extremes over a painting review? Luckily, neither of us was killed and I only wounded him slightly. Now we both agree now the whole affair was completely silly. Too much absinthe at Café Guerbois, I think.'

Édouard turned away to speak to some others who had arrived.

'I'm glad he has stopped going to that dreadful café,' his mother said to Cornélie. 'He has such a volatile personality. He gets into trouble so easily.'

Louise watched Édouard closely; he was charming and intelligent, and attractive, like an older version of Paul with the same confidence.

The butler arrived with the drinks tray again. Louise was

overcoming her nerves by drinking champagne. The butler had become her friend. She found herself chatting to Suzanne who was warm and relaxed, very different from her husband.

Occasionally, Louise looked over at Berthe. She always seemed to be at Édouard's side, eyes sparkling. Louise had not seen her so animated before. They seemed to be discussing art. Cornélie occasionally tried to interrupt their tête à tête.

'Berthe, we're just discussing the new department store, *Le Bon Marché*. Would you like to come with us to see the latest fashions?'

Berthe ignored her mother and continued talking to Édouard while Suzanne carried on chatting to Louise. She didn't seem to mind Berthe monopolising her husband.

Édouard's mother called Suzanne over to talk to someone and Louise was left on her own. She stared into her champagne glass. The bubbles swirled up, fizzed and popped. They looked like the way the inside of her head felt.

Will I just pop, disappear into the air any minute? Back to Mum's cottage? That would be good.

'You look like you'd like to dive in there.'

Louise jerked her head up and blushed.

'Eugène,' he said with a little bow. 'And you are Louise, from Brittany.'

'Yes.'

'Have you been in Paris long?

'Er, no. I just arrived yesterday.'

'And how is Brittany this summer?'

'Em, fine.'

Louise didn't know anything about Brittany. She swallowed and tried to think of something to say to Eugène. To fill the space, she started talking about how she loved the sea (Brittany was on the sea, wasn't it?) and about her attempts to paint it. Eugène said he did a bit of painting himself, but he wasn't very good. He knew what she meant about the difficulty of capturing light on the water. They chatted about painting for a while and Louise found herself telling him about her boyfriend – why did she not say "husband"? – and how he'd left her for another woman. Why was she telling him this?

'I cannot believe anyone would leave you,' Eugène said, twinkling at her again. He refilled her glass and Louise felt her cheeks warm. Surely she wasn't blushing? How embarrassing! Her fingers started tingling. Was she beginning to disappear?

'Can you still see me?' she said.

'Eh, yes,' Eugène said, staring at her.

'Good,' she said. The tingling in her hands faded.

Cornélie called them to the drawing room. It was time to listen to Suzanne playing the piano: Chopin. Eugène sat next to Louise, who was having trouble focusing. Suzanne was becoming a bit blurry. Now she seemed to be playing a duet with herself.

'She's very good,' Louise said, too loudly.

'She used to be our piano teacher, mine and Édouard's,' Eugène whispered.

'What? Édouard married his piano teacher?'

'Shh,' Cornélie said from the front row.

*

At the end of the evening, the family and Louise stood in the hallway, saying farewell to the guests.

'Édouard, may I bring Louise to your studio tomorrow?' Berthe said. 'She'd love to see your work. She does some painting herself.'

Louise looked at Berthe. Surely this was overstating things.

'Of course, that would be lovely,' Édouard said. 'Come in the morning.'

'I'll come along, too,' Eugène said, smiling at Louise.

*

Louise struggled up the wobbly staircase to her room and flopped onto her sumptuous bed. The opulent bedroom spun gently around her. How fascinating all these people were: Berthe, Cornélie, Tiburce, Édouard, Suzanne, Eugène. They were loads more interesting than her own friends at home, the few she had left.

Berthe's family was so kind and welcoming. She couldn't believe they'd accepted her, welcomed her. It was so nice to be part of a family, a real family. She was the only particle in her quantum family now. Now her mum had died. She sighed. *What a day!* Seeing the city, the soirée. Eugène was nice. And he seemed to like her. At least one man paid her some attention. *Eugène.* Maybe she could stay here and marry him. She wouldn't need to divorce Paul because it was 1871 and she hadn't married him yet! She could hide out here. She wouldn't need to deal with anything – especially Paul. 'To hell with Paul,' she said to the nineteenth-century bedroom. She took off her wedding ring and stuffed it in the back of the drawer of the bedside table.

CHAPTER 9

ÉDOUARD'S STUDIO

Louise sleepily stretched her hand over the bed to touch Paul's warm body. She liked to stroke his chest, his stomach, and down to the soft fur beneath his navel.

Her hand searched, but of course, he wasn't there. She remembered that lately Paul had been turning away from her, pretending to be asleep. She should have recognised the signs.

She rubbed her head and blinked. She was still in Paris, in 1871. When was she going to go home? What would she say to Paul when she got back? He'd never believe her. But he was having an affair so he wouldn't care.

Her head throbbed. Why had she drunk so much champagne?

After breakfast, Berthe was in a hurry to get to Édouard's studio. Giselle crammed Louise into the blue outfit from the previous day and Berthe bustled her into the carriage. Louise sat with her head pounding. Her right hand kept drifting over to her left hand and fiddling with her ring finger. It was empty, sad, and exposed. *I should have put my ring back on.*

It was her first day as Berthe's chaperone. All she had to do was fit in, be invisible, do whatever Berthe wanted. It would be easy.

'I am excited for you to see his paintings,' Berthe said, rubbing her gloved hands together. She was in a very good mood today. 'Édouard is such a wonderful artist. I have not been able to go to his studio since before the war. I am so looking forward to seeing his new work.'

Louise sighed quietly. She hated going to look at other people's art, trying to be polite when it was so often terrible. It was hard to know what to say. "That's interesting" was often the best she could manage. It was worse when people insisted on looking at *her* paintings. They'd say: "I like the way you've done the mountains", pointing to what was supposed to be clouds or "I like that bit", pointing to one tiny area in a corner. Even worse, they said nothing at all and there was an excruciating silence.

The carriage clopped along the cobbles from Passy to Clichy. Louise assumed they were heading for some tiny attic studio, perhaps in Montmartre. They reached the Place d'Étoile and turned into a smart new boulevard, Rue de Saint-Petersbourg, then stopped at a grand entrance. They climbed down from the carriage, and went up the stairs to a first-floor apartment where they entered an elegant hallway. *An art studio? Here?*

Suzanne was just leaving. She greeted them and introduced Louise to a handsome young man in his late teens. He was smartly dressed in a black jacket, light yellow trousers, and a straw hat with a black band. He would fit in as a hipster in London today, she thought.

'This is Léon, my brother,' Suzanne said. 'We're going shopping. You must come with me one day, Louise. You'll love our new shops.'

Berthe and Louise entered Édouard's studio. It was huge, a vast room with floor to ceiling windows leading onto a balcony overlooking the boulevard. The room was packed: paintings hung on every wall or stacked on the floor. Several easels held half-finished paintings, the tables covered in paints and brushes. Shiny helmets, feathers of all shapes and sizes, Spanish clothes, guitars, swords, coloured drapes, hats of all kinds, jackets and uniforms, vases full of flowers, silver pots and plants – so much stuff scattered around. Chairs and a chaise longue were crammed in beside a long table which was set with water, glasses, fruit and pastries.

'Wow!' Louise said.

'First you must see this one,' Berthe said, pulling Louise along for what seemed like a mile across the studio.

'This is ...'

'*Olympia*!' Louise said, putting her hand over her mouth. 'Oh my God!'

She was looking at one of the most famous paintings ever. A naked woman lying on a chaise longue, staring directly out of the scene, her hand strategically placed over her crotch. She had a pink flower in her hair and a black neck ribbon. One of her slippers was off, the other teasingly balanced on her toes. A black maid emerged from the dark background with a newly delivered bouquet of flowers. But it is the naked woman who is most striking: her unashamed pose, her challenging gaze, as if to say: "Yes, I'm naked, so what?" To see it so close, so directly, was astonishing.

Louise slowly turned to Édouard.

'What, er, what is your surname?' she asked in a faint voice.

'Oh, didn't I tell you last night? It's Manet. I am Édouard Manet,' he said with a little bow and a smile.

Édouard Manet!

Louise thumped down into the nearest chair, put her head in her hands and heard herself made a strange, choking sound.

'Are you all right?' Édouard said.

'I think perhaps her, er, clothes are a bit too tight,' Berthe said, coming over to Louise. She gave her a little shake, pulled her up and started explaining the painting *Olympia* to her with great enthusiasm.

'You see, she's like a classical painting, like Titian's *Venus of Urbino* but she is clearly Victorine, Édouard's model. She's posing as a professional prostitute, a courtesan, having flowers delivered from a client. And look, the cat is brilliant.'

A black cat arched its back at the end of the bed. It glared out of the painting, flicking its tail.

'I painted the tail suggestively raised,' Édouard laughed. 'And Victorine, I painted as herself, charming and confident, not like those ridiculously submissive naked women in the Salon named after some

Greek Goddess or other. There's always a crowd of men peering at them closely, ogling them.'

'Édouard is so modern! He thinks about the woman's point of view,' Berthe said. 'But *Olympia* shocked everyone. They said she was shameless and vulgar. There was complete uproar!'

'They had to put guards next to it to protect it,' Édouard said.

'Édouard is mocking the hypocrisy of society, you see, the men who pretend not to visit prostitutes. The critics were too stupid to see this, of course.' Berthe smiled at Édouard.

'Actually, no one appreciated her at all,' he said. 'I was quite hurt.'

'He even stopped going out for a while, can you believe it?' Berthe said, putting her arm through Édouard's.

Louise stared at them open-mouthed.

Berthe disentangled herself from Édouard and dragged Louise to the other side of the studio.

'Now look at this one. '

Louise gasped. *Le Déjeuner sur L'Herbe*! Two fully clothed men sitting in a park having a picnic with a naked woman; the men, in black, are chatting together, the one on the right making a point with an outstretched arm. A woman in a white diaphanous gown crouches in the background. She's too big, too high, out of proportion and perspective with the rest of the painting. The gleaming bright figure of the naked woman in the foreground stands out against the darkness of the men and the background. She's sitting with her hand on her chin, turned to the viewer, as if to say: "Yes, just sitting here, got a problem?" It's a bizarre scene.

'This was rejected by the Salon,' Édouard said. 'Along with two thousand eight hundred others.'

This was rejected? One of the most famous paintings in the world?

'The Salon said this painting was not good enough for them,' Édouard said. 'They just want the same old boring traditional paintings all the time. They all look like brown sauce to me.'

He turned away in disgust.

'The problem is,' Berthe said to Louise, 'that woman seems to have just taken off her clothes in the park!'

'Yes, yes,' Louise said, pointing to the painting, 'and there are all sorts of spatial problems. The woman in background is way too big and ...'

Louise stopped. They were staring at her.

'Er, yes,' Berthe said, looking at Édouard who raised his eyebrows.

Oops. It was a bit unlikely that a young woman from Brittany would know this sort of thing. She clamped her lips shut.

'I called it *The Bath*,' Édouard said. 'Everyone else called it *Le Déjeuner sur L'Herbe*. It's true there's no bathing going on, but no one is having lunch, either,' he said. He laughed and wiped his brow.

'It caused a storm of controversy,' Berthe said. 'People said it was obscene. A man even hit it with his stick, did he not, Édouard? Men hurried their wives and children past it.'

'Then returned to stare at it alone,' Édouard said. 'Anyway, the Salon thought it was a provocative taunt. They thought I had deliberately insulted the traditions of the Academy, but I really didn't intend that.'

'Édouard is notorious now,' Berthe said, glowing.

'Yes, notorious, but not a good artist apparently,' Édouard said.

He turned to Louise.

'Well, what do you think?' he asked her. 'You're very quiet. Oh, I suppose I've offended you too, like all the others.'

Louise put her hand to her mouth. She hadn't said a word about his paintings. He thought she didn't like them!

'Oh no, yes, I mean, they're wonderful, totally brilliant! I love them,' she said, waving her arms around at the paintings.

'I'm so pleased,' Édouard said, now looking a bit confused by this country woman's great enthusiasm.

'But can you explain,' Louise said, 'what is the Salon? Why do you care about them?'

'They are the arbiters of everything, the old dodderers,' Édouard said.

'They are the official government art establishment,' Berthe said. 'The academic jury chooses the so-called *best* art every year for their exhibition, two dozen rooms crammed with paintings, hung according to their importance. But the jury is *so* old fashioned. All they want is historical, mythical and biblical scenes with a moral lesson, or celebrating the glory of France.'

'Yet it is the only place to exhibit,' Édouard said. 'Your reputation is established there. It is where you find buyers.'

He took them over to another painting.

'Look, here's one with Berthe. I did this a couple of years ago. It's called *The Balcony.*'

Louise didn't know this one: three figures on a balcony, framed by the strong green of the window shutters and the metal struts of the balcony. A man and a woman are standing behind Berthe who is sitting holding a fan, leaning forward over the balcony, preoccupied with her own thoughts. It looks like she has nothing in common with the flighty, trivial people behind her. She looks out over the boulevard, confined behind the bars of the balcony.

'It's Berthe with Fanny; they didn't get on,' Édouard said. 'That's why they're looking away from each other so grimly.'

'You made us pose at least fifteen times – no wonder I look jaded,' Berthe said.

'Oh, you were in a bad mood because Edma had fallen in love with my friend, Adolphe, and was going to leave you at home with your mother,' Édouard said.

'Huh,' Berthe said.

'You are always a delight to paint, my dear Berthe,' Édouard said, taking her arm.

Berthe glowed a little more.

'This one got into the Salon exhibition,' Berthe said, 'but Édouard was so nervous, he could not move. What a state he was in! First he was told his painting was dreadful, then the next minute he was told they were sure it would be very successful.'

Berthe looked around the room.

'Where is the latest one you did of me? *Repose?*' she asked Édouard.

'Ah, I lent it to Durand-Ruel. I'm hoping he'll buy it. It is a faint hope. Shall I get it back so Louise can see it?'

'Yes, please,' Berthe said.

Louise nodded. Why would Édouard Manet want to show her one of his paintings?

They were interrupted by a clomping of footsteps. A very well-dressed man stepped into the room: black frock coat with lace handkerchief in its pocket, blue neckerchief, stovepipe hat, walking stick and dark eyes.

'Edgar! Lovely to see you.' Édouard and Berthe went over to greet him.

'You must meet Louise. This is Louise from Brittany,' Édouard said. 'Louise, this is Edgar.'

'Nice to meet you, Edgar,' Louise said and took a deep breath. 'And may I ask – what's your surname?'

'Degas. I am Edgar Degas,' he said, with a little tilt of his chin.

'Ah, *Degas!*' Louise tried to stifle a hysterical giggle.

'Do you find my name funny?' said Edgar Degas, insulted.

'No, it's just ...' Louise made an odd squeaky sound.

'Louise has just arrived from the country,' Berthe said. 'I think she's a bit overawed by the city.' She glared at Louise.

Édouard, Edgar and Berthe walked around the studio talking about the paintings. Louise shook her head and tried to pull herself together. Manet, Degas and Morisot, in one room, with her.

Unbelievable! She closed her eyes and pinched herself hard. She opened her eyes. They were all still there. *Don't let me disappear now. This is fascinating. If only Mum was here, she'd absolutely love this.*

She went over to find that they were talking about the Salon.

'I don't believe there will be an exhibition this year, it's too soon after the siege, but we should start thinking about next year,' Édouard said.

'What will you paint for it? Something that will be passed by the jury this time?' Edgar said.

'I don't know. It's so frustrating. I really think it is time to reform the Salon, the jury system. Bring it up to date,' Édouard said. 'I don't believe the jury should be the arbiters. They reject too much good art.'

'I agree,' Berthe said.

'Our paintings are all hung right next to each other, far too close, jammed up all around the walls,' Edgar said. 'It's a terrible display. I mean, *we* are the artists, so we should be able to place them as *we* like. Even a shoemaker can display his shoes as he wants. It's not as if there is not enough room in there.'

'Yes, there's plenty of room, rooms of room,' Édouard said.

'My painting of Edma was hung so high no one could see it,' Berthe said. 'It was impossible to come to any sort of judgment about it. They are *our* paintings. We have a right to have them displayed properly.'

These artists couldn't have their work displayed as they wished? Louise scratched her head. Weren't they famous yet, in 1871? She clearly didn't know enough about art history.

The discussion about the Salon exhibition continued until Eugène arrived. He came straight over to Louise's side, smiling. He suggested they all go out, but Berthe had arranged to meet her mother, to visit some cousin or other; she couldn't get out of it.

Louise looked at her. 'Berthe? Would it be all right if I went?'

Berthe reluctantly agreed. She would meet Louise back at the studio later in the afternoon. Edgar would not come; he had work to do, so Eugène and Édouard would take Louise, the country bumpkin, out and about in the city.

CHAPTER 10

CAFÉ GUERBOIS

L ouise stepped out onto the street with Édouard and Eugène. Her heart was racing! Surely there was no better company in all of Paris. She wanted to see as much as possible – this was Paris, in 1871!

It was a busy day in The City of Light. Well-dressed men ambled along the boulevards, twirling their canes, some tipping their hats to Louise.

'It looks like they're parading,' she said.

'Ah yes,' Édouard said. 'The *flâneur* is the new thing. Paris is the theatre. What you must decide is which one you want to be, *flâneur* or viewer. I think it is best to be both.'

They strolled along and Édouard told Louise how he had found inspiration for many of his paintings in the streets of Paris.

'I first saw Victorine coming out of a café with her guitar and drew her on the spot. Then there was the ragpicker, and an old musician I painted. This is the best place to find subjects.'

An old woman was sitting on the ground selling apples from a basket. Édouard went over and crouched down to talk to her. He pulled out his sketchbook and began drawing her. The woman looked at him, confused at the attention. Louise watched him. It was fascinating to see him in action.

'How did Édouard first become an artist?' she asked Eugène.

'Well, it was quite a struggle for him. Father did not approve at all.'

Eugène explained that their father had been a decorated, highly regarded official in the Ministry of Justice. He had wanted Édouard, his eldest son, to follow him into the legal profession.

'Édouard wasn't interested. He persuaded Father that he should take up a naval career instead. He failed those exams because he didn't bother studying, then he went on a training ship to Rio de Janeiro just before his seventeenth birthday. He sailed for seven months, watching the changing colours of the sky mostly, and arrived in time to enjoy the Rio carnival. But he didn't get into the naval school.'

'He didn't care, I suppose.'

Eugène nodded. 'Eventually, Father gave up and allowed him to become an art student. But Édouard always felt that Father was disappointed in him, that he thought that art was not a respectable profession.'

'And you, you paint too, you said?' Louise said.

'Yes, a little, but how can I compete with that?'

They looked over at Édouard. He was charming a young woman into posing for him.

'I take care of the business side of the family,' said Eugène, 'and trying to keep Édouard out of trouble.'

'It must be difficult having a brother like that.'

Eugène looked at Louise in surprise.

'You have understood the struggle of my entire life in a moment,' he said and offered her his arm. 'Sometimes I feel like I'm a small sapling in the shadow of a tall oak, struggling for light,' he said with a smile.

Louise happily took his arm. *He doesn't take himself too seriously,* she thought.

Men and women rode by on elegant horses. One woman riding side-saddle was swathed in layers of fabric and ribbons with feathers in her hair.

'How much material can one woman wear?' Louise said. 'How can she ride in all that?'

'She has at least four skirts on. And look!'

Eugène pointed to a man walking a turtle on a leash.

'He is trying too hard.' Eugène picked up a cabbage from a stall next to them and balanced it on top of his top hat. 'How about that? Anything for attention!' he said and twirled around.

Louise laughed.

'Oi. Put that back if you're not buying it,' the stall owner said.

Eugène put the cabbage back and did a little dance along the pavement, whirling his cane. He swung around a lamppost.

'Ha, you're just like Gene Kelly,' Louise said smiling. 'Shame it's not raining.'

'What? Who's that?'

'Oh, er, never mind.' She watched Eugène walking along with his top hat and cane. Wasn't Gene Kelly's first name Eugène? This Eugène was just like him. He was probably a good dancer, too.

'I should call you "Gene",' Louise said. 'It suits you.'

'Whatever you wish, Louise,' Gene said. 'I've been called worse.' He smiled at her and tipped his hat, exactly like Gene Kelly. How did he know to do that?

Édouard caught up with them, stuffing his sketchbook into his pocket.

'Let's show Louise the new station,' he said.

They walked along the Rue de Rocher to the Gare St Lazare. Louise looked around the vast space and at the huge roof held up by iron columns. The sunlight beamed through the enormous skylights and filtered through the steam and grey smoke.

'It's like a cathedral,' Édouard said. 'A cathedral to progress, to the steam engine, our new god.'

'This is such an exciting time,' Gene said to Louise. 'You won't have seen this in Brittany, but the progress, the new inventions … It's incredible what's happening now.'

A train started up and there was a cacophony of hissing steam and clanging iron. The engine rumbled and the ground trembled. Crowds of travellers, porters and coalmen milled around. Dirty children in rags tried to sell them newspapers, fruit or bread.

'Look at that huge new clock,' Gene said. 'It's enormous! Well, I suppose you don't want to miss your train, Édouard.'

'They will have to organise time better right across the country so everyone will know what time the trains run. No one need ever be late for anything again,' Édouard said.

'Organise time? Isn't it already? Organised, I mean?' Louise said.

'Do *you* pay much attention to the time?' Édouard said. 'I know I don't.'

'We'll all need to get clocks and watches now,' Gene said.

'Ah, yes,' Édouard said. 'Time will become our other new god. We'll become slaves to its ticking hands.'

Louise glanced around her. People hadn't really been bothered about the exact time until now because they hadn't needed to. They had used the sun's slow movements. Time had moved gently across the sundial, through the days, months and seasons. That must be so relaxing. There must be such a freedom to life like that, without the tyranny of time dictating every moment.

A whistle blasted. She jumped. Now the steam engine had been invented, days would be punctuated by the demands of whistles and flags. Time would be grabbed by the scruff of the neck, sliced into hours, minutes and seconds. Hung, drawn and quartered, thrown into prison – time serving time.

'Louise,' Gene said.

She jerked around to face him. 'Yes?'

'We were saying how unusual it is that the classes are mixed up here – the bourgeois, the workers, the poor. I've only ever seen that here.'

'But everyone is ignoring each other. Look, pretending the others don't exist,' Édouard said. 'It's very strange.'

He took out his sketch book and started drawing the disconnected crowd.

A train made a loud snort and released a cloud of dirty smoke. It was like an angry dragon, impatient to get going. The air around them clogged with the acrid smell of burning coal.

'A cathedral, yes, a cathedral to climate change,' Louise said, coughing, wrinkling her nose. 'This is how it all begins: fossil fuels, pollution, global warming, melting ice caps, species extinction ...'

Gene was staring at her.

'What?' he said. 'What's climate change? And those other things?'

'Oh, em, never mind,' Louise said. She put her hand over her mouth. 'Can we go outside? I can't breathe.'

They left Édouard sketching in the station and went back out onto the boulevard. Louise took a deep breath of fresh air, cramming it into her crushed, corseted lungs. They were so excited about progress, so full of hope for the future but they had no idea how badly the future would let them down.

'Édouard will catch up with us,' said Gene, taking her arm. They wandered past some stalls set up to entice the passing travellers with fruit and pastries. A little boy in rags with bare feet was sitting crying under an empty stall.

'What's the matter, little fellow?' Gene said, crouching down to him. Through his sobs, the little boy told them that he had lost his mother. Gene took his hand and they set off to find her. She wasn't far, just at a stall round the corner. She thanked them for bringing him back. They walked on and heard her scolding him.

'He was lucky,' Gene said. 'A lot of children are abandoned, left to fend for themselves on the street. It's an outrage. You'd think we would be more civilised in this day and age.'

'Really? Abandoned? In Paris? That's awful.'

They walked on, but Louise was now dragging her feet, exhausted from carrying her curtains around.

'Let's go to a café. I'm tired,' she said.

'Well, respectable women don't go to cafés in Paris, Louise.'

'Oh, I know, but that's stupid.'

Gene paused. 'Yes, it is, isn't it? Why not? Times are changing. We'll go to Café Guerbois.'

'Is that the one Édouard mentioned last night? I thought he'd stopped going there.'

'That's what his mother thinks. He has two tables reserved every afternoon. We'll see him there.'

They walked up Avenue du Clichy to Café Guerbois. A few empty tables sat outside on the pavement. Inside, it was tiny. Lace curtains decorated the windows, and a line of pegs ran along the wall at the entrance, some holding shiny top hats. The friendly, fat proprietress, wearing a black dress and white apron, welcomed them. Two men already sat at a white-clothed table to the left of the door.

'Come and meet Émile. We were talking about him last night,' Gene said.

Émile Zola, the author! Louise had read *Thérèse Raquin,* his scandalous story about adultery and murder. How exciting to actually meet him!

'Émile, good to see you,' Gene said. 'This is Louise, she's visiting from Brittany.'

'Louise, lovely to meet you,' Émile said, getting up. He had a big bushy brown beard and a high forehead. His eyes were piercing, but warm.

'It's an absolute honour to meet you, Monsieur Zola,' she said.

Émile looked bemused at her enthusiasm.

'And this is Paul,' Émile said. 'He's also visiting from the country.'

Paul stood clumsily, nearly pushing his chair over, and nodded at her, not making eye contact. He was a young man, tall, round-shouldered, awkward. He had dark skin and, already, a receding hairline. His dirty crumpled blue trousers were held up with string.

'If you don't mind me asking, what's your surname?' Louise said. She had decided that she would check everyone's surname now.

'Cézanne,' Paul replied.

He sat down grumpily, leaving Louise standing with her mouth open. *Cézanne!*

Gene got a chair for her and encouraged her to sit.

'Paul is in Paris to sell some paintings,' Émile said.

'How many have you sold so far?' Louise said. She couldn't believe she was talking to Paul Cézanne!

'Pfff! None,' Paul said. 'I'll never sell anything. It's hopeless. I should have been a banker like my father said. I'm going to give it all up.'

'Oh no!' Louise said, putting her hand on his arm. 'You can't do that!'

Paul raised an eyebrow at her and glowered down at the table.

'You are a good painter, Paul,' Gene said. 'It's just a matter of time.'

Émile and Gene started talking about the critics. Émile launched into a tirade about the savaging they'd given him for *Thérèse Raquin*.

'They said it was pornography, depraved, disgusting. They called me hysterical. I admit there was adultery and murder in my novel but, really, the critics were offensive.'

Louise was only half listening. She was watching Paul Cézanne, trying to remember her art history. He was important for Cubism; hadn't Picasso called him "The Father of Us All"? That must have been later. This young man looked impoverished and dejected, uninterested in the conversation. He fiddled with his glass, moved the white milk jug a couple of inches to the left and the vase of flowers behind the salt and pepper pots. He turned his head to look at the arrangement from different angles and kept rearranging the objects, creating forms, and analysing shapes. He was oblivious to

Louise staring at him.

'Auguste, over here,' Camille said, waving to a man in the doorway.

'Louise, this is Auguste,' Gene said.

'Hallo, pleased to meet you,' Louise said. 'Please, if you don't mind me asking, what's your surname?'

'Renoir,' he said with a little bow.

Louise gazed at the young man – the wonderful Auguste Renoir! He was young, with a beard, a flat cap and gentle eyes. His jacket was old and worn, his shirt collar frayed. Auguste pulled up a chair.

'You had a narrow escape, I hear,' Gene said to him.

'Yes, the rebels of the Commune thought I was a spy when they found me painting by the Seine. They nearly threw me in the river. Luckily, one of the men recognised me and saved me at the last minute. It was a close thing.'

Renoir almost killed – that would have been a tragedy!

'Claude, come and meet Louise, our daring new friend,' Gene said, waving at another young man entering the café. 'Louise, this is Claude.'

'What's ...'

'*Monet!*' everyone said for Louise's benefit, laughing. Claude Monet, perhaps the most famous of them all. Louise gave him a strained smile, trying to hide her shock.

She sat and gazed at the men around the table. These painters had all known each other; that's what made this such an exceptional time in art history. They encouraged each other, supported each other, made leaps in their art that would have taken them much longer if they'd worked alone. Impressionism was born in this creative hot-house of artists. She'd always thought that this must have been one of the best times ever to be alive – Paris in the 1870s. Was that why she'd been transported here, to this time?

But they were so young, so poor! Claude's clothes were threadbare. He was handsome with a bushy black beard and beret, but he looked thin and haggard. Was he ill?

Gene ordered Claude a beer. 'You went to London to escape the war?' he asked him.

'Yes, and then to the Netherlands where I did twenty-five paintings,' Claude said.

'It's so good to see you again,' Auguste said. 'Maybe we could work together again. I enjoyed the time we spent painting at La Grenouillère last summer.'

La Grenouillère. Louise dragged a bit of art history up from the depths of her memory. Renoir and Monet's paintings of La Grenouillère, a fashionable bathing spot near Paris, had been groundbreaking.

'It's a boating resort,' Gene said to Louise.

'I know,' Louise said. 'Shhh.'

Gene raised his eyebrows.

Bit abrupt. 'Sorry,' Louise said.

'We were experimenting,' Auguste said. 'Claude's water was very good. He really captured the light.'

'I used large brushstrokes in three tones, greenish black, greenish brown and bluey white. It's so difficult to pin down the shimmer of light on water,' Claude said.

'Yes,' Louise said under her breath. She should have looked at a Monet when she was trying to paint the light on the sea in Luskentyre.

'I think the atmosphere there affected us, all the people, the loud parties. I'd never painted anything like that before,' Claude said.

'I'm painting the women of Montmartre now, at least the cheerful ones, in the dance halls,' Auguste said.

The Moulin de La Galette – was he painting that?

'You don't like serious subjects, do you?' Gene said to Auguste.

'Why paint miserable scenes? I would not enjoy that. That would be pointless,' said Auguste.

'And how is your family, Auguste?' Émile said.

'Fine,' he said.

'Is your father still a tailor in Montmartre? Are you living there?'

'Yes, it's the cheapest,' Auguste said. 'And you, Paul? Are you staying in Paris?'

'Ah, I don't have any money. I'll be forced to re-join my rotten family in Aix soon,' Paul said. 'They are boring beyond measure, the most disgusting people in the world.'

The others laughed but Paul was serious. He scowled into his beer.

'Why do we do it?' Auguste said. 'I'd make more money painting porcelain in a factory. We try to create something new, something to capture the beauty of the world, but no one wants to buy our art. I will have to go back to the factory soon, to survive.'

'And I have no more money for paint,' Claude said. 'I saw some of Constable and Turner's paintings in London. They see the sky, the water, so clearly; they paint with such wonderful freedom and lightness of touch. I want to paint like that, too.' He sighed. 'But I need to eat. My family needs fed. So, I am looking for work.'

'We make a new type of art for this new era,' Auguste said, 'but no one is interested.' He put his arm around Claude. 'Maybe one day someone will like our paintings, Claude.'

Louise sat back. She couldn't believe her ears. These brilliant artists were starving. They were desperate, hopeless.

All heads turned – Édouard Manet was entering the café. It was his appointed hour, late afternoon. Édouard was impressed to see Louise there.

'Well, Louise is fitting right in,' he said, 'even drinking beer in a café. We had better not tell Cornélie!'

Édouard joined the discussion about art. Louise sat quietly, hanging on every word. She seemed to be at the reunion of the future greatest artists of the nineteenth century. Painters at the cutting edge of art and none of them knew it. The Impressionists – they were light years ahead of their time. When did people begin to see it, to appreciate them? She wished once again that she had her phone; she'd love to take a selfie with them.

Now they were talking about Haussmann's changes to the city. Édouard, urbane, charming and charismatic, was holding court with his distinctive cracked voice.

'They are wiping out the homes of the poor, destroying communities to create grand homes for the bourgeoisie,' Édouard said. 'The delights of wandering through the maze of alleys in the old city will be no more. These modern boulevards are just vulgar materialism.'

'Haussmann's structures are so cold. The buildings are lined up like soldiers at review,' Auguste said. 'But I do like the light and air he has brought into the streets.'

The proprietress brought over some more beer.

'We have clean water and a sewage system now in this street,' she said. 'It used to be infested with rats, filth, hovels, shanties, full of thieves and beggars. I much prefer this.'

'But the poor suffer,' Émile said. 'The Commune was a result of that, the establishment ignoring them. No wonder they fought.'

Gene turned to Louise. 'What do you think of our new Paris, Louise? It must be quite a change from Brittany.'

Louise didn't answer.

'Louise?'

'Well, those old areas are unsanitary. So many people crammed together with no fresh water or sewage system. They're ideal environments for the spread of epidemics like cholera, typhus, TB.'

'Oh, is that right? I did not know,' Gene said. He looked astonished. Louise had said too much, again. She sat back in her chair and tried to make herself invisible.

'Have you heard about the church they're going to build on Montmartre? A huge, white building to dominate the city,' Édouard said.

'They want to destroy the Commune,' Claude said. 'This church has nothing to do with God, it's the establishment exerting their power. What we need is another revolution.'

Everyone stared into their beers.

'Well, it's nearly *the green hour*,' Édouard said, breaking the mood. 'Who's for an absinthe?'

'I'll have one,' Louise said, eager to experience everything of this new life.

'Are you sure?' Gene said. 'It's not called "the Goddess with Green Eyes" for nothing.'

'Or "The Green Fairy" because you go away with the fairies!' Auguste said.

'I've never tried it before,' Louise said. She felt herself blush. These people must think she was a bit mad; she veered from awkwardness to enthusiasm in a minute. It was so hard to figure out how to behave.

Gene left her side to order from the proprietress at the bar.

Édouard came over, pulled out Gene's chair and sat down beside her. Louise turned to him and took a deep breath. His eyes seemed to bore right into her, to her very soul. The intensity of his attention was unnerving.

'You know, I'm a keen observer of people, Louise, and there's something strange, something different about you,' he said quietly.

'You have no idea,' Louise said, meeting his gaze.

'No, but I'll enjoy finding out,' he said, smiling. He reached for her left hand and took her fingers into his. 'You've taken off your wedding ring. Now, why would you do that?'

Louise stared at him. Even Berthe hadn't noticed that. She struggled to think of an answer.

'Excuse me,' Gene said to Édouard. 'I was sitting there.'

Édouard smiled at Louise and got up without a word. Gene looked furious.

'Here you are, Louise,' he said, giving her the absinthe. 'Better drink up. We must go back and meet Berthe. She should at the studio by now.'

Louise gulped down a little of her drink – it was strong and pretty disgusting – and jumped up, glad to escape Édouard. She had better avoid him. He was too astute and too attractive. Dangerous.

They walked back to the studio and Gene took Louise's arm. Her mind was racing. Meeting these amazing artists, hearing them talking about their paintings, their ideas – her mother would have been fascinated. Louise bit her lip to stop herself from crying.

'How do you know so much about them?' Gene said.

'What? Who?'

'You seem to know a little about Claude, Auguste and Paul.'

'Er, I don't really. I was just interested in what they were saying.'

'It's a shame they struggle so much. Did you know that Claude tried to kill himself a few years ago?'

'What? Monet did?'

'Yes, Claude; he threw himself in the Seine. His son had just been born and he despaired that he could not support his family.'

'That's awful!'

'Yes, I worry for him. He's such a good painter but so poor. He can't sell anything.'

Louise tried to imagine a world without Monet's waterlilies, his cathedrals and haystacks. Impossible.

CHAPTER 11

EVA

B erthe was at the studio.

'I have been waiting a very long time.'

Louise looked at her wrist to check the time, but of course she didn't have her watch. Anyway, it turned out that Berthe had only arrived ten minutes earlier. Louise sat quietly at the table beside her.

Adèle, Édouard's maid, produced wine, bread and cheese from a room at the back. The smells of cheese merged with those of turpentine and paint.

'You went to Café Guerbois?' Berthe said to Louise. 'Oh I wish I could have come with you! But you must not tell Mother, she would not approve. Who was there?'

Louise told her about Monet, Renoir, Cézanne and Zola, hardly believing her own words. Berthe knew them all. She was especially fond of Auguste Renoir.

'Were you with Édouard?' Berthe said.

'Gene mostly, Eugène. Why?'

'Nothing. I so wish I could go to the café.'

'Well, why not come next time?' Would there be a next time?

'I couldn't. Really. I could not be seen there,' Berthe said.

Édouard arrived then, with a few absinthes inside him it seemed. He went straight over to his easel, picked up a brush and started painting with great exuberance. An audience clearly didn't put him off. He was re-working a very dark painting of a man with a black cloak wrapped around him, wearing a battered top hat. The man was leaning against a dark wall. Beside him, a glass of green liquid – absinthe.

'Maybe I can sell this one,' he said. 'I simply have to raise some cash; this dreadful war has ruined me for years to come I'm afraid.'

'This painting was inspired by Velázquez, wasn't it?' Berthe said.

'Yes, rejected by the Salon a few years ago. "Who wants a drunk?" they said. Now I've added a bit on the bottom of the canvas. I don't know why I cut him off at the knees. It'll look better like this. I'll call it *The Absinthe Drinker.*'

The man's new left leg was at a strange angle, but Louise didn't dare say anything.

'It is so dark, Édouard, why not give it some light?' Berthe said.

'It's supposed to be dark,' Édouard said.

A small young woman appeared at the doorway.

'Ah, Victorine,' Édouard said. 'Come in.'

Berthe introduced Louise to Victorine. This was the famous Victorine, model for *Olympia*. She had bright red hair, a cleft chin, and a square jaw. She was tiny. Louise knew that she was nicknamed "the shrimp".

'It's an honour to meet you,' Louise said, shaking her hand.

'Who, *me*?' said Victorine, looking around her.

'Yes, you.'

Victorine laughed. 'That's a joke!'

'Are you here to model?' asked Louise.

'No. Just here for some paints. Édouard, you said you'd look out some old paints for me.'

To Louise she said, 'I'm doing some painting myself but can't afford the paint. Édouard said he'd give me some of his.'

'Yes, I'm sorry, I forgot,' Édouard said. 'But I will get some organised for you. Come to the house sometime.'

Victorine left with a shrug. She didn't seem convinced. Perhaps he'd promised before.

'Look at the time,' Édouard said. 'I need to prepare the still life.'

He called on Adèle to bring out a salmon and some grapes. He draped a table with a white cloth and arranged them.

As they watched, Gene asked Berthe what she was painting at the moment. She described an idea she had for a woman and little girl standing on a balcony looking over the bright Paris skyline, admiring the new city. Gene was listening closely. Berthe told him she had found the perfect spot to set it but was frustrated as she couldn't go and paint there alone. Gene offered to accompany her; Berthe didn't answer him.

Louise stared at her. She could be quite rude sometimes.

'And I've been doing one of Louise,' Berthe said and smiled at her.

They started talking about some people she hadn't heard of, so Louise got up and wandered over to the window to look out over the Place de L'Europe. A puff of steam rose from a train as it set off from the Gare Saint Lazare. The floor trembled. She turned and walked around the studio, gazing at the paintings. It was like being in the best chocolate shop in the world. There was *The Spanish Singer* and *Mademoiselle V. in the Costume of an Espada,* Victorine as a matador.

'Were these inspired by Velázquez too?' Louise said to Édouard who had abandoned his still life to join her on her tour of his work.

'Yes, I met him in Madrid a few years ago. Velázquez, the greatest artist there has ever been.'

She moved along the wall. Here was a picture of soldiers with rifles pointed, ready to shoot a rebel fighter who was standing behind a barricade made of rubble in a narrow street. Next to it was a lithograph of a dead revolutionary in uniform, a white flag of surrender in his hand.

'Oh, these are awful,' she said. 'I mean ...'

'Yes, it was awful. This was the end of the Commune. But these will never be shown. The government will never allow it, the horror, the disgrace.'

Louise remembered how Édouard upset had been about the war, so she moved on. She found a portrait of Émile Zola sitting reading beside a table covered in books and papers. She had seen it before, in the future, in an art gallery. On the wall behind Zola in the painting was a sketch of *Olympia* and a Japanese print, and a Japanese screen to his left. A flash of art history came back to Louise. At this time, art from the Far East was revolutionising European painting with its exaggerated foreshortening, asymmetry and flat colour.

'You like the flattened perspective in Japanese art, don't you?' Louise said.

'Yes, I used that idea in *Le Déjeuner sur L'Herbe*. That's why people think it looks so strange.' Édouard peered into the painting of Zola, as if re-evaluating it.

Louise realised she had the chance to ask *the* Édouard Manet, the father of modern art, anything! How had he come up with such revolutionary ideas about perspective? In *Le Déjeuner sur L'Herbe* he had painted the people at the picnic as if from several different points of view. He was playing with space and perspective long before Einstein came up with the idea of relativity. How did he know how our view of the world would change so much?

'In *Le Déjeuner*,' she said, turning to indicate the giant masterpiece, 'why did you make the woman at the back so big, so out of perspective with the rest?'

'Well, there's more than one way to see the world,' Édouard said. He turned to look at the painting with her. 'We've been constrained by tradition for too long. It is time to shake things up, to try something different, something new, to match our times.'

'Yes, but how did you know —'

'You seem very well informed about my art,' Édouard said. He looked deep into her eyes. 'And how do you know about perspective?'

'Well ... I read books ...' She turned back to the Zola painting. 'Is

Émile a friend of yours?' What books could she possibly have been reading in Brittany?

'Yes. He's been my constant supporter. Look on the table.' He pointed at the table in the painting. 'That's the article he wrote defending me. I painted this to thank him. I'm going to give it to him.'

Édouard went back to his display and Louise continued her tour. There was a painting of a woman who was herself painting a still-life. The woman was dark-haired, wearing an elaborate white dress with a black belt, and no apron. She was sitting, reaching out awkwardly to paint some flowers in a vase. Her dress was so full she looked like she'd sat on a large white meringue. Not exactly dressed for oil painting. And she'd casually thrown some matching flowers on the floor beside her.

'Who's this?' she said to Édouard.

'That is Eva, my student, and, for that painting, also my model. But you will meet her, she should be here any moment. It's her I am preparing for.'

At that moment, a dark, spirited young woman swirled in, followed by her maid.

'Ah, Eva, we were just talking about you,' Édouard said, going over to greet her.

'That's good to hear,' Eva said with a simpering smile.

Édouard introduced Louise to Eva, and Berthe greeted Eva with some coolness. Berthe turned away, shooting a dark look at Louise.

Eva settled down with a fuss, arranging herself in front of Édouard's table of salmon and grapes. She was ready to learn, focused, as eager as a puppy, and Édouard was fired up with his mission to teach her how to paint a still-life. She bathed in the glow of his attention.

'Get it down quickly,' Édouard said. 'Don't worry about the background. Just go for the tonal values. You see? When you look at it, you don't see the lines on the paper over there, do you?'

'No, no,' Eva said.

'You don't try to count the scales on the salmon, of course you don't. You see them as little silver pearls against grey and pink, don't you?'

'Yes, yes.'

'Look at the pink of the salmon, with the bone appearing white in the centre and then the greys, like the shades of mother of pearl. And the grapes; now, do you count each grape? No, of course not. What you notice is their clear amber colour and the bloom that models the form by softening it.'

Louise gazed at them, fascinated by this masterclass in still-life by Édouard Manet. Berthe rolled her eyes at her.

'What you have to decide with the cloth is where the highlights come. The folds will come by themselves if you put them in the right place. Most of all, keep your colours fresh!'

After several more minutes of this, Berthe said, 'We should go. Come on, Louise.' And she ushered her away down the stairs into the carriage. They settled into their seats and set off.

'I was enjoying that. Édouard is so talented,' Louise said, 'and so famous. Well, in my day he is.'

'Yes, he is most definitely a genius, but he has not sold a painting in a very long time. He would be destitute if it were not for his family's money.'

'Really?' Louise said. 'Destitute?'

'What were you talking to him about?' Berthe said.

'His paintings. Why?'

Berthe didn't answer. She turned away.

'Who is this Eva person?' Louise said.

'Oh, Eva, Eva. She's his only pupil,' Berthe said. 'He will not even have me as a pupil. She is his star: she has poise, perseverance, she can get her things finished, whereas I am incapable of doing anything properly, apparently.'

'So, he teaches only her?'

'Yes, and paints her. He has started her portrait again, for the twenty-fifth time. She poses every day, and every night he rubs out her head so he can start again. She has all the virtues, all the charms. She is an accomplished woman, according to Mother. Where it seems I am not. I do not know why I bother.'

She paused in her tirade, frowning.

'Have you heard of her? Eva? Eva Gonzáles?' Berthe said.

'No.'

'Good,' Berthe turned away.

Louise stared at Berthe; she was jealous, definitely jealous.

CHAPTER 12

THE GIFTS

Back to Berthe's studio and a cup of tea with madeleines. Berthe asked Louise to tell her more about the meeting at the café. Louise told her that Auguste, Claude and Paul said that they had sold nothing and had no money, that Auguste was going to go back to work in the pottery, and that Claude looked thin and ill.

'Claude says he's going to have to stop painting too and find some work.' Louise rubbed her head. How would Monet become famous if he stopped painting?

'No. Impossible,' Berthe said, crashing down her cup. 'He cannot stop! He, Auguste – they are all brilliant painters. It would be a tragedy if they stopped!'

'Yes, I know, I don't understand …' Louise said.

'What can be done?' Berthe said. She stared glumly out of the window. 'I do not have any money of my own. I do not have anything I can give to help them.'

Louise looked around the bedroom, to the elegant dressing table. Amongst the paints and brushes was some of Berthe's jewellery.

'Well, you do.'

'What?'

'You have loads of jewellery.'

'Yes, yes! My jewellery! I can give them my jewellery.' Berthe jumped up. 'I will do that. And they can sell it, buy food, paint, keep painting.'

'Well, not all of it, Berthe,' Louise said. 'Even a few bits would be a lot for them.'

'It is an excellent idea. They cannot stop painting. It would be a crime to lose their talent.'

She rummaged through her jewellery box and picked out some gold earrings and a brooch with emeralds.

'What about these?'

Louise nodded. 'They must be worth a good deal.'

'Yes. That is the point, is it not?'

'But won't your mother notice?'

'Who cares? I will tell her I lost them. She already thinks I am useless. It will not matter.

'Oh, Berthe she doesn't.'

'She does. Anyway, I will not miss them. I have others.'

'But –'

'You do not understand, Louise. It is not just for them. It is for *me*. I am being selfish in fact. If Claude and Auguste stop painting, what hope do I have? We need to forge a path forward together.'

'But how will we get the jewellery to them? Shall I take it?'

'No, you doing so would be too obvious. Go down to the kitchen and ask Giselle to come up. Tell her to bring a basket and some rolls. We will take out the middle of the rolls and hide the jewellery inside. Giselle can take them. She knows Montmartre well.'

*

After dinner, Louise excused herself. She went into Berthe's room to find a book to read. She needed a distraction. On the shelf were rows of Shakespeare books, then she found *Madame Bovary*. She'd read it before … or in the future. It would be interesting to read it in its own time. That would do nicely. She took it to her room and put it on the bedside table.

She changed into her nightdress and brushed her hair. How kindly Gene had looked after that lost little boy today. Was Gene interested in her? Was she attracted to him? He was very different from her usual type. Her past boyfriends, her husband, were all a bit wild, handsome, edgy, more like Édouard than Gene. Édouard was dangerously just her type. Gene was handsome too, but clearly the younger brother, in Édouard's shadow. But he was funny, tender, kind and interesting.

But no, what was she thinking? She couldn't get involved with anyone. She was in enough trouble as it was. But maybe she could make Paul jealous if she told him when she got back. Would he care? Probably not. He'd be too busy with his girlfriend.

Louise got into bed and opened *Madame Bovary*. It fell open at a page where a passage was underlined in pencil:

"She was not happy -- she never had been. Whence came this insufficiency in life -- this instantaneous turning to decay of everything on which she leaned? But if there were somewhere a being strong and beautiful, a valiant nature, full at once of exaltation and refinement, a poet's heart in an angel's form, a lyre with sounding chords ringing out elegiac epithalamia to heaven, why, perchance, should she not find him? Ah! How impossible! Besides, nothing was worth the trouble of seeking it; everything was a lie. Every smile hid a yawn of boredom, every joy a curse, all pleasure satiety, and the sweetest kisses left upon your lips only the unattainable desire for a greater delight."

And then a marker on another page, this passage underlined:

"Love, she thought, must come suddenly, with great outbursts and lightnings, -- a hurricane of the skies, which falls upon life, revolutionises it, roots up the will like a leaf, and sweeps the whole heart into the abyss."

And another page, this one with double underline:

"The smooth folds of her dress concealed a tumultuous heart, and her modest lips told nothing of her torment. She was in love."

Louise slowly closed the book. Berthe! Berthe was in love. Who was she thinking of? Louise could guess. She put the book on the bedside table; she shouldn't be reading this.

CHAPTER 13

LE BON MARCHÉ

What day was it? Thursday. This time last week she'd been in London drying her hair. This time last Thursday she'd found out Paul was having an affair. Where did Paul think she was now? He would never believe she was here. She hardly did herself. She hoped he was worried about her, that he had confessed to his boss that he had stolen her idea, dumped his mistress, and was sitting anxiously at home by his phone waiting for her to call. *No, probably not.*

Louise got up, dressed and brushed her hair. She had settled into the routine of the Morisots' house. It seemed that not much happened most days. And so far she had managed not to annoy Berthe. She enjoyed watching her paint. It was a very quiet life compared to her previous one.

At breakfast, Cornélie announced that Suzanne had sent a message: she was coming to take Louise out shopping.

'Why don't you go too?' Cornélie asked Berthe.

'It is a waste of my time,' Berthe said. She was in a dark mood, fiddling with her fruit, not eating anything as usual. *She's like a thoroughbred racehorse*, Louise thought. A beautiful black mare, pawing the ground, straining at the reins.

'Anyway, I have to paint,' Berthe said.

'Really, I do not know why you cannot go shopping like ordinary women,' Cornélie said. 'And stop frowning. Do you think a husband wants a face like that? Why can't you smile?'

Berthe got up from the table and left the room, slamming the door.

Cornélie shrugged. 'You had better get ready, Louise. Suzanne will be here in no time.'

*

Louise wasn't keen on shopping either, but she liked Suzanne. It would be interesting to go out with her. She got dressed. Her mind turned to time; time is everywhere in our language. You can waste time, take time, save time, spend time, buy time, make time. Have it, need it, lose it, use it, run out of it. Pass time, give it, borrow it, squander it … So many things you can do with time.

And time has its own agency, too; it can fly, drag, march, stand still, even heal, they say. But to move through time, like she had, how did that work? Why had she come now? *Why here? Why her?* Had it happened because of her mental state at the cottage? She had been fragile, breaking, falling apart when she started painting Berthe's painting. That was the moment she'd been transported.

You can kill time or save time, but time had saved her. It had taken her out of her distress and despair and brought her here. To distract her from her grief over her mum? Or was she supposed to do something here? But the first rule of time travel was that you don't interfere. You never interfere. She had to be careful of every step she took, everything she said. It was a huge responsibility.

She called for Giselle to help tighten her corset.

*

Suzanne arrived – Louise had run out of time. She jammed on her hat and went downstairs to greet her.

In the carriage, she sat back into the comfortable padded seat. The plodding of the horses, the sway as they made their way along the boulevard was so soothing. Time was certainly gentler here. It was a relief from the hustle and bustle of her century.

'Have you heard of *Le Bon Marché*?' Suzanne said.

'You were talking about it at the soirée, weren't you?' Louise said. 'The new shop?'

'Yes, it's the most wonderful shop. It's actually a very big "department store" as they call it. You can get *everything* there, all the latest fashions.'

Louise had always enjoyed shopping with her mother. Sometimes they'd go and try on really expensive clothes just for the fun of it. Her mother would put on some fancy sequined evening gown and ask Louise's opinion. Then, very seriously, say it wasn't quite right for the occasion she'd just invented, and Louise would stifle her giggles.

Louise turned away from Suzanne to hide her tears. She wiped her eyes. Another thing she'd never do with her mother again.

The carriage trundled on across the river to *Le Bon Marché* and drew up outside an enormous five-storey building. It took up an entire block and had huge bay windows showing elaborate displays of clothes and household goods. A queue of carriages lined up, waiting to drop people off, horses and carriage drivers jostling for position.

'Good, it's not too busy today,' Suzanne said.

A buxom flower girl in a low-cut dress provocatively offered her blooms to a passing gentleman. Was she really a flower girl? Another girl offered a man postcards. Louise could see that there were naked women on them. A maid festooned with boxes struggled out of the big heavy door, following her mistress. She held colourful parcels wrapped in string, boxes of all sizes, huge to tiny, hanging from her shoulders, arms and hands. Covered in cubes, she looked like a cubist painting which had been transformed into real life.

Inside the shop, a grand staircase wound up through the centre of a huge hall. Light filtered in through enormous coloured cupolas in the ceiling. Balconies surrounded the hall for three stories up. People were everywhere, up and down the staircases, all along the balconies. Women mostly, in flounces, pleats, ruffles and frills.

Suzanne led Louise through the crowd. It was hard to move, and to breathe. Louise was smothered by the fuss and frippery, crushings and crumplings. Smart staff in uniforms displayed lace, parasols, gloves, fans, buttons, chokers, hats and hair decorations on long counters.

'Look at all the things you can buy! You can touch things. And try them on!' Suzanne said.

Louise gazed over the sea of accessories. The intoxication of shopping was beginning in Paris. Here and now.

'The new fashion is for a more tight-fitting silhouette, a long waisted bodice. You need a longer corset, of course,' Suzanne said. 'That would suit you nicely. You're so slim. Not me, I'm a bit too round for that. Édouard says I should exercise ... Maybe I should get a new dress for the masked ball. Are you going?'

'I don't know. I haven't heard about it,' Louise said, looking around at the mayhem.

'It's the event of the year,' Suzanne said. 'I'm really looking forward to it. I could get a new dress. They have thirty different kinds of silk here, you know. Or I could get some more lace and add it to that white one I have. Look at this pink. Do you think I should get this pink or the blue?'

Louise shrugged. She had no opinion on the lace.

'I'll get both. They'll look nice together, don't you think, across the skirt and the bodice?'

Louise couldn't imagine what this dress would look like. She nodded.

'Marie, our maid, can sew it on. She's really good at sewing. Would you like to buy something?'

'Em, no,' Louise looked away. She didn't have any money.

'What about this?' Suzanne, picked up a beautiful lace handkerchief with an *L* on it. She understood; she had once been in Louise's position. 'I'll get it for you.'

Louise accepted gratefully. Suzanne bought a few more things and they climbed up the stairs to a beautiful, ornate café. Louise was hit by a cacophony of clattering cutlery, dishes, and women's voices. Suzanne took them over to a table near the window and sat plumply amidst her frills. She ordered coffee and cake.

'You're from Holland, aren't you?' Louise said, trying to find a neutral topic which wouldn't reveal too much about herself.

'Yes. Delft. Have you heard of it?'

'Yes, Delft,' Louise rummaged around in her brain. 'Pottery, blue pottery, ceramics, tiles. Is that right?' Had she got the time period right?

'Yes, it's famous for that, but my father is a church organist. He's getting old now. His hands are starting to shake. I don't know how they're going to manage when he can't play anymore. I try to send them money sometimes.'

'How did you first come to Paris?'

'I was sent to improve my music. I was nineteen. I was always good at the piano; Mother got me lessons. It is my only talent. I studied but I had to work too, teaching. I was very lonely here at first.'

'And then you met Édouard? You were his teacher, weren't you?'

'Yes. Édouard's father heard me play one evening and hired me to teach Édouard and Eugène. It was good money for me to send back to the family. But the boys weren't particularly good. They were teenagers and not interested. Édouard just wanted to paint.'

Suzanne had met Édouard when he was a teenager? What an unusual relationship.

'What do you think of his paintings? Édouard's, I mean?' Louise asked.

'To be honest, I don't really understand them. They're so strange. I don't know why he doesn't do normal paintings. You know, portraits or still lives, subjects people like. Then he could sell them, and then he maybe wouldn't be so upset and depressed.'

'But it's really important what he's doing. He's changing art, for the future.'

'Oh, do you think so?'

'Yes. Have faith.'

'It would be nice if he wanted to paint me sometimes,' Suzanne said sadly. She signalled to the waiter and asked for more cake. She took solace in cake.

Louise sat back and fiddled with her teaspoon. When did fame come to Édouard Manet? Was it in his lifetime? She didn't know. Did Suzanne suspect Berthe had a crush on Édouard? Perhaps she was reading too much into the *Madame Bovary* passages.

'What about you?' Suzanne said. 'How do you like Paris?'

'It's wonderful. It's an amazing time to be here. The boulevards, the City of Light.'

'Aren't you missing home, your family in Brittany, your friends? It's hard being away from home.'

'A little,' Louise said. She looked around the café at the friends chatting, mothers laughing with their daughters. She suddenly felt so heavy, so tired. She'd never have tea with her mother again. Paul — he'd be having tea with someone else now. She was completely alone. 'But the Morisots have been so kind,' she said, dragging herself back into the present moment.

'We have a lot in common then; the Manets have been so very kind to me. And Paris is much more interesting that Delft.'

'And Brittany,' Louise said. They laughed.

'The men are more handsome too,' Louise said. 'Tell me about Gene. Does he have a girlfriend, someone he's interested in?'

'Well, I used to think he liked Berthe, but I don't know. Every man seems to like Berthe.' She took another piece of cake. 'He seems to have cheered up a lot since you arrived,' Suzanne said, smiling at Louise.

Louise quickly changed the subject back to the latest fashions. Suzanne knew a great deal about the subject. She was very entertaining about the right hats, the wrong ribbons, the perfect size of bustle, what to wear for what occasion. It was fascinating. She wished she could take notes.

The café bustled, and Louise relaxed in Suzanne's company. If

Berthe was a racehorse, Suzanne was like a friendly pony. She was easy to be with, much easier than Berthe.

It was late afternoon when Louise returned to the Morisots'. She went straight up to the studio where Berthe was concentrating on getting exactly the right shade of blue for a shadow in her painting. She seemed uninterested in Louise's day out with Suzanne.

'Did she have anything stimulating to say or was it all about buttons and bows?' Berthe said, and carried on painting.

'We had a nice chat,' Louise said. Had Berthe talked to Suzanne at all at the soirée? Louise didn't think so; Berthe could be pretty imperious at times. Strange, that she was jealous of Eva, but seemed unconcerned about Édouard's wife. Maybe her interest in Édouard was just about the art.

As Berthe painted, Louise looked through her bookshelves. She found Victor Hugo's *The Hunchback of Notre Dame* and settled down to read it. It was weird going even further back in time to medieval Paris.

As the afternoon wore on, it became hot and stuffy in the studio. It was hard to concentrate. Berthe put down her brush and grabbed her fan.

'I feel like I will melt. I think the paint is going to drip off the canvas,' she said.

Louise put her book down and looked at Berthe's painting. It was of the garden through the window. Flowers were in bloom. Berthe had captured the light and the colours perfectly, the bright yellow of the irises, the subtle lavenders in the folds of the petals, the glow of the red in the roses, and the deep blues in the green of the leaves. The colours vibrated and bounced off the canvas. Louise could see more of the garden in the painting than out of the window.

Berthe fanned herself violently. She picked up her freshly painted canvas from the easel and threw it to the back of the room. It fell face down and smeared paint across the floor.

'Berthe, your painting!' Louise said.

'Oh, it was terrible!' Berthe walked out of the room in disgust.

Louise went over to the canvas and propped it against the wall. Maybe it could be saved. She got an old painting cloth and cleaned up the wet paint on the floorboards. Berthe was as explosive as a firework, with a very short fuse. She would have to be careful. One false step and she would be out on the streets.

CHAPTER 14

REPOSE

This morning they were going to Édouard's studio, with Louise as chaperone. So far her job was easy. She didn't have to do anything except be with Berthe, and that was usually interesting. Perhaps Gene would be at the studio. She was surprised to realise how much she wanted to see him again.

Berthe was rushing around, hurrying Louise to get ready. Giselle struggled to get Louise into her layers of clothes.

'Stay still, Mademoiselle Louise,' she said as she pulled the corset tighter.

'Call me, Louise, Giselle, please,' Louise gasped. 'And maybe not so tight. These corsets are such a ridiculous fashion.'

Louise didn't like the idea of having servants looking after her, especially Giselle with whom she had more in common than anyone else in the house. And she was increasingly irritated by all of the bourgeois nonsense, stuck in her nest of petticoats, especially on a warm day like this. She longed for Lycra, to pull on some running shorts and trainers, and go pounding off down the boulevards.

*

Édouard was in a high mood when they got to the studio. He greeted them with great enthusiasm, and some questions for Louise.

'Ah, mysterious Louise, the young woman from the country who isn't shocked by my paintings and drinks beer in a café. Who *are* you?'

Louise stared back at him and said nothing. He turned to Berthe.

'Berthe, dear, where on earth did you find her?'

'She came all by herself,' Berthe said, and quickly changed the subject. 'What have you been doing, Édouard?'

Édouard stood up and whisked the cover off the painting of Berthe he'd got back for Louise to see.

'And now, I give you – *Repose*! Ta ra!'

Louise squinted at the painting. She had expected a conventional portrait of Berthe, perhaps posed as a demure, bourgeoise young woman. But nothing about this was normal. Berthe was flung across a sofa looking very fed up, arms wide. She wore a white patterned dress with a full skirt, a black belt and a neck ribbon. Her dark hair was partly tied up, some falling over her shoulders. Her pose and her expression were so unusual, so striking. She looked fed up, pained, anxious.

'Oh,' Louise said. 'How ... interesting.'

'I remember when I sketched this,' Édouard said to Berthe. 'You'd come in, so frustrated about all the talk of war.'

'Well, men and their wars. It is endless! Where is the beauty in them?' Berthe said.

'You were only worried it would disturb your painting.'

'Yes, that is true too,' Berthe said, laughing.

'And you threw yourself onto the sofa in disgust.'

'And you said, "Don't move – that's perfect" and grabbed your sketchbook. I was just collapsed there. It really is not a proper pose.'

'You were a picture of Paris; you captured the mood of sorrow and hopelessness pervading the city. I thought of calling it *Melancholia*, but I think *Repose* is better. No one will think it is a portrait of you.'

'You see, it is not a respectable attitude for a lady,' Berthe said to Louise. 'Not that I mind.'

'Berthe is a wonderful model,' Édouard said to Louise. 'Look at her now, in that deep black dress with her fan. Let me sketch you,' he said to Berthe.

'Oh, you are always drawing me,' Berthe said, smiling, willing. She went over to a gold chair, sat down and swung her right leg over the left. With her legs crossed, her dress didn't fully cover her elegant ankles and her right foot pointed out at an angle. She was wearing pretty pink silk slippers. It was probably quite a provocative pose at a time when women were supposed to cover their ankles. Berthe wiggled the slipper around on her toes and flicked her fan open in front of her face.

'Now you cannot draw me,' Berthe giggled. *What a surprising sound.*

'Yes, I can,' Édouard said, getting his pencil and sketchbook. 'Stay like that. You know you can tell so much about a woman from the way she carries herself. Women with a seductive personality always point their feet out.'

Louise watched, mesmerised, as Berthe sped from the end of Édouard's pencil. She could almost see the electric sparks flying from Berthe, into Édouard's eyes, down his pencil, onto the paper. Édouard focused on Berthe while she played provocatively with her fan. His pencil got to her ankle and foot, and he stopped, threw down the pencil and paper, went over to Berthe, and took her hand.

'Berthe and I have to go out now, Louise. We'll be back in a few hours. Make yourself at home.'

'What? What do you mean?' Louise said.

Berthe left with Édouard, laughing, without a backward glance to Louise.

'But Berthe, I'm supposed to be your chaperone ...' Louise said to an empty room.

Louise went over to the abandoned sketch. It was a wonderful lively image of Berthe with the fan in front of her face, the slipper and ankle standing out against the dark black of her dress. All done in about a minute. Where were they going? Louise had no idea. What were they doing? She did have an idea about that.

She wandered around the huge studio. What was she supposed to do now? It wasn't very nice to dump her like this. She paced around, frowning, until it dawned on her that it was only her here, with *Olympia*.

When her mother took her to the Musée D'Orsay, they'd peered through crowds of tourists trying to get a glimpse of just a corner of this masterpiece. Now she was alone with it. She stepped up to it and touched the paint, very gently, on the right-hand corner. *Look, Mum*, she whispered. *I'm touching Olympia*.

And there were so many more: *The Ragpicker*, a man in dirty, ragged clothes with a scraggly beard and rubbish at his feet. This must have been shocking – a large portrait of someone with "no worth" to society. This was totally against the traditions of the art world.

Here were the paintings of *The Execution of Maximillian*, several of them in a row along the wall. His execution by the Mexicans had been a huge embarrassment for France. Hadn't the government forbidden Édouard to exhibit this painting?

There were paintings of horse races. The horses' legs extended out to the front and the back. Édouard wouldn't yet have seen film of how horses really gallop. That must come later.

And here was Victorine as *The Street Singer*, caught in the moment of emerging from a café eating grapes with a guitar under her arm.

More wonderful still-lifes, drawings, and paintings, all of them just hanging there. Unsold. She rubbed her hands over her eyes. Were people blind?

At the far corner at the back of the studio, she discovered a table with a large pile of Édouard's sketchbooks. She flicked through them and found a sketch of Berthe, then another, and another. There were endless sketches of Berthe in different poses, different clothes, page after page of them, in sketchbook after sketchbook.

My God, Édouard is infatuated with Berthe, she thought.

Footsteps. Coming up the stairs. She closed the sketchbooks and stepped away from the table. Gene stepped into the studio.

'Hallo, Louise. How nice to see you. What are you doing here, all alone?'

'Just waiting for Berthe. I'm, er, meeting her here later.' This sounded a bit feeble but that was all she could think to say.

Gene looked mystified. He gazed around the studio.

'I came to talk to Édouard, but I see he's not here either.'

'Please don't tell Cornélie, I mean Madame Morisot, that I'm not with Berthe. I'm supposed to be her chaperone.'

'No, of course not. But where are Berthe and Édouard?' Gene's face clouded over.

Did he know? Suspect? Louise turned away to avoid his gaze and fiddled with some paint brushes on the table. If he told Cornélie about this, she'd be thrown out of the house, for sure. Onto the streets.

'Please don't say to Cornélie,' she said again.

'Hmm,' he said. Then he turned to her and smiled. 'Of course I won't say anything. Do not worry. Now, shall we go out for a walk together? I don't think you mind being unchaperoned with me, do you? It is a lovely day.'

'Yes, let's,' Louise said.

They walked down the boulevards in the sunshine, Parisian style, forgetting Berthe and Édouard, watching the world watching them. Gene took her arm and Louise relaxed in his company.

At Café Guerbois, they found Edgar sitting at a table outside in the sun. They joined him and ordered coffee. Louise sat back and watched the passers-by while Edgar and Gene talked about what he and the other painters were working on, and what a struggle it was to sell in these times. Edgar hadn't sold any paintings. Gene told him that Édouard was also struggling. There just wasn't a market now.

'But at least we have some money,' Gene said. 'Auguste and Claude have nothing. They are so poor. It would be crime if they gave up painting.'

Louise took a sip of coffee. *Not as poor as they used to be,* she thought. Berthe's jewellery would help them for some time.

'It's odd how Monet and Manet's names are so similar,' Louise said. 'Claude and Édouard, do people ever get them confused?'

'Oh yes, I have a great story about that,' Edgar said. 'Claude's portrait of Camille at the '66 exhibition was quite impressive and there was a cartoon in the paper poking fun at it, saying something like, "Is it Monet or Manet? Monet! But surely we owe Monet to Manet. Well done, Monet! And cheers Manet!"'

'Édouard was impressed with Monet, Claude's painting,' Gene said, 'but he didn't think the satire was funny. He said: "Who is this Monet with a name so similar to mine? He's taking advantage of my fame."'

'Yes, but he was intrigued,' Edgar said. 'Édouard invited Claude to meet him at Café de Bade. They got on very well. That's when I met Claude too. Édouard introduced us. I went to see his seascapes in his studio, but I didn't take to them. I said, "I'm off, all these *reflet d'eaux* are making my eyes hurt." It was full of draughts. A few more and I'd have pulled the collar of my jacket up.'

Louise and Gene laughed.

'Actually, my eyes seem to be hurting a lot these days,' said Edgar, blinking into the sun.

At that moment, a young women strolled past the café, arm in arm with an elegant man. She was dressed in the latest fashion, swathed in red ruffles with matching hat and parasol, talking about the new styles. The conversation had obviously been going on for a while. The man was gazing off, disinterested.

'Wow, look at her!' Louise said. 'She looks amazing.'

'Pah, what a display,' Edgar said. 'Fashion! I sometimes wonder … what would happen if there were no fashions? How would women spend their time? What would they have to talk about? Life would be unbearable for us men. The government would have to step in.'

'We're not *all* like that,' Louise said.

But Edgar was on a roll. He was twirling his coffee spoon around his fingers.

'Women think in little packages. I understand nothing about the way their minds work. They put every subject into an envelope, label it and it's finished. Little packages. Little packages. Actually, I think the chief charm of a woman is to know how to listen. There are some women who should barely be spoken to, they should only be caressed.'

'Oh, for goodness' sake,' Louise said. 'That's so stupid. What about Berthe?'

'She makes paintings as she would hats.'

'What!' said Louise, slamming down her cup. 'She does not. Don't be absurd. I thought you were her friend?'

'If I did not treat people as I do,' Edgar said, 'I would never have a minute to myself to work. But I am really timid by nature, I have to force myself continually.'

He smirked at Louise.

Louise snorted back.

'Gene, I think it's time to leave,' she said, getting up and looking at her bare wrist again.

'What is so interesting about your left wrist?' asked Gene as they walked back to the studio. 'Does it hold the meaning of life or something?'

'Oh, never mind, you wouldn't understand,' Louise said. 'Edgar! He makes me furious. He's a misogynist pig.'

'What?'

'Misogynist pig. Edgar hates women.'

'Yes but is he just pretending? Sometimes I wonder.'

Louise tried to stomp along the street in petticoats. It was quite difficult.

'I've been wondering about you,' Gene said. 'You're a very unusual young woman. Tell me about your life in Brittany. And why did you come to Paris?'

'I like to travel, from time to time ... Why I came? It's not very interesting,' Louise said. *Actually, it's very interesting but you'd never believe me.*

'Well, don't take Edgar so seriously. He doesn't mean half what he says. He thinks he's being entertaining.'

'Well, *I* don't find it funny.'

They walked on.

'Look, Louise,' Gene said. 'I enjoy your company. You're different, interesting. I would like to see you again. Would you come out with me for a drive sometime?'

Louise imagined driving through Paris in a red convertible with the warm wind in her hair. *Oh, a carriage drive, he means.* She fidgeted with her gloves.

'Yes, I mean, I'll have to check what Berthe's doing. You know, I'm her, er, chaperone.'

Could she go out with Gene? Would it matter? It would just be a drive. He is very attractive. Why was she hesitating? Paul wouldn't care. She took his arm.

'That would be nice, to go out again.'

'Let me know when suits you. Send a messenger with a note. I can make myself available any time.' Gene smiled warmly at her.

*

Berthe and Édouard were back in the studio when they returned. Berthe was looking a little flushed. She quickly made her excuses to Gene and ushered Louise into the carriage.

'So, you went to the café?' Berthe said.

'Yes.'

'Who was there?'

'Just Edgar.'

The carriage rocked them home and they sat in silence. Louise looked at Berthe's rosy cheeks and dived straight in.

'So, are you and Édouard having an affair?'

'I suppose that was a bit obvious today,' Berthe in a soft voice. 'Do you think anyone else knows?'

'No, I don't think so. I don't know. How would I know?'

'Oh, please do not tell anyone. Please!' Berthe said, grabbing Louise's hand. 'It is so difficult, so hard for us to find the time to be alone together. Mother does not approve of me going to Édouard's studio. I think she suspects. Well, I *know* she does. But you can help, like today, help us be together. Will you? Please?'

'As your pretend chaperone?'

'Mother will never know. We leave the house together and return together. Please!'

'What about Suzanne?'

'Oh, she doesn't know. Please do not tell her.'

'No, I won't but …'

'It would be so wonderful if you could do this small thing for me.'

Louise looked out at the boulevards rolling past. Berthe had taken her in, saved her, become her friend. She had nowhere else to go, no money. She was totally dependent on her, on the Morisots. What else could she do? But what was she getting into – becoming complicit in this affair? Suzanne, the innocent wife, so kind, and so in the dark, deceived. Just as she had been.

They got back to the house and Louise went straight her room, saying she needed a rest. She sat on the bed and took her wedding ring out of the bedside table. She slipped it on and twisted it around her finger. What was Paul doing now? Had he forgotten about her? Probably. She'd given him a free reign to carry on with his mistress now. She sighed, took the ring off, and put it back in the drawer.

She had no alternative. She had nowhere to go. She would have to help Berthe have her affair.

CHAPTER 15

TIBURCE

It was early. For the last few nights, Louise had had trouble sleeping. It was like she had jet leg, or perhaps 'painting-lag' from changing time zones. If you fly around the world, you can arrive in another day, but she'd slipped through a painting and arrived in another century. No wonder she couldn't sleep.

As the light came up, a gentle breeze swayed the thin lace curtains. *There's only a diaphanous veil between past, present and future,* she thought. It seems it's easy to slip through it. That oak tree in the garden, it might live another hundred and fifty years. The furniture in this room, Berthe's paintings on the wall, could all survive into her time. She could probably go and see *Thatched Cottage in Normandy* in an art gallery when she went back. If she went back.

If.

Could she stay here? She hated the idea of deceiving Suzanne by being Berthe's chaperone, but she was getting comfortable here, settling into this new life. If her mum had still been alive, she'd have someone to go back for. But now, there was no one. She shivered. There was only pain back in her old life.

She got out of bed, dressed and was down early to breakfast. Tiburce was sitting at the table reading his papers before going to work. The early sun slanted through the long windows and the smell of fresh coffee and croissants mingled. Tiburce's papers rustled. It was calm and peaceful. Louise read the newspaper and drank her coffee.

After a while, Tiburce put down his papers and smiled at Louise. She asked him what he was working on. He said that he was reviewing some of the issues in his precinct. He was concerned about Paris; there were so many problems.

Louise asked questions and Tiburce seemed happy to answer. There were the difficulties of putting the city back on its feet after the siege, the need to move people to new neighbourhoods as areas were knocked down for the boulevards, the need to feed the population, and to avoid another revolution.

Louise swung into full journalist mode. She knew she sometimes irritated people by going too far, asking too many questions, like a dog worrying a bone, but Tiburce didn't seem annoyed. He talked freely. She wished she had a notebook with her. Or her phone.

'I usually protect Cornélie and Berthe from the difficulties of my job,' Tiburce said. 'They are not very interested. But you, you have many questions.'

'Yes, I find it very interesting.'

'I think you are a good companion for Berthe,' he said. 'I like your curiosity, your desire to understand. Tell me, how do you think Berthe is? I know she can be, well, difficult at times.'

'I think she's fine. Painting furiously, never satisfied with her work, it seems. I don't know why. I think she's brilliant.'

'Yes, she is, isn't she? I like to think she gets it from me. I used to paint when I was young, when I was studying architecture. No time for that now, but I've always encouraged her, supported her. I built her a studio in the garden, but it was destroyed in the siege.'

'Did you?' So it wasn't only been Cornélie who supported Berthe.

'Berthe has always been unusual, unsettled, unsatisfied, in a rush, even as a child. I want her to be happy. I'm pleased if she wants to paint. She doesn't need to get married if she doesn't want to. Her mother doesn't agree, of course. She's worried about our social position.' He sighed. 'I often think it would be easier for Berthe if she'd been born a male. It's so hard for women. She's so constrained. She was born like that, you know, a bundle of energy with little shining eyes, as if lit from within. It was my idea to name her Berthe.

It means "bright".'

Louise gazed at Tiburce. He understood his daughter so well, loved her so much. It was such a pleasure to sit in his company. Her heart swelled – and her throat tightened. What a wonderful father! She had never known such a thing. Tears sprang to her eyes. She dropped her napkin on the floor. Bending under the table, she dried her eyes quickly, hoping Tiburce wouldn't notice.

'Are you alright, Louise?' Tiburce said.

'Yes.'

'What's wrong?'

'It's just ... Well, I never really had a father.'

'What happened to him?'

'He left. My mother and me.'

'I'm sorry.'

'And your mother now?'

'She ... died.'

'Oh, I'm so sorry.'

'And my boyfriend – why could she never say "husband"? – he's having an affair!' Louise struggled not to cry.

'Oh dear, that's very sad. Unfaithful men. That is our greatest weakness. But you must not take it personally. I'm sure it was nothing to do with you. Do not let the vagaries of men affect you. You are a beautiful, intelligent young woman. You will easily find a husband.'

Louise grimaced.

'If you want to, of course,' Tiburce said and smiled. 'You have to find your own way. Give it time. For now, you can relax. You're welcome to stay here as long as you want.'

'Thank you, thank you so much.'

*

After breakfast, Louise skipped to the kitchen. She could stay as long as she wanted, Tiburce had said.

The kitchen was her favourite place in the house, warm and cosy. She took a deep breath of the smells of baking bread mixed with whiffs from the onions, herbs and garlic hanging up to dry. She sat at the big wooden table with Giselle. She was teaching her to read and write between chores. That was one useful thing she could do here.

They could only do their lessons when Nanette went out to the market, but she spent a suspiciously long time there. According to Giselle, Nanette fancied the butcher.

Giselle was keen to learn. She'd had no education at all, but she was like a seedling ready to shoot up, open into the light, and suck up knowledge. She was particularly good at numbers. Louise had started with addition and subtraction, using the potatoes as props, lining them up on the table in rows, adding some, taking some away. Now they were on fractions, and Louise was cutting potatoes into halves, quarters, and thirds. Giselle picked it all up easily.

'You're good at this, Giselle,' Louise said.

'Am I? I like the patterns the numbers make in my head,' Giselle said. Then, after a moment, 'I want to ask you, Mademoiselle Louise, why is Mademoiselle Berthe so cross? She has so much, everything you could ever need, but she snaps at me sometimes.'

'It's not about you, Giselle,' Louise said. 'Berthe is frustrated. It's because she's not taken seriously. She wants to be an artist, but she feels excluded, cut off, from the male art world.'

'But is it proper for a woman to be an artist? Why doesn't she get married? She's quite old now.'

'Old? No, she's not old. And of course it's proper: women *can* be artists. We can do anything a man can do. Or we should be able to. We just need the opportunity. Berthe wants to be taken seriously. You know, now you've learned arithmetic, counting, you could get a better job, in a shop maybe.'

'A shop! I'd love to work in a shop. A clothes shop. *Le Bon Marché* …'

'Yes. You'd have more money for clothes, food.'

'And for my family.'

'Education's really important, for girls, women especially.'

'Is that why you're teaching me?'

'Yes, and you're a very good learner.'

'I could teach my little brothers and sisters too.'

'Yes, you could. That's a great idea.'

At that moment Nanette burst in with her baskets and bags. She saw all the potatoes lined up along the table, cut into halves, quarters and eighths.

'What on earth are you doing?' she asked.

'We're, em, organising the potatoes,' Louise said. Giselle giggled.

'My potatoes don't need organised, they need peeled,' Nanette said.

Louise left Giselle to prepare the lunch. How would Giselle get a job in *Le Bon Marché*? Did they do interviews in these days? Maybe she could help Giselle, give her some confidence, though she was hardly an expert in that.

In her bedroom, Louise started washing out her giant underwear. The pantaloons had a gap, so she supposed they were healthier than her usual tight underwear but still, she had to be careful. She was terrified of getting cystitis. She'd had it before, and the pain was intense. You couldn't get antibiotics here, so she'd probably die! She scrubbed away with the sliver of hard soap.

Her own last interview had been a total disaster. It was the week after that horrible barbeque and her confidence had drained away, slipped down around her ankles like a pair of old knickers. That day she'd put on her best underwear and tried to talk her confidence up from her feet, thinking about her past successes, her films which had won awards. Her confidence climbed to her knees. Her recent series had been well received and got good audience figures; it reached her hips. Praise from her last boss, and her confidence hugged her around her waist. Her mother telling her how wonderful she was, and it swelled her heart. She would not be pathetic: she would get this job. She had played Beyoncé's *Run the world Girls* and put on her smart suit and a bright scarf.

Louise wrung out the pantaloons and looked for somewhere to dry them. Not over that beautiful hardwood chair, it might damage the wood. She found what passed for a towel, a thin, crusty thing, and laid it on the floor by the window. She spread the underwear on top and sat beside it, as if looking after a baby sleeping in the sun.

She remembered walking to the Underground in her best heels – not too high – and she had felt like Beyoncé, strong and proud. They'd be fools not to hire her. She danced up the escalator and along the corridor to the offices of the top independent production company, got her badge from the glamorous receptionist, and sat down in the colourful little lounge with its lime green and purple sofas. Glittering awards lined the walls. She had to wait a long time.

A woman and a man interviewed her. She was a fierce, high-powered exec who'd been responsible for some great programmes, and he was in HR. The job was for the producer of a science documentary series. It had started well enough: they asked her about her latest series, and she enthused about it, managing to describe her role, her ideas. Then the exec asked her how she'd handled the presenter she'd worked with. He was notorious for being difficult to work with, opinionated and inflexible. It had always been a nightmare trying to stop him taking over the production. He was a lot older than Louise and regarded himself as "the expert"; he wasn't impressed by being told what to do by a young woman. He talked down to her, embarrassed her in front of the crew, and tried to change the agreed script all the time. It had been a constant battle.

Louise searched for a way to answer the question and her confidence started to slip away. She blustered through a feeble reply. Then: "What is your greatest weakness?" Oh no! "My lack of confidence" she had nearly said. Instead, she wittered on about being a perfectionist, organising, scheduling, attention to detail, getting the facts right. She sounded really boring. Gravity was now overcoming Beyoncé. Her confidence slipped down her legs into her feet. It oozed out over her shoes, flowed under the door, down the stairs and got on the bus to John O'Groats. She watched the attention drift out of the exec's eyes. The interview shuddered to a halt, and she crawled back to the underground tunnels of London.

*

Louise watched the birds settling in the garden below her. Giselle had put some breadcrumbs out for them. How could she teach Giselle confidence when she had none herself? When she felt strong, it was like she was walking on springs, like Tigger, but she hadn't felt like that for a while. In London, instead of Tigger, she was a small grey slug, slithering around underground stations. On the way back to the flat that day, she had stood in a corner of the Underground station watching swarms of bright busy-bee people buzzing past her. Did any of them feel like her? It didn't look like it. A woman her own age, fashionably dressed for business, was checking her phone while buying a cappuccino with oat milk, not even looking at the barista. So solid, focused and certain, such strength – a strong inner core. The type who did the plank every morning for five minutes. Her core must be made of wood – a plank of hardwood, oak maybe. Louise could only manage one minute. Her core was hollow, like a dead tree, or a brandy snap.

She sat staring out the window. When had she become so pathetic? What had happened to her old bright self? She had slowly evaporated in London. No one ever said "hello". She often had the feeling of not being seen, of disappearing. Sitting with a group of Paul's friends in the pub she couldn't hold anyone's attention. She would watch their eyes; they never met hers, rarely sought her out. Was she really there? Maybe no one could see her.

She'd read that there was no such thing as a *self*, an *I*. It's just a trick of consciousness, neuroscientists said, memories strung together to give the impression of a self. Yet it *felt* like she was here, now, otherwise who or what was thinking about this stuff? But consciousness was nowhere to be found in the brain. They've rummaged around in there and found nothing. There's no one in. The *I* that makes you *you*, that feels things – it's not there. It, too, is invisible.

That day of the interview Louise had trudged whatever her *self* was back to the tiny flat and sat at her laptop, trying to arrange some letters of the alphabet to rewrite her CV. Letters were like atoms, words like molecules, sentences like cells; a page was an organ of the body like a heart or a lung. A CV became the whole person. She tried to write herself into existence as a credible person.

Louise slumped into the armchair by the window and sighed. Maybe TV hadn't been the right career for her after all. It was so difficult. You were only as good as your last programme. You got the next job if the boss liked it, or liked you, if you fitted in. Schmoozing, claiming credit for someone else's work – it wasn't her. She was as smart as her colleagues but was often passed over. Some man blustering with confidence would step in and snatch the project she longed for.

Well, no wonder: she never stood up for herself. Why had she accepted a researcher's job, two grades below what she deserved? Why did she never fight for herself?

CHAPTER 16

CHAPERONE

At lunchtime, Berthe was subdued, and Cornélie quiet for once. Had they had another argument? To break the uncomfortable silence, Louise asked Cornélie how Berthe had started painting.

'Well,' Cornélie said. 'It was my idea. I wanted the girls to draw some pictures for Tiburce, so I got them lessons with a well-known painter, Chocarne –'

'He was so boring,' Berthe interrupted. 'He had his latest Salon entry displayed on an easel all the time. Always a tedious portrait of a woman in classical drapery.'

'Tiburce would go to collect them and find Berthe reduced to a stupor by his classes, but the girls were nonetheless interested in painting. But they needed a new teacher, so I asked Joseph Guicard to teach them. He took them to the Louvre to copy famous works, the old masters.'

'Titian, Veronese –' Berthe said.

'Joseph warned about getting the girls lessons,' Cornélie said. 'He said that it would risk them actually becoming painters. And that, in my social circle would be a revolution. A catastrophe, even.'

Cornélie looked at Berthe.

'Sometimes I think I should have listened to him. It *has* been a catastrophe. Berthe is now obsessed with painting to the exclusion of all else.'

Berthe ignored her and turned to Louise.

'We got tired of the Louvre and wanted to paint *en plein air* –

plants, people, life, not stuffy old antiques. We were desperate for light and colour.'

'So Camille Corot took them to paint in the countryside,' Cornélie said, 'and Achille Oudinot taught them too.'

'We had a wonderful time,' Berthe said.

'And have you exhibited many, Berthe?' Louise said.

'The place to show your work is the Salon,' Cornélie said, 'and in 1863 Berthe had two landscapes displayed, as did Edma.'

'One was *The Old Lane in Auvers*,' Berthe said.

'Tiburce built them a studio in the garden. I was surprised he was so supportive,' Cornélie said.

'But it was burnt down in the siege,' Berthe said, 'that's why I paint in my bedroom now.'

'And when did you meet Édouard?' Louise said to Berthe. She put her hand over her mouth. Oh, maybe she shouldn't have mentioned Édouard, but Cornélie didn't react and Berthe continued.

'Three years ago, when I was in the Louvre copying a Rubens,' Berthe said.

'They have a lot in common; the art of course, but he's the reason Berthe started doing these very peculiar paintings. She certainly has talent, but I don't believe there is any demand for that type of work.'

'Edgar Degas is hugely complimentary as you know, Mother, and I have sold two. Anyway, it is up to me what I paint.' She got up, abandoning her uneaten food, and left the room.

Cornélie sighed. 'Her head has been turned by a little bit of praise from some of her artist friends. Are these compliments really genuine? One praised her work as being so subtle and distinguished that it makes other artists jealous. Is it really that good? And anyway, what has this to do with her prospects for marriage?'

'But she's very good, so talented,' Louise said.

'When she paints, she looks so anxious and unhappy. Her life has become that of an incarcerated prisoner. And I do not wish to have this tension around me all the time. At my time of life I want some peace.'

Cornélie folded her napkin and firmly placed it on the table. She turned to Louise. 'It's good that you're here. Go with her when she goes out, go everywhere with her. Do not let her out of your sight. I don't know how things are in Brittany but it's important in Paris that a young woman of social standing is never left alone with a man. It can ruin her reputation. We don't want that happening to Berthe, especially at this crucial stage.'

Louise gripped her chair under the table. Now Cornélie was recruiting her to become part of a controlling operation, tightening Berthe's cage further. But how could she refuse? Cornélie was clothing her and feeding her. Was it to stop her affair with Édouard? Perhaps this was Cornélie's deal – look after Berthe's reputation and she would be allowed to stay.

'Yes of course,' Louise said. She tried to smile at Cornélie. Now she was working for both mother and daughter.

'Good,' Cornélie said. She looked like she was going to say something else. Louise waited, dreading whatever was to come next. But Cornélie decided against it and rang for Giselle to clear the lunch.

With a sense of doom, Louise climbed the stairs to Berthe's room. Now she was working for both Cornélie and Berthe.

She found Berthe rummaging around at the back of the room, looking for a blank canvas.

'I cannot tolerate the way she goes on,' Berthe said. 'Nagging all the time. If it is not about what I should paint, it is that I should get married.'

'Yes, but she did get you painting lessons,' Louise said. 'It sounds like it was a bit risky for your mother, with her social position, but she did help you.' What she wanted to say was: "Appreciate your mother while you have her. You'll feel like you've had a limb torn off when she's gone."

It pained Louise to see Berthe and Cornélie arguing so much. They were like two squabbling chickens trapped in a tiny coop. Compared to them, she and her mother had had a good relationship. Her mother had always supported her, and Louise had tried to help her as much as possible, knowing that she worked so hard to keep their little family together. The only time they'd really argued was when she had wanted to go to art school and her mother had insisted she go to university. Perhaps it was a pattern: mothers and daughters disagreeing about art.

Berthe settled down to paint a vase of roses on the table by the window. Louise sat down to watch. Her mother would be fascinated to see how Berthe painted, how she started, her technique. She would have had so many questions for her. Louise felt her chest tighten. She closed her eyes. Why hadn't she gone to see her mother that weekend? Maybe her mum would have told her she felt unwell, and she could have taken her to a doctor, to a hospital, in time to have her heart checked. She could have saved her. Her mum would still be alive. Louise wrapped her arms tightly around her stomach and tried to stop herself crying. She took some deep breaths and concentrated on Berthe painting to calm herself down.

'I enjoyed looking at Manet's paintings at his studio,' she said after a while.

'Why do you always call him by his second name? His name is Édouard.'

'I suppose it's because that's how he's know in my time: Manet, the Father of Modern Art.'

'What!' Berthe said, turning to her. 'That is an incredible title. Is it true? Do you think we should tell him? He would most definitely be amazed, and maybe a little less depressed about his painting.'

'No, I think we'd better not talk about my secret to anyone,' Louise said. She looked at Berthe's painting of her, the one she'd travelled through, sitting stacked against the wall. 'It was funny how you mentioned this painting of me the other day. You know, if you ever did finish it, I might vanish back to my own time. Maybe that's how it works – when you finish it, I disappear.'

'Yes, so it will never be finished,' Berthe said with a smile. 'You know, I did not realise how lonely I was until you arrived. It is so very nice having you here.'

Louise smiled at Berthe. She liked having her here – that was wonderful to hear! She sat back in her chair.

'Your style is so different from Manet's, I mean Édouard's,' she said. '*Olympia, Le Déjeuner,* they're quite ... I don't know. And that one of you on the balcony ...'

'People called me a *femme fatale* after seeing that. Mother refused to look at it. Édouard told her someone had asked the price of it, and she said they had only asked to make fun of him.'

'It is quite an odd painting ...'

'Well, *I* look odd. I look more strange than ugly in it. I think his pictures produce something of the impression of a wild or unripe fruit.'

'I know what you mean. But your paintings, they are so light and free, full of movement. I think it's the way you paint light, things are sort of fragmented.' Louise paused. 'Have you heard of photons?'

'What?' Berthe said, preparing her canvas, only half listening.

'Photons. Physicists, scientists, have discovered that light is made of photons. Light behaves like a wave and a particle at the same time. It's weird. Something about the way you paint ... I don't know.'

'Tell me about these *photons,*' Berthe said.

How could Louise explain physics and light to someone in 1871? She launched in.

'Well, light travels in a wave, very fast. It's the fastest thing in the universe. You can't see it, of course, but it's made up of these tiny little packets, photons. And photons can act as a wave and particles at the same time. It's strange.'

'Where do they come from, these photons?'

'Light is from the energy produced in the heart of the sun by nuclear fusion.'

'Nuclear fusion?'

'Yes, but don't ask me to explain that.'

'So light is a wave and a particle at the same time. I can almost imagine it waving and bouncing,' Berthe said, waving her paintbrush around. 'It is funny, when I paint, when I focus on something, everything disappears except the light. I do not even see the thing I am painting any more. That is why I did not see you at first when you appeared. Remember, it took me a while to recognise you were there?'

'Yes, and I just sat there, dumbly.'

'Look, come over here; do you see the light on that rose?' Berthe said.

Louise peered deep into the rose and smelt its sweetness.

'It looks red,' Berthe said, 'but there are blues and lavenders too. It changes in the light all the time.'

'Yes, I see what you mean.'

'It is like the light shimmers and pops through it … like a wave and a particle,' Berthe said, 'just like you said.'

Louise stared at Berthe, amazed how she seemed to understand this concept.

'You know, I have often wondered where the colours go when it gets dark,' Berthe said. 'Are they still there and we cannot see them, or do they disappear?'

'Let's see, colours are produced by light. The wavelengths of light are reflected off the object, so a green leaf absorbs all the colours *except* green. It reflects the green back into our eyes. So, if there no light, there's no colour. There are no colours when it's dark.'

'Oh, so things do not have their own colour?' Berthe said. She seemed disappointed. 'But I see it is because of the light. That makes perfect sense. Things only live in the light.'

Louise nodded. 'And they discovered, I don't know when, that all the colours together make up white light. You know how in a rainbow you can see all the separate colours? If you put them back together, you get white light. Some artists, it must be about now, I suppose, came up with this idea of using just points of pure colour straight onto the canvas to make up a scene. Dots of pure colour. It makes the colours seem stronger. It's called Pointillism. I can't remember when that happened, or happens.'

'Dots of colour? I do not like that idea at all,' Berthe grimaced. 'I heard there is a way to make light out of air, not from burning a candle or gas, but in the air somehow. Do you know what that is?'

What could she be thinking of …?

'Ah, electricity!' Louise said.

'Electricity?'

'Yes, we have it everywhere, in my time. You just flick a switch on the wall and the light comes on.'

'Really? That is amazing. Like magic.'

'I suppose it is.' Louise had obviously taken electricity for granted.

'So, maybe you travelled on light, on a light wave, to get here?'

'Hah, maybe. I don't know. I don't know how it happened. I don't know if there's any science for it, for travelling through a painting, through time.' She paused. 'But maybe time doesn't even exist. Some scientists say that it's just a trick of our perception.'

'A trick?'

'That we just imagine it. That time isn't real.'

Louise had a sudden idea. 'Do you have a pack of cards? Have they been invented yet?'

'Yes, of course. Why?'

'I want to show you something.'

Berthe dragged some cards out from the back of a drawer and gave them to her. Louise fanned them out on the table.

'OK, so how could you order these cards?'

'Well, let's see. You could put them all in number order, aces, two, threes, etcetera.'

'One suit at a time?'

'Yes, all the hearts, ace to king, then all the clubs and so on.'

'OK.' Louise started putting the cards in that order. 'And how else could you order them? Is there another way?'

'I suppose you could put all the numbers together, like all four aces from all the four suits, then all the twos together, the threes, and so on.'

Louise started doing that.

'How else?'

'I do not know. Perhaps you could put the suits in different orders, like the two red suits, hearts and diamonds, then the black suits, clubs and spades ... or maybe put them in reverse number order.'

'You agree there are quite a few different ways to organise these cards?' Louise said.

'Yes, I suppose ...'

'Well, that's like time. Maybe we can only see one way the cards can be organised. We don't see other possible ways. Our brains, the way our biology is set up, means we are not able to see the other ways that time might be organised. Time could be completely different from what we think. Or it may just be an illusion, something our mind has created.'

'Really? No time? I cannot imagine that.'

'That's the point, I suppose – you can't imagine it. It's like before we used to think that the earth was flat. It seemed that way to us because that's what we could see. But now we know it's round.' Louise stopped. 'You do know that, don't you?'

'Yes, of course!'

'And we used to think the sun went round the earth but now we know the earth goes round the sun. You know that too, right?' Louise said with a giggle. 'But it doesn't feel like we're moving at all. So that's like time. We see it one way but maybe it actually works differently.'

Berthe leaned forward, grabbed the cards from the table and threw them all up in the air. They fluttered down and landed on the floor, all mixed up.

'Maybe that is how you came here. Someone threw all the cards up in the air!'

She went over to her paints, picked up her brush and threw some wild brush strokes onto the canvas. At that moment, Cornélie came in.

'What on earth are you doing, Berthe? Trying to impress your friends? You really need to stop this experimental nonsense.'

Berthe sighed. Cornélie walked round the studio, examining Berthe's paintings, shaking her head. She picked up a conventional portrait.

'This is the kind of thing you should be focusing on. Don't turn away from popular subjects like this. You need to make sure that people who are not well-versed in art are able to appreciate it. If you want to be successful, you must pay attention to public taste. These other paintings look incomplete, you'll never be able to sell them. Honestly, praise from a few other artists has gone to your head.'

Berthe glared at her. Cornélie went to the door.

'Oh, some news. A boy delivered a message: Pierre Puvis de Chavannes,' she said with a flourish, 'will call next week.' And she left the room.

Louise looked at Berthe, who turned away, frowning.

Who on earth was Pierre Puvis de Chavannes?

CHAPTER 17

PARALLEL UNIVERSE

Dawn was breaking over the city skyline. Louise had slept well for once. She sat up in bed and looked out at the trees in the garden. They were reaching up to the light. Their branches extended like arms, arms turning into hands, fingers becoming leaves, stretching and opening to gather up the sunlight. That image – she had seen it so vividly before.

She was twenty, driving with her friends out to the countryside. They had found a remote beach on Loch Lomond with a view of the mountains. She was apprehensive – she'd heard stories of people seeing melting walls and giant black spiders. But her first tab of acid opened up a beautiful world to her, as if she had gone through a door into a magical new reality. She could see the trees reaching up to grasp life with their hands and fingers. She could see life everywhere: in the vibrant pulsing energy throbbing through the veins of a leaf, and there in her own hand, in her own veins, clear, bright, and strong. She could see the intense, vibrating energy of life itself.

Louise went to the open window and breathed in the fresh morning air. LSD and magic mushrooms; it was like having your blinkers removed. Is it always there and we just can't see it? That universe just out of sight, only a shimmer away from our normal? It just needs a tiny chemical to open the gates in our brain and let it all flood in. Open the prison of your mind and the solidity of things melts away into thin air. It's like looking right through things into the quantum world.

Maybe that was why she liked the Impressionists so much. They caught a glimpse of the energy of life. Their perception was freed too; it was looking let loose.

That day she'd felt she understood time for the first time. She had picked up a stone from the beach and held its weight in her hand. It was heavy and ageless. She gazed at the solidity of the mountains around her. Human beings had toiled in their foothills, struggling to grow crops for centuries. Later, she and the others had trudged up the slopes in lines of bright colourful Gore-Tex to eat sandwiches on their tops. The mountains stood solid, oblivious to the furious activity as millennia passed. Their time moved infinitely slowly. And she was just a firefly, a brief speck of bright life in the endless age of the world. She felt her ego, her *self*, dissolve. Time and space disappeared, and she felt at one with everything.

That experience altered her. She had never forgotten the eternity of the mountains and the shimmer of energy and light beyond her visible reality. That sense of mystery. She'd tried to describe it once to Paul, but it was so hard to find the right words. He'd scoffed and made fun of her.

Louise looked out at the orange glow of the sunrise warming this Paris morning. She, her *self*, had dissolved through Berthe's painting. She had slipped through time from one energy, one world, to another. Was this a parallel world?

Quantum physics had a theory about parallel worlds. The world splits every time you make a decision. There's a world where you make one decision and another world where you make the opposite one. Two parallel worlds are created every time you decide something. These alternate universes lie alongside each other, unknown to you. There must be hundreds, millions, an infinite number of parallel worlds. They create a multiverse – everything possible happens somewhere. Everything, everywhere, all at once.

Maybe I'm in a parallel universe now, she thought. *Maybe I left a version of myself in Mum's cottage in Harris.* If so, what was *that* Louise doing now? Had she cleared the house for sale?

Or maybe, in another universe, Paul had guessed where she was and rushed up to tell her he loved her, begged her to take him back ... She sighed. She wanted that – him to want her, to beg her. But he didn't care anymore. Back at the cottage before she came here, she had felt desperate about his affair. Perhaps in that universe the glinting broken glass had proved too enticing, and she had slit her wrists. She was dead on the carpet, being nibbled by the mice.

What would happen if she went back? Would she merge into the original Louise? Or would there be two of them? What if she was dead? When she went back, would she just die? Or maybe in the other universe she was already dead, and she would get stuck in the painting for ever, between two worlds.

There were endless parallel universes, endless possibilities, like an infinitely branching tree. What would happen to her? Louise's heart started thumping. Panic churned up inside her. She had to stop thinking about all this stuff. She was safe here. Staying here was a much better option than confronting any of that. She looked at herself in the mirror.

I don't want to go back. I can't.

She went to the basin and splashed cold water on her face.

*

Louise dressed and skipped down the stairs, happy with the world she found herself in this morning. *Sometimes I believe as many as six impossible things before breakfast,* she thought.

There was no one in the dining room. She'd spent so long gazing out the window thinking about her trips, she had missed breakfast. That was annoying; she'd wanted to see if she could do something for Berthe, but Berthe must have gone out with Cornélie.

There would be food downstairs. She went down the stone staircase and along the dark corridor into the kitchen. Giselle was there, alone. She quickly put something behind her back.

'What are you doing?' Louise asked.

'Oh Mademoiselle Louise, I'm sorry, so sorry. I was just going to take this to my family.' She produced half a loaf of bread. 'It's an old loaf, it's stale, they would just throw it out. I'm not stealing!'

'I'm sure you're not, Giselle. Don't worry. It's fine. And do call me Louise. Where do your family live?'

'Montmartre.'

'How many of you are there?'

'My mother, my two brothers, two sisters.'

'Are they hungry?'

'Yes, all the time,' Giselle said.

'Well, let's see what else there is.' Louise looked around the kitchen.

'But Mademoiselle Louise, I can't take any more.'

'Of course you can. They'll never miss it.'

Louise rummaged around and filled two baskets with fruit, vegetables and more bread.

'You can't carry all this by yourself; I'll come with you,' Louise said.

'You! Oh no, you can't!' Giselle said.

'Why not?'

'It's not right, for a lady.'

'If you can go, so can I.' Louise picked up a basket.

'But I'm walking there.'

'Good. We'll walk together.'

They set off along the clean tree-lined pavements of Passy, carrying one heaped basket each. As they walked, Louise asked Giselle how she had become a maid for the Morisots. Giselle said that Nanette, the cook, had got her the job. Nanette was a friend of her mother's in Montmartre and had persuaded Madame Morisot to give her a chance. Nanette was teaching Giselle how to be a maid.

'I think Madame was sorry for me when Nanette told her about my circumstances,' Giselle said.

'Was she?' Louise said. It seemed that Cornélie had a heart after all.

Giselle's father had been killed in the war and her littlest sister, Amélie, had died of malnutrition during the siege.

'She was only three,' Giselle said and started crying quietly.

Louise shifted her basket to her other hand and took Giselle's arm. She sighed. She understood that grief. The pain for her mother was always there, just beneath her skin. It could lurch up and overwhelm her at any moment. And with the grief, a tidal wave of guilt could surge up and crush her without warning. She had not been there for her mother when she needed her most. She had failed her.

Louise clenched her teeth tightly and walked slowly on, dragging her grief and guilt behind her. After a few steps, she looked over at Giselle, who was wiping away her tears, looking back at her, confused; she was not used to people being nice to her; she was only a servant. Louise squeezed her hand.

Montmartre was further than Louise expected. It was getting hot. She started sweating under her layers of clothing. They had only reached the bright new Arc de Triomphe, and she was already tired. Then she saw Gene coming towards them, a knight in a shiny carriage.

'Gene!' she called out.

'Louise, what on earth are you doing here?' Gene said. The carriage pulled up beside them.

'We're going to Giselle's family in Montmartre, taking them some food,' Louise said.

Giselle lowered her eyes, sure that she would get into trouble now.

'It's quite far,' Gene said, 'and those baskets look heavy. Why don't I take you?'

They climbed in. Giselle had never been in a carriage before. She held on tightly and gazed around her in excitement.

They neared the foot of Montmartre and Gene said the horses wouldn't be able to get up the steep hill. He'd walk up with them. He took Giselle's basket.

Montmartre – Louise couldn't wait to see it again. She loved it in her time. It was her favourite area of Paris. Eagerly, she started the steep climb up the hill. She looked up and marvelled at the pretty old windmills and gardens. It was such a shame they hadn't kept them. But when she looked down at the streets, the thrill left her. Buildings were broken and crumbling, dirty listless children in rags sat on the ground, women getting water from crowded pumps stared at them with surly faces. Policemen and soldiers stood at every corner, watching. An ugly silence hung over the place, a sense of despair.

'They've imposed martial law on Montmartre since the Commune,' Gene said. 'There's a curfew, a crackdown on drunken disorderliness.'

They walked up to the Place du Tertre. Louise stopped, open-mouthed. It was unrecognisable from the last time she had been here, one hundred and fifty years in the future. Then, it was always thronging with tourists, artists drawing surprisingly good caricatures, endless shops with Impressionist paintings on magnets, mugs, aprons. People sitting in cafés eating crepes, taking selfies, laughing, chatting, with the white Sacré-Cœur gleaming over them.

But now it was a mess. Gene pointed out some abandoned cannons. The Commune had seized them from the army, he said, and refused to let the army recover them after the siege. They were lying broken on the ground. Like the people.

Giselle led them on through the dirty alleys to her home in Rue Cortot. The building which would become Renoir's studio was on this same street.

Giselle explained that her mother did laundry to try to feed the children. She hesitated at a low door.

She doesn't want us to see inside, Louise thought and began putting her basket down.

But Giselle's mother opened the door, drying her hands on her skirt.

'They've brought us some food,' Giselle said to her mother.

'Oh Mademoiselle, Monsieur,' her mother said, 'so much food! How kind of you. Do come in. May I get you something to drink?'

She ushered them in, squeezing them through the tiny doorway. There was one dark room with a bare floor. Beds were crammed at one end and laundry piled in a corner next to basins of hot water in the middle of the room. It smelt of grime and soap. Two dirty little boys and two skinny girls looked at them in terror from the corner. Louise took some apples from a basket and held them out to the children. They grabbed them and ate them straight away.

'It's nice to meet you but I'm sorry, we can't stay,' Louise said.

Giselle and her mother thanked Louise and Gene over and over. The children started unpacking the baskets to see what they'd got, squealing with delight.

Louise crouched down through the door and stepped out into the light. She put her head back to feel the warmth of the sun and closed her eyes against the brightness. This was exactly the same sun that shone on her in the future but here, now, everything was different. She'd seen poverty in India and Nepal, but it was strange to see it in Paris, in Montmartre. And such a contrast from the Morisot house. London, Glasgow, most cities in Europe would be like this, at this time. Squalid. She squeezed her eyes closed.

'Are you all right?' Gene said.

'Yes, it's just shocking, the poverty.' Louise took his arm.

They walked slowly down to La Place de Pigalle to meet the carriage, stepping over the piles of rubbish and holes in the streets.

'I know,' Gene said. 'Many of these people were forced out of the city by Haussmann's changes. Is it any wonder they wanted a revolution? It's even worse for them now, after the disaster of the Commune. While we wander along our bright new boulevards, they starve.'

They walked in silence and entered the square, Place de Pigalle.

'There was a battle here, the government against the Commune,' Gene said. 'It's hard to believe that was only a few months ago.'

It was late afternoon, and the square was busy. Louise gazed around – what on earth? Young women were standing around the fountain in the middle. But what women! Some wore silk dresses gleaming with jewels and heavy brocade, their hair gathered up into magnificent chignons under feathered hats. Others seemed to be in fancy dress as ancient heroines, mythical deities or biblical figures. Many were draped in some semi-transparent material. Clouds of musk and patchouli drifted over to Louise and Gene.

'What are they wearing?' Louise said. 'Are they prostitutes?'

'No,' laughed Gene, 'Artists' models. This is the marketplace for models. They're posing as figures from paintings.'

She could see now. Young men were chatting to the women, appraising them, sketching them.

'Well, that one looks like a prostitute,' she said, indicating a woman wearing next to nothing, lifting her skirt to a group of admiring young men.

'Yes, she probably is,' Gene said. 'There's a thin line sometimes. So many prostitutes in Paris now. They are supposed to be registered with the police and have, er, physical inspections, to check for syphilis.'

'Really? That's disgusting.'

'Yes, it is. But it's hard sometimes to tell the prostitutes from "respectable women."'

'Why don't they check the men?'

'What?'

'For syphilis?'

'Oh. Yes, I suppose they should,' Gene said. 'I don't know. I'm sorry, all this must be very shocking for you.'

'Well these women have no money, no education, no *access* to education, no vote, no rights, nothing. What are they supposed to do? Starve? I would do the same in their position.'

'I suppose you're right,' Gene said. He helped her into the carriage and looked closely at her. 'You are very different, Louise. Most women try their hardest to ignore these things.'

'Is there a big problem with STDs, I mean, syphilis, then?' Louise said, settling onto her seat.

'Syphilis? Er, yes. There is. Actually, my father had it.' Gene looked away, embarrassed. 'I don't know why I told you that; it's supposed to be a secret.'

'I'm sorry about your father.'

'Yes, it is a horrible disease. They pretended it wasn't that, of course, they said it was a stroke. A respectable judge with syphilis? Impossible for a man of his standing, his reputation.'

'Maybe he should have thought about that before … Oh, I'm sorry.'

'No, you're quite right. It's disgraceful. Some men behave very badly, even my father.'

'Wasn't your mother angry?'

'Probably, but she never talked about it. No one did. Our family secret, our family shame. Well, one of them.'

The carriage rumbled back to Passy. The sun was going down and a warm pink glow lit the boulevards. She looked at Gene. His face was tinged with the rosy colour of the sunset.

'I think you and I are a bit alike actually,' she said. 'You know how you were saying how you feel next to Édouard? I feel a bit, well, faded sometimes next to Berthe.'

'Ah, Berthe! So talented. I doff my hat to the beautiful artist,' Gene said. 'But she has a difficult time as a woman. You're good for her, though. She's definitely brightened up since you came. And you are not at all faded. Not at all. Ridiculous idea.'

'I suppose it's like you said – you feel, with Édouard, like a sapling in the shade.'

'Yes,' Gene said. 'So, do you want to be an artist too, like Berthe?'

'I'd like to be. But I don't think I'm good enough. I don't really know what I want. Lots of things. I have so many ideas, things I want to do. I don't seem to be able to do any of them, though.' Louise looked out over the boulevards.

'It's hard for women.'

'No, it's not that. It's me. I stop myself somehow.' The voice in her head telling her she was worthless, the echoing sound of an absent father. 'But what about you? What do you want from life, Gene?'

'Me? Well, I don't have any particular talent. I like to paint, you know, write a bit of poetry, but I'm not a star, not like Édouard, or the others. I just want a quiet life, I think, to be settled one day, wife and children, you know.' He paused. 'You didn't get in touch. I was hoping for a message from you, asking to meet me.'

'Sorry, I've been a bit busy,' Louise said. *Pathetic!* How could she be busy?

'Is it your boyfriend? Do you think he will come back? Do you want him to?'

Boyfriend, husband – Paul. The sting of betrayal stabbed her in the heart, and she clenched her fists. Years of love cancelled out.

'No, not really. He's far away, and I like it here.'

Gene took her hand. She took off her glove and wrapped her fingers around his. It felt like a very daring thing to do.

CHAPTER 18

EN PLEIN AIR

Six weeks ago since she'd left London. Four weeks since she'd come through the painting. The last month and a half had been a blur. Louise had been Berthe's pretend chaperone several times, waiting for her at the studio while she went off with Édouard. She passed the time by gazing at his paintings, trying to understand the techniques he used to paint them.

She'd been out shopping with Suzanne a few times. She enjoyed the trips for a while, but Suzanne was only really interested in fashion, and Louise got bored. She missed Chloe. She'd like to tell her about these women's lives, how restricted they were. And she'd like to tell Chloe about Gene – what would she think of him, and whatever was going on between them?

Louise had managed to meet Gene only three times. She could only see him when Berthe and Cornélie went out. She listened closely to Berthe and her mother as they made their arrangements – would there be a chance to see Gene today, or tomorrow? Organising a meeting was difficult. No text messages. She had to ask Giselle to get a boy to send a note to him. As she waited for opportunities, Louise found herself wanting to see him more and more.

But this morning Louise had a job as chaperone. She, Berthe and Édouard were going painting. They took the carriage to the Bois de Boulogne, met Édouard, and set up their easels under some trees.

'I bumped into George Seurat yesterday,' Édouard said as he put out his paints. 'He was at the Louvre. He had ventured out of his studio for the one half hour he allows himself a week. He's become fascinated with the new scientific discoveries about light.'

Édouard turned to Louise. 'Do you know they've found that white light is made up of all the colours: red, blue, green, yellow? They all add up to white light. Isn't that amazing?'

And to Berthe he said, 'George is thinking about making a painting using just pure colours, no mixing – which he says just muddies them – just small points of different colours on the canvas to make up a scene. He thinks it'll be more vibrant.'

Berthe swung round to Louise. Louise shrugged and smiled at her. Berthe shook her head in disbelief.

'Yes, I know. Ridiculous isn't it?' Édouard said. 'It'll take him hours, days, weeks, years! I don't see the point of it – ha ha!' He squeezed out some paint. 'Look, Louise, have you seen our new paint tubes? They make it so much easier to paint outside. We used to have to carry paint in pigs' bladders. Do you remember, Berthe?'

'And they would dry out, or burst – such a mess,' Berthe said.

'These little tin tubes are wonderful,' Édouard said.

'And the new colours,' Berthe said, looking through her paints. 'Chrome yellow, emerald-green. We have wonderful new pigments now.'

'Look at this viridian, it's a vibrant green,' Édouard said, showing Louise a tube, 'and ultramarine, such a beautiful blue. It used to be they had to make it from lapis lazuli, now they make it in factories.'

'Alizarin, that is most definitely my favourite,' Berthe said. 'Violet. It used to come from a plant, madder, I think.'

Louise tried to express the appropriate amount of awe at the paint tubes and the colours, for Édouard's sake.

Their paints prepared, Berthe and Édouard started painting. But Louise froze. How could she paint with Édouard Manet here? She couldn't put a single dab of paint on the canvas.

She watched Berthe and Édouard begin in their very different ways. Berthe put in white for the background first; she said it made colours brighter. Édouard began with black shadows. Louise found herself taking mental notes of what exactly they were doing, then realised she was doing this so she could tell her mum. Her mother had loved going to classes, learning new painting techniques. But of course, she wouldn't be able to tell her mother anything. Louise took a deep breath. The pain stabbed her in the heart again.

'I think you use too much black,' Berthe said to Édouard. 'Why not let some light in?'

'But I like black,' Édouard said.

'Yes, you love it! Black, black, everywhere. But look at that shadow under the tree – it's lavender, blue, violet. Add some colour. Use the complementary colours next to each other for extra intensity.'

'I do know that,' Édouard said. 'I'll think of adding some colour if you add some contrast. Look, there are no strong accents to your shapes. The balance is wrong.'

'You are so formal with your rigid, defined shapes,' Berthe said. 'Loosen up a little. The city is full of light now.'

Louise smiled. Berthe and Édouard. They were so right for each other. She picked up her brush and tried her best to paint the park landscape.

All was peaceful until, after five minutes, Édouard threw down his brushes and said, 'I can't paint this. It's boring. I need people!' He went off with his sketch book to find some new subjects.

Louise and Berthe continued contentedly, Berthe occasionally coming over to give Louise suggestions. She was teaching Louise to see light and colour. Louise painted the lake through the trees: light dappling through the leaves, the water a shimmer of blue, the rowing boats just a gentle stroke from a heavily laden brush. It was exhilarating when you got it right. Her painting had improved a great deal.

After about an hour, Édouard announced it was time to leave. He wanted to go back to his studio. They piled into the carriage and trundled through the boulevards. Louise breathed in the first scents of autumn. It was September, and the trees lining the pavements were beginning to be tinged with gold, bronze and coppers. Time was passing.

Edgar was waiting at the studio, lounging on a chaise.

'Where have you all been?' he said, 'I've been waiting for ages.'

'Painting *en plein air*, at the Bois de Boulogne,' Berthe said, putting down her bags.

'Oh, *en plein air!*' Edgar said. 'Never say *en plein air* to me again! You know what I think of people who work out in the open? If I were the government, I would have a special brigade of gendarmes to keep an eye on artists who paint nature landscapes. Oh, I don't mean to kill anyone, just a little dose of birdshot now and then as a warning. Women painting outdoors? Even worse.'

'Do you like women at all?' Louise said. No one ever challenged Edgar's ridiculous statements.

'Hah, I'm not sure he does,' Édouard said. 'A while ago, I was convinced he must be sleeping with Clotide, his attractive young housemaid. I asked her and she said she went into his bedroom once while he was changing his shirt and he shouted, "Get out you miserable creature!"'

'Well, I have no desire to marry, for sure,' Edgar said. 'What would I want with a wife? Imagine having someone around who at the end of a gruelling day in the studio said, "That's a nice painting, dear."'

They laughed, Louise despite herself, and Edgar continued. He twirled the end of his moustache. 'All these glamorous bejewelled women with bare shoulders and plunging necklines, hauled by their husbands from salons to opera boxes and glittering dinner parties. I was seated next to one lady at dinner one evening, past her prime, shall we say, she was practically naked. I could not take my eyes off her. Suddenly she turned and asked: "Are you staring at me?" "Good Lord, Madame, I wish I had the choice!" I said.'

'So, you have no interest in women,' Louise said. 'You don't have a girlfriend?'

Maybe he was gay.

'The artist must live apart. His private life should be unknown,' Edgar said.

'I've heard him,' Édouard said. 'When his work is going well, he sings a little song to himself: "I'd rather keep a hundred sheep than one outspoken girl." He punched Edgar playfully on the arm.

'I have locked away my heart in a pink satin slipper,' Edgar said, crossing his arms over his chest.

Louise looked at him and smiled to herself; her mum would never have believed what Edgar Degas was like.

CHAPTER 19

PIERRE PUVIS DE CHAVANNES

At breakfast, Cornélie announced that Pierre Puvis de Chavannes was coming to visit. *What a ridiculous name*, Louise thought, but it seemed that he was an important visitor. Cornélie fussed over what Berthe would wear. Demure, frills, not the newest fashion, she insisted.

'He's a traditional man. You must make a good impression.'

Why? Louise wondered.

At eleven am exactly, Giselle showed Pierre into the drawing room where Cornélie, Berthe and Louise were sitting waiting. Louise was not impressed. Pierre was in his late sixties, balding, with a carefully groomed beard and a large middle-aged spread. He had an arrogant air about him. Cornélie introduced Louise, but he looked right past her, not interested in a girl from Brittany.

Cornélie started her carefully choreographed monologue. She praised Pierre's work and asked him about his latest projects. He was doing very well, thank you. He had completed murals in Amiens, Marseille, Poitiers and Lyon. Of particular importance, he said, was the cycle at the Palais de Beaux Arts in Lyon. People were very keen on his allegorical pieces and idealised themes from antiquity, he explained to the women.

Louise stifled a yawn.

'I am working now on *Le Pigeon*,' Pierre said. 'Remember during the siege we used pigeons to carry messages? In my painting, a woman is in mourning. She is St Genevieve; she embodies Paris itself. She is protecting a white pigeon from an eagle. It is a painting of hope – the hope that Paris will become reunified.'

'I like how your work is full of symbolism,' Berthe said, 'and so independent of artistic currents today.'

Louise looked at Berthe. She *liked* his work?

'But Berthe, you must let me see your latest paintings, my dear,' Pierre said.

Louise trailed after them up the stairs to Berthe's room. At Cornélie's insistence, Berthe had cleaned it up and put away some of her more "experimental" work. On show on the easel was *The Harbour at Cherbourg*, a long harbour leading into the distance with a cart, a few figures and sailing boats moored alongside. Louise hadn't seen it before.

Pierre examined it closely.

'That's a very promising beginning,' he said. 'You do have some talent, Berthe.'

Louise stifled a scoff and turned it into a cough. Pierre noticed and frowned at her.

'You do not think it finished?' Berthe said.

'No, it's a good sketch but the cart looks too light, not very solid. The painting needs more detail, especially in the foreground. You should finish it off like this.'

Pierre picked up one of Berthe's brushes and started putting in details on the cart, the bags on the harbour, the boats.

'But that's Berthe's painting,' Louise said. 'You can't do that!'

Berthe stood watching. She was gritting her teeth, but she didn't say a word.

'Yes, exactly,' Cornélie said, leaning in to watch Pierre. 'That's much better, just what I've been telling her.'

'It was better the way it was,' Louise said. This imperious, pompous old man was ruining Berthe's painting.

Everyone ignored her.

'And what's the story?' said Pierre, laying down the brush. 'Try to give every painting a narrative for the audience to interact with. Put some emotion into it and I think it will be much better. Do you understand what I'm saying?'

Louise glared at him as he turned to Cornélie.

'I will return when Tiburce is here,' he said. 'There is something I wish to discuss with him.'

He leered at Berthe. Louise stared at her and her friend lowered her eyes. Why was she being so submissive? What was going on here?

As he turned to leave, Pierre Puvis de Chavannes gave Louise a thin smile; it was more like a grimace.

CHAPTER 20

MERE DAUBS

Lunch, served up with bread, cheese and fruit; more tension between mother and daughter. Berthe, as usual, ate next to nothing. Was she anorexic?

'So, Berthe are you going to marry Pierre Puvis de Chavannes?' Cornélie said. 'He will no doubt want to discuss it with Tiburce when he calls.'

Louise spluttered into her glass of water and looked at Berthe. *Marry Pierre Puvis de Chavannes, that old buffoon? Surely not!*

'I shall be brutal,' Cornélie said. 'You are nearly thirty and your looks are fading.'

'But you will still love me!' Berthe said, smiling at her mother.

'You are making a huge sacrifice for an unnecessary profession. Why do it?' Cornélie said.

'Do what?'

'Inflict this pain on yourself. I really don't think there is any point to it. You'll never achieve the success you wish.'

Berthe sighed.

'I do like some, many, of your paintings but you're not selling any. And your artist friends will move on in time,' Cornélie said.

'You mean men.'

'Yes, men. My greatest wish is for you to be content and settled, Berthe. Continue like this and you will become more irritable than you already are. You will have less freedom than if you followed the

141

traditions you so greatly detest. And yes, I mean marriage.'

'Stop,' Berthe said. 'That is enough. I respect you as best as I can, but ...' She pushed back her chair, got up and left the room, slamming the door.

Cornélie sighed.

'You see Louise, I'm trying my best to get her to understand, to help her. And yes, I am thinking of myself too, but as time passes, her youthfulness, her looks, will slip away and the people she believes to be her friends will not be around anymore.'

She brushed some crumbs off the table.

'I understand she is attracted to the glamour of Paris, the art, the excitement of the exhibitions, but it is just a fantasy, an illusion. If she were to settle down, I believe she would be much happier. I wish she were past having these wild ideas.'

'But Berthe is so good,' Louise said. 'She's a wonderful painter. I'm sure she'll be a successful artist.'

Louise watched Cornélie sharply cut up her cheese. It was hopeless. How could she, as a young woman from Brittany, convince Cornélie that Berthe would become a famous artist?

'These artists are not known for their reliability,' Cornélie said. 'Édouard is like a weathervane; he uses other people to entertain himself. Madame Manet says she's worried that he is on a destructive path – he has no prospect of success with his unconventional work. I've heard that people stay away from him to avoid talking about his paintings. Poor Suzanne, having to put up with it all. I heard he just painted a portrait of her, which I think was high time.'

Had he? Louise hadn't seen any painting of Suzanne in Édouard's studio.

'It is generally accepted that it is preferable to enter into a marriage,' Cornélie said, 'rather than to remain single and in limbo.'

Louise sighed. Cornélie was not interested in anything she had to say. She sat through the rest of her monologue until she could escape to find Berthe.

*

Louise went up the stairs, opened the door to the studio, and gasped. The room was full of smoke. Berthe was ripping up paintings and throwing canvases onto a fire. The smell of burning oil paint was choking. Louise saw a beautiful garden scene dissolve into black smoke. Others were already ashes.

'Stop, Berthe! What are you doing?'

'They are terrible!' Berthe said. 'I am not an artist! I am fooling myself. I will never be good enough. I should marry Pierre. Forget about all of this.'

Berthe picked up the painting of Louise, the one she'd travelled through, and took it towards the fire.

'No!' Louise lurched forward and grabbed it from her. 'No, you can't destroy this, or any of them. You're a wonderful artist. You're in a book in the future. Remember, I saw this in a book, and it's in lots of other books too!'

She looked around for some of the other paintings she'd seen. They weren't there. Had Berthe destroyed them already? Or maybe she hadn't painted them yet.

'My paintings are mere daubs,' Berthe said with tears in her eyes.

'No, no, they're not.'

Gently, Louise took Berthe's arm and pulled her over to sit on the chaise.

'You're an amazing artist, Berthe. Don't listen to Pierre, or your mother. You're at the beginning of a something new, a new style, a new type of art. People just don't recognise it yet, but you will be famous. There will be exhibitions of your paintings in Paris, and around the world.'

'If only that were true,' Berthe said. 'I wish I could believe you.'

'Well, just imagine, for a moment, that I'm right. Isn't it worth carrying on, just in case?'

'But I will never be accepted.' Berthe put her head in her hands. 'Those men are all against me. I cannot go to the school to study. I cannot get proper training. I cannot draw nudes. I want to understand human anatomy, to learn.'

'Why can't you?'

'Women of society are not allowed into the schools,' Berthe said. She looked longingly out of the window at the city. 'My mother believes it is not right or safe for me to be out on my own. It's so frustrating. I wish I could wander about and paint as I please, like a man. I yearn to be able to go wherever I want, take a seat in the Luxembourg Gardens, look at the artwork in shops, see the churches and museums, explore the old alleys at night. That is what I crave, and it is that freedom I need to become a true artist.'

She got up and walked to the window.

'I am stuck, trapped in this house, in this woman's body, in the monotony of daily life. I have been trained to do the same things over and over again – embroider, play the piano, visit other women with whom I have nothing in common. I am so bored! I say "I'm bored" to myself twenty times a day. And I feel so lonely without Edma; there's a huge emptiness in my heart since she left.'

Louise felt her heart breaking for Berthe.

'I know but I'm here now. I'll keep you company,' she said. How could she make Berthe see what a good painter she was? She looked around at the beautiful paintings and went over to one hanging on the wall. A young woman sat at a window in a white tea dress, distractedly fiddling with a fan, gazing into nothing. Blurry figures stood on distant balconies in houses opposite.

'Look at this painting, for example – it's wonderful.'

'That is Edma,' Berthe said. 'I painted that when I visited her in Lorient. It was not long after she was married. She was, is, so bored, stranded in the country with nothing to do. A wife.'

'But you've captured that perfectly – a woman excluded. Real life happening out there on the street, and she's stuck inside, unable to join in.'

'Confined to the house and sentenced to a life of boredom. So called *respectable* women cannot go to public spaces, the street can only be seen from the protective cocoon of home, through the window, or from a balcony. Male and female spaces are worlds apart.'

'You show that brilliantly, how trapped she feels,' Louise peered into Berthe's sister's face.

'I can only paint my mother or sister, or the maid or anyone I can persuade to sit still for a minute,' Berthe said.

'You paint a woman's experience.'

They looked at the sad painting of trapped Edma.

'I exhibited that painting at the Salon last year,' Berthe said. 'That is the one that was hung so high up that nobody noticed it.'

Louise went over to another painting of a young woman and an older woman sitting on a floral patterned sofa.

'And this one – is this Edma and your mother?'

'Yes. I did that a few years ago.'

Cornélie was in a dark black dress, black hair with black scarf, white cuffs and neck frill. She was concentrating on reading a book. Edma sat beside her, dressed in white, hands clasped in her lap, staring blankly in front of her. The black swathe of Cornélie's dress cut diagonally across the foreground of the painting dominated. Edma looked smothered and trapped by the dark presence of her mother.

'Edma looks sad, like she'd rather be anywhere else,' Louise said.

'Yes, she was bored then too.' Berthe said. 'I should have burnt this one. I was so annoyed; Pierre Puvis de Chavannes, you know, my *suitor*, well, a few years ago he came in when I was painting this and started examining one of the figures. He said it was completely wrong and I should start all over again.'

Louise tensed up. The arrogant Pierre! He was like Paul, taking over, destroying a woman's confidence.

Berthe came over to look at the painting with Louise.

'I was so distressed, I asked Édouard to come and give me his opinion. He came the next day, which was the final day to submit the painting to the Salon. He thought it was good, except for the bottom of the dress, which he started painting over. But then he couldn't stop himself from adding more and more to the painting, to the dress, to the hair, all in a complete frenzy. He thought it was hilarious. By five o'clock that evening, we had a ridiculous caricature. That is why the painting is so dark.'

Louise looked more closely.

'I think it's quite good.'

'I did send it to the Salon, but I became so distressed I had to get it back. Mother retrieved it, but then we couldn't think of anything to say to Édouard, so we resubmitted it.'

'Was it well received?'

'It was quite a success, but it was not my painting anymore. You can see Édouard's work all over it, in Mother's face and dress. Only the upholstery and reflections in the mirror above Edma's head are mine. Then Pierre ruins my Cherbourg harbour! I will never ask anyone for an opinion of my painting again.'

'You didn't even ask for his opinion!'

'No. I will fix it later, put it back how it was. Come, look at this one.'

Berthe took Louise out to the hallway and into Edma's bedroom where a large painting of a young woman hung on the wall.

'It's you.'

'Yes. Edma did that of me when I was twenty-four.'

The painting was of Berthe painting; it was dark and intense like Berthe herself. Berthe was balancing her palette on her left arm, and held brushes and a rag in her left hand. In her right hand, she held a paintbrush. She was concentrating hard. The deep brown background, her brown coat, hair tied back with a red band, framed the brightness of her attention. It captured Berthe totally – serious, focused.

'Edma is so talented,' Berthe said. 'She was a better painter than me. All our teachers said so. They tried to be kind to me, but it was clear that they thought so. That was very painful for me, but it was true. Now she does not paint any more. It is a great loss, such a waste. She wrote to me today. I have the letter here.'

Berthe took the letter out of her pocket and started reading it.

'She says she is totally bored. It is raining all the time.'

'Oh dear,' Louise said.

'I do not know. I think she has a better life now. Her husband loves her. Painting is just such a frustration. Perhaps she is better off without it.'

'But I don't understand. Why can't she still paint when she's married?'

'She says she has too much to do: entertaining, sewing. Her husband of course feels like he should be enough for her. I could not do it. Despite what I just did,' Berthe said with a smile, 'really, I could not stop painting – I think it would kill me. Luckily for Edma, she has been blessed with two daughters; motherhood is a perfect fit for her.'

Berthe put the letter back in her pocket.

'But in some ways I feel I *would* like her life. When her little daughter comes to visit, she is so sweet the way she plays with me. It is so confusing. I feel the urge to have a baby now – but that is the last thing I need!'

So Berthe wanted a baby too! Louise looked at the conflict on her face. She knew exactly how she felt.

Berthe put the letter away and they went back to her bedroom. They sat together by the window.

'So, Pierre Puvis de Chavannes?' Louise said. 'What a name!'

'Yes I know. But he is a wonderful artist.'

'He's old.'

'He is a bit older.'

'How much?'

'About twenty years.'

'Twenty years!'

'He is in demand,' Berthe said, 'as an artist all over the country. He is called "the Painter for France". But if I married him, my life as an artist would be over. I would be his wife. I would not be able to keep painting.'

'In my time, women keep their careers when they marry. We can be totally independent. Our own jobs, money. We can buy our own houses …'

She stopped talking mid-sentence. Her stomach knotted up – her flat in London, which she co-owned with Paul. If they split up, they would have to sell it. How would she get enough money to buy another one on her own in London? Was Paul thinking about any of this while he was having his nice affair? Her life back home would be complete turmoil when she went back.

'To be independent,' Berthe said, 'that must be wonderful – to be free! But I have no money of my own. I am totally dependent. Now, on my father, and if I married, it would be on my husband.'

Louise dragged herself back into the room, and the present.

'We can keep our careers after marriage,' she said, '*and* after we have children. We are equal to men, except, well, we still don't have equal pay. Actually, we're not really equal in lots of things yet but we've come a long way. And we have contraception. That has helped a lot.'

'What is that?'

'You can take get a pill to stop you getting pregnant when you have sex. You can control when and if you have children.'

'Really? A pill? Is everyone, you know, making love all the time then?'

'It's a lot easier for women than now, I imagine. But it's still usually the woman's responsibility. So, not completely equal.'

'Have you had many boyfriends?' Berthe said.

'I suppose I've had quite a few.' Louise started counting in her head.

'And some, er, experience, then?'

'You mean sex? Yes I suppose so. I'm married now, you know.'

No: why had she said that? She clenched her fists – she did not want to talk about Paul.

'Oh, are you?' Berthe turned to face her. Louise looked away.

'But I did not know! Why did you not tell me?' Berthe said. 'You are married! Do you not miss him?'

'No,' Louise said. She changed the subject. 'What about you? Have you had many boyfriends, before Édouard?'

'Me? No.' Now it was Berthe's turn to look away, embarrassed. 'You have to be so careful, your reputation. If you got caught …'

'Your social position, yes, it's difficult for you,' Louise said. 'You know we have lots of single women, working, bringing up their children.'

'Goodness! Here only poor women do that. Women actually *choose* to do that?'

'Sometimes. It's perfectly possible if you have the money. And we can vote.'

'Vote?'

'Yes. Women with property got the vote in 1918, that's about, fifty years from now.' She tried to remember when women got the vote in France. 'I think it was quite a bit later in France.'

'What a surprise,' Berthe said. She looked at Louise closely. 'You are remarkably interesting, Louise.'

'Thanks. Have you heard of feminism? No, probably not,' Louise said.

'What is that?'

'It's a movement which starts a bit later than this. A feminist believes women are equal to men. Who wouldn't want to believe that? Some people still don't, I don't know why. You are definitely as good an artist as a man, better than most. Édouard thinks you're a good painter, doesn't he?'

'Yes, he does, that's true.' Berthe smiled.

'And he's a genius, you agree?'

'Yes,' Berthe said, smiling. 'I showed him one of my paintings, *Vue du petit port de Lorient,* and he announced that I had made a masterpiece without suspecting it! I was amazed. I could not even laugh when he said that. I gave it to him immediately. And Camille Pissarro bought *Vue de Tivoli* several years ago. Pierre has bought one too.'

'So, several purchases by excellent artists.'

'Yes, I suppose so.'

'So, not "mere daubs"?'

'Maybe not,' Berthe said, now laughing at herself.

*

That night, Louise tugged her huge frilly nightdress over her head and thought back over the day. *How can Berthe not see how talented she was?* She had stood by and watched Pierre ruin her painting. And she had been so close to destroying her wonderful paintings. She had so little faith in herself, and so little opportunity to shine. She was like a bright bird flapping against the bars of her gilded cage. It was cruel to keep such a fierce intelligence and talent trapped like this.

Louise paused, frozen in mid ruffle. But what had she done? She had stopped Berthe burning her paintings – she had interfered, broken the time-travel rule.

She tugged down her nightdress. But maybe Berthe's art existed *because* she had stopped her burning them. Surely that was a good thing? The paintings she'd seen in that book in her mum's cottage in the future, she hadn't seen any of them here. Maybe Berthe hadn't painted them yet, but would now, *because* she had interfered.

Pierre would stop her painting, suffocate her even more. Berthe's future would be ruined if she married him. Maybe that was why she was here – to stop Berthe marrying Pierre!

CHAPTER 21

LIGHT IS EVERYTHING

Louise hadn't slept well. Her mind was racing, trying to figure out how she could stop Berthe marrying Pierre. To try to relax, she started doing yoga. She was upside down in a downward dog when Berthe knocked and came into her room.

'I found this dress for you ...' Berthe said. 'What on earth are you doing?'

'Yoga.'

'What is that?'

'Stretching, breathing exercises.'

'You look ridiculous.'

'It's good for you. Come and try. You could do with it.'

'What do you mean?'

'You're stiff. Stiff as a board. You could do with a stretch.'

'Well, thank you.'

Louise got up. 'Look, I'll teach you.'

She positioned Berthe in the centre of the room.

'Stand up straight, shoulders back. Now breathe in and stretch your arms up, up as high as you can. Breathe out and stretch slowly over to the side, like this. Further.'

'I could not do this wearing a corset,' Berthe said. She was wearing a tea dress.

'It's better in just underwear. Now, the other side. Good. Take in a deep breath, and stretch up and over then touch your toes.'

Berthe took a shallow breath and bent forward until she was at about a forty-five-degree angle.

'Is that as far as you can go?'

'Yes, I think so.'

'Gosh, you're so inflexible,' Louise said. 'It must be all those corsets. They are not good for you. It would be better if you took your dress off.

'Really, should I?'

'There's no one here.'

Berthe took off her tea dress.

'Now, sit on the floor, here.' Louise patted the floor beside her. 'Reach up as high as you can and bend over and touch your toes.'

Louise folded over and wrapped her fingers around her toes. Berthe could not get anywhere near her ankles.

'How can you do that? I cannot get any further,' Berthe said.

'Practise.'

'But what is the point?'

'It makes you feel better. Let's try something else.' Louise got into a plank position, balancing herself on her elbows, forearms, and toes.

'Oh, I am sure I cannot do that,' Berthe said.

'Just try. It's good for your core strength.'

'What is this "core"?'

'Your muscles inside.'

Berthe pushed herself up into plank position, managed to hold it for about five seconds and collapsed.

'This is ridiculous. I cannot do any of it!'

Louise reached out and patted her on the back.

'You're a bit weak, that's all. You'll get better.'

'I will be aching tomorrow,' Berthe said, sitting up, rubbing her sides.

'Let's try some relaxing breathing exercises. Lie down, make yourself comfortable.'

'Comfortable? On the floor?'

'Yes.' Louise lay beside her. 'Take a deep breath in.'

Berthe took a shallow breath.

'Deeper. Fill your lungs as full as possible, then breathe out, and push your stomach out with the air.'

'I had bronchitis last year,' Berthe said, wheezing a little.

'Close your eyes. Imagine you're breathing in light. Fill yourself with warm sunlight. Breathe it in slowly, down to your toes, from your toes to your knees, up your legs. That's it, the light is filling you with warmth. Until your body is completely full. Now, breathe out slowly. Breathe out calm, blue air.'

Berthe breathed.

'That's it, lovely, and again. Keep doing that,' Louise said. She watched Berthe breathing deeper and deeper. A calm Berthe – a novel sight. 'Let your thoughts drift off, like passing clouds. Empty your mind.'

For ten minutes the room filled with the sound of gentle breathing, and the occasional little wheeze.

'This is so good for you,' Louise said.

'Yes, I like it,' Berthe said, opening her eyes. 'It is really peaceful. I felt like I was beginning to disappear.'

'Yes, it's good for when you get stressed about things, when you can't make a decision ...'

Louise paused and looked at Berthe closely.

'You know, a decision about whether to marry someone, like Pierre Puvis de Chavannes.'

'I do not know. I do not know,' Berthe sat up. 'Mother is putting a lot of pressure on me.'

'Well, you don't have to decide right now,' Louise said.

'No.'

Silently, they put their dresses back on.

'I felt like I was disappearing there,' Berthe said, 'when we were breathing. It is like you kind of fade away as your thoughts drift past. One of the thoughts that came to me was about you, and about how you appeared in my painting.'

'It must have been very strange for you.'

'Yes. You appeared when I painted you. I was wondering what would happen if I painted you again, on the painting you came through. Do you think you would go back to your time?'

'I don't know.'

'Shall we try, to see what happens?'

Louise hesitated – was Berthe trying to get rid of her?

'Do you want me to go back?' Louise said.

'No, of course not,' Berthe said. 'I most definitely do not want you to leave. Just to try. An experiment. If you start to disappear, I will stop straight away. I promise.'

'I don't know.' Louise got up and started pacing around the room. If she went back, she'd get out of this mess of being a chaperone and deceiving Suzanne. But then she'd have to deal with Paul and his affair.

Her pulse started racing. *How could she face him?*

'Come on, let us try,' Berthe said.

They went to Berthe's room where Berthe put the painting of Louise on the easel and squeezed some paints onto her palette – whites, blues and greens.

Louise sat in the chair by the window in front of the garden, exactly as she'd been when she'd arrived, nervously fingering her tea dress.

'There is too much here,' Berthe said, scraping some paint off the canvas. She turned it upside down. 'And here.' She put it back the right way up. 'Right.'

She looked closely at Louise, mixed up shades of greens and yellows, and started to paint, getting lost in the shifting colours.

Nothing happened for a few minutes. It wasn't going to work. Louise relaxed a little. But then her fingers started to tingle, and she began to feel dizzy.

'Stop! Stop now!' Louise said. She jumped up off the chair. Berthe dropped her brush. The tingling stopped.

Louise gasped. 'Yes, that works. I think I would go back, but I don't want to, not yet. I can't, I can't go back.'

She stepped away from the chair, terrified about being thrown back into her old – future – life. She wiped her shaking hands on her dress. She couldn't go back. She couldn't bear to see Paul. She'd never forgive him for betraying her and she couldn't face living there without her mum.

A sob burst out of her. She turned away from Berthe.

'What is the matter?' Berthe said.

'No, nothing,' Louise said. 'I'm, em, having such a good time here I'm not ready to go back yet.'

There was an awkward silence.

'Maybe we should paint together?' Berthe said gently. 'Why don't you find something you would like to paint?' She indicated around the room.

Berthe picked up the Cherbourg Harbour painting that Pierre had ruined and started to fix it. Louise wandered around, picking things up and putting them down. Gradually, her breathing slowed, and her heart stopped thumping. She spotted some dried flowers on the top of the wardrobe and reached up for them. There were grasses, brown ferns, red berries, honesty and feathers, all woven together into a sort of crown with white ribbons to tie under the chin.

'Look,' she said to Berthe. 'A crown of flowers.'

'I had forgotten about that,' Berthe said, coming over to her. 'Oh, but the flowers have dried up. I made this when I was a little girl playing in the garden. I would wear it for hours – I was the queen, there was no king of course. And no rules in my kingdom. I never had to sew, practise the piano, sit still. I ran barefoot and played out all day. It was wonderful! I loved that time. Until I was sixteen. Then the silky threads of convention wound around me, like a spider trapping its prey in a web.'

Berthe wove her fingers together, clenched her hands, and sighed.

Louise looked down at the delicate crown in her hands. She placed it gently over Berthe's dark, shining hair, tied the ribbons under her chin and stepped back.

'There. You *are* the queen. Berthe – Queen of Painting!'

Berthe smiled at her. 'You are a good friend, Louise. I am so very glad you are here. Truly, I am not ready for you to leave.'

They spent the afternoon painting. Louise attempting to paint the crown of flowers, Berthe coming over every now and then to make suggestions.

'Look at the shadows – there are blues, purples, reds. And the white ribbon – it has yellows and lavenders in it. Loosen up your brushstrokes, look carefully at the light. Light is colour, movement, life – everything. In fact, light is the subject of every painting.'

CHAPTER 22

PIERRE PERSISTS

Cornélie was out on her endless morning social rounds and Berthe and Louise were reading when Giselle knocked and came in.

'Er, Pierre Puvis de Chavannes is here, Mademoiselle Berthe,' she said.

'Oh, but mother is out,' Berthe said.

'He says he came by to give you something.'

Louise put down her book. He was trying to catch Berthe alone.

Luckily, I'm here – her chaperone.

'Show him up,' Berthe said, and raised her eyebrows at Louise.

Pierre strode into the room with a small bunch of flowers and a package for Berthe.

'I've brought you some presents, my dear,' he said.

Louise squirmed.

Pierre didn't give Berthe the package but unwrapped it himself.

'It's a preliminary sketch of my latest work. I thought you would like it.'

'A sketch?' Louise said.

'Yes,' Pierre said, glaring at her. 'It will become a very important work. This sketch will be very valuable one day.'

'Thank you,' Berthe said, 'that is very thoughtful of you. It is lovely, but I must get Giselle to put these flowers in water.' She left the room to call Giselle.

'So where exactly in Brittany did you say you were from?' Pierre hissed at Louise.

'I didn't.'

'No. You didn't. I know Brittany rather well. I've done several commissions there.'

'How nice for you.'

'Yes, so what town or village are you from?'

Louise didn't answer.

'Hmm. Are you from Brittany at all?' Pierre said. 'I have my doubts. Your accent is strange. Why are you here exactly?'

He saw that Berthe was coming back in, leant forward and whispered.

'You're just in the way.'

Berthe sat on the sofa and Louise sat beside her, glowering at Pierre.

He droned on for a while. He was like a pig, a boar, boring. Every now and then he looked at Louise and flicked his eyes towards the door. She sat tight. There was no way she was going to leave Berthe alone with him. She would be a *good* chaperone on *this* occasion.

Eventually, Pierre gave up and stood to leave. Berthe went to ring for Giselle, and he turned to Louise.

'I believe that I will tell Cornélie that you're not from Brittany at all, that you are an imposter. I'm sure she would not be happy to be hosting a liar in her home.'

'Go ahead,' Louise said. Her stomach lurched. Would Cornélie believe him? If so, she might be thrown out onto the streets!

When he'd gone, Louise turned to Berthe.

'Really, he is too awful, isn't he?'

Berthe didn't answer. She turned away.

'You're not actually thinking of marrying him, are you? He would destroy you, and your painting career.'

'I do not love him, it is true,' Berthe said, 'but it is probably my last chance to marry.'

'But *him*? And you love Édouard!'

'Édouard, Édouard. Yes. That is the problem. Édouard has this hold over me. I am desperate to be with him, near him, all the time. It is like a kaleidoscope of colour when we are together.' Berthe paused and turned to Louise. 'Have you ever felt like that? Like all the colours of the world fall around him, and the rest of the world disappears.'

Louise rubbed her chin and thought of Paul, Antoine, her past boyfriends.

'No,' she said.

'I despair when we are apart,' Berthe said. 'I know I should keep away from Édouard but no one else comes close to him. I have tried to be interested in other men, but they are just pale shadows compared to him. But sometimes I wonder: do I love him or want to *be* him?'

'Who would not want to be him? He is a remarkable man.'

'But he is married. We cannot be together.'

'But Pierre? You can't marry him. He's an old bore.'

'But ... I do so wish to have a baby.'

Louise was silent. What would a woman put up with to have a baby? An oaf like Pierre? An unfaithful husband like Paul?

CHAPTER 23

LE CORPS DE BALLET

Cornélie was insisting Berthe accompany her to visit relatives. Berthe didn't want to go. She rolled her eyes.

'Who would think I was nearly thirty?' Berthe said. 'I have no control over my own life.'

Louise was not expected to go with them. She hadn't told Berthe, but Gene was coming to take her out. Why she was keeping her friendship, her relationship, with Gene a secret? Perhaps Berthe might laugh at her. She had no interest in Gene; he was invisible to her.

Gene arrived in his carriage with a bunch of colourful dahlias he'd picked from his garden.

'So, where would you like to go?' he said. 'Down to the river for a stroll, or to the park for a drive, perhaps?'

It sounded a bit boring.

'Of course, we're a bit limited,' he said. 'You can't really experience Paris like you could if you were a man.'

Louise looked at him in his elegant coat and hat, then down at her ridiculous layers of petticoats and skirts, pink today.

'Well, I'll be one then. You must have some clothes I could borrow?'

'Don't be ridiculous! Dress as a man?' He looked her up and down.

'What about Édouard's studio? He's got lots of old clothes. I bet I could find something to wear there.'

They took the carriage to the studio. Édouard wasn't there, only Adèle. She was used to all sorts of strange things happening at the studio and rummaged around until she found some men's clothes. In the backroom, Louise tore off her layers of petticoats and, with Adèle's help, the suffocating corset. She sighed with relief – a prisoner escaping her cell. Adèle handed her a white shirt and a slim, smart black suit. It fitted her well. Finally, Adèle popped a top hat on her head.

Louise bounced into the studio.

'Ta ra!'

Gene applauded. 'You look wonderful!' he said. 'Even better, if that's possible!'

They set off on foot, Louise striding at his side.

'Wow, this is great. Free at last!' she said. She twirled her cane as they went down the street. Gene laughed. They would go to Café Guerbois to see who they could surprise.

Edgar, as ever, was there, and he was delighted with her transformation.

'Well, you look terrific,' he said. 'Who needs convention? Perhaps all women should dress as men.'

Edgar told them he was going to the ballet rehearsals and asked if they would like to come with him.

'Definitely!' Louise said. As much as Edgar annoyed her, she loved the ballet.

'We'll introduce you as *Louis*,' he said.

They arrived at the Salle Le Peletier, the home of Paris Opera, on the Rue Le Peletier. It was a grand building with large arched windows and columns. To Louise's surprise, they didn't go in the main entrance but walked round the side to the stage door. People were rushing in with musical instruments and armfuls of costumes. Edgar seemed to know everyone: the musicians, dancers, teachers and composers.

Edgar introduced Louise to his friend, Ludovic Havely, and the ballet teacher, Francois Merante.

'This is my nephew, Louis,' he said. 'He's visiting from the country. He's very shy.'

Louise looked down and shuffled her feet, getting in character.

They went into the rehearsal room, a big high-ceilinged room lined with mirrors. About a dozen men in top hats and fur-collared overcoats, middle-aged, balding, fat, were spread around at the edge of the room, waiting.

An avalanche of dancers tumbled down the spiral staircase: fifteen or so young girls, dressed in silk and satin tutus, chatting and arguing. They were young, thirteen, fourteen, some even younger. But they were not fit, healthy and athletic as Louise had expected but small and scrawny. Far too thin. Louise looked over at the men. They were leering at the girls, at their forbidden exposed legs.

'Who are these men?' she said to Edgar.

'Well, he's a financier,' Edgar said, 'that one's in the government. They're mostly members of the Jockey Club at Longchamps, the racecourse. They are allowed in here if they take out a subscription for three seats a week in the theatre.'

The men in black went over to the young girls, looming over them, looking them up and down, and whispering to them.

'Are they *choosing* them?' Louise said.

'Yes, they pick a mistress for later on,' Edgar said, 'take them out for dinner, then come back to watch them dance at the interlude in the opera. This is really the prelude for their real business later tonight.'

'They're *choosing* them?'

'Well, we call the men the *lions* and this is their *game* I suppose,' Edgar chuckled. 'This is their pitiful weakness. It's all the rage. It seems everyone has a dancer for a mistress these days, even Baron Haussmann has a mistress from the ballet corps.'

'But they're treating them like commodities! Most of those girls are underage!'

'Commodities? Well, that man's a stockbroker, he should know about commodities,' Edgar said. 'Underage? What do you mean?'

Maybe they don't have the concept of underage yet ... but still. Louise shook her head in disbelief.

'I call the girls the *petit rats*,' Edgar said, 'because I expect they're riddled with syphilis. Look at their poses and movement. Actually, they're more like little monkeys.'

'This is disgusting,' Louise said. She turned and strode out of the room.

In the corridor, a ruddy-faced woman was fussing over a girl, her daughter, probably. She was straightening her seams, fluffing up her thin pink tutu, adjusting her hair. The mother looked ill and the daughter was haggard, frail and exhausted. She was a tiny thing, painted with sticky cosmetics, sweaty and haggard after her last performance. The mother caught Louise's arm.

'How do you like my pretty girl?' she said. 'Odette, shoulders back!'

Odette looked at Louise and forced a strained smile. She'd lost a tooth.

Louise pulled her arm back and turned away.

'But monsieur, she's very supple,' the mother said.

Louise felt sick, but she could only go back to rehearsal room and stand next to Gene and Edgar. The girls started their stretching exercises.

'Look at the beautiful shapes they make, the angles, their pretty skirts,' Edgar said.

'Yes, I'm sure they would make lovely paintings,' Louise said sarcastically.

Edgar stared at her and raised his eyebrows. He walked to the other side of the rehearsal room. When she next looked over at him, he was sketching on a scrap of paper.

'He's a pig,' she said to Gene. 'Has he never had a girlfriend, a relationship with a woman?'

'Oh, I think he's celibate. He had a bad experience when he was younger. Rumour is that he got syphilis from a prostitute. And I think he believes sex would ruin his art, steal his creativity somehow. He loves to look, but never touches.'

Louise watched and sighed.

'I'm sorry,' Gene said. 'I had no idea it would be like this. I'm ashamed to be seen in the company of these men. I even met someone I know.'

Louise stared at the predatory men in black. This is the society Berthe lives in. She has to socialise with these men. They know her father. And they treat women, girls, like this!

Eventually the session ended, and Edgar came back over to them.

'So, would you like to go and see some more dancing, somewhere we can have a bit more fun?' he said.

Louise didn't answer. This place was disgusting – what would the next one be like? But she did want to talk to Edgar. He knew everyone, so perhaps he knew Pierre Puvis de Chavannes. Maybe she could find out something about him to stop Berthe marrying him.

'Where were you thinking?' Gene said to Edgar.

'Well, we could go to see some can-can perhaps?' Edgar said.

'Can-can? At the Moulin Rouge? Can we go to the Moulin Rouge?' Louise said. 'That would be amazing!'

'Where?' Edgar and Gene said, staring at her.

'Oh. Er, never mind,' she said. Maybe it hadn't been built yet.

'How about the Jardin Mabille? We could show Louise another side of the city,' Edgar said.

'Are you sure?' Gene said. 'Isn't that a bit, well, disreputable these days?'

'Well, everything is disreputable these days,' Edgar said. 'Paris is in heat. Excess and desire are everywhere. But she's dressed as a man, no one will recognise her. It would be interesting for her, I think.'

'Yes, let's go,' Louise said, tugging Gene's arm.

It was getting dark as they took the carriage to Rue Montaigne, just off the Champs Élysées. The Jardin Mabille had a beautiful entrance with ornate archways. Louise had never seen it before. This surely didn't exist anymore, or she would know it.

It was a sort of enchanted garden with sand paths, lawns, trees, shrubs, baskets of flowers and imitation grottoes. There were thousands of gas lamps, some in the form of palm trees. Coloured-glass globes, strings of lights and chandeliers were suspended from branches. Trees, benches and vases glistened with gold, silver and precious stones.

'Oh, it's beautiful,' Louise said.

There were some well-to-do gentlemen mingling amongst the less well-dressed women.

'The garden had a reputation as a place for gentlemen to meet prostitutes,' Edgar said.

'Another one,' Louise said.

'The women pay less to get in,' Gene said.

'It's not as good as it used to be,' Edgar said. 'There used to be gorgeous women here. These now are the poor relations. The velvets and satins, cashmeres and lace shawls, brocades, jewels, feathers and flowers are all gone. Do you know the can-can was invented here?'

'Will Marguerite Badel be on tonight, do you think?' Gene said.

'I doubt it,' Edgar said, 'but we'll see. Look, it's starting.'

They went over to join the crowd gathered under a mock Chinese pavilion. An orchestra was starting up.

'Look closely when they kick up their legs,' Edgar said to Louise.

Has he forgotten I'm a woman?

Four women rushed onto the stage to raucous applause and the orchestra began. The dancers kicked their legs in an exuberant can-can, swishing their skirts around, the flurry of white petticoats contrasting with their black stockings. They kicked higher and higher until Louise could see the full pantaloons, and a flash of skin – the gap in their pantaloons.

'My God, is that what the men are here for?' she said.

'Yes! Ha Ha!' laughed Edgar. 'It's the poor man's dance. The can-can is to dance what slang is to language.'

Gene looked embarrassed. The dancers turned their backs and threw their skirts over their heads to great whoops of applause.

Gene went off to get them some more wine, and Louise took her chance.

'Do you know Pierre Puvis de Chavannes?' she asked Edgar.

'Pierre Puvis de Chavannes!' Edgar said. 'He with the pretentious name. Do you know he added "de Chavannes"? It's not even his name. The Painter for France, they call him. Huh. All those lovely, perfect nymphs in their gardens of Eden. He's painting them all over the walls of villages and towns. He does it very well, of course, but it's all so very tedious.'

'Yes, but do you know anything about his personal life?'

'I know he had an affair with his model in Montmartre. And of course, there's his Romanian princess. What's her name? Marie Cantacuzène. He's been seeing her for years. I'm sure he thinks no one knows but of course everyone does.'

Berthe doesn't.

'Are you interested in him?' Edgar said with a suggestive leer.

'No. Just wondering.'

Pierre has a mistress! As soon as she got home, she would tell Berthe.

At that moment, Gene returned with glasses of wine.

A dancer come over to them.

'I bet I can take your hat off without using my hands,' she said to

Louise.

'Let's see you try,' Louise laughed. They were standing up. It seemed unlikely. She looked to Gene who nodded in agreement. She didn't have any money.

The dancer kicked up her leg and her foot perfectly caught the rim of Louise's hat and sent it spinning to the ground.

'Hah!' she said. Louise applauded and Gene settled the bet. The dancer looked a bit disappointed.

'I don't think that's all she wants from you,' Edgar said.

'Ah but I'm not equipped,' Louise said to the dancer who looked her up and down and smiled.

'I don't mind,' she said.

Louise laughed. 'Not today, thank you.'

'You looked like you were actually considering that offer,' Gene said.

'Yes, but I like you better,' Louise said, hooking her arm through his.

They drank and watched the crowd. Louise's mind whirred. *Pierre has a mistress.* Surely that would stop Berthe marrying him?

There was a roar from the crowd as the band came on again. It was time for the audience to dance. People rushed onto the floor.

'Let's dance!' Gene said. He pulled her up and swirled her around. Edgar, as ever, watched. No one batted an eye at two young men dancing together; they weren't the only ones. A group of people pulled them into a line to dance the can-can, kicking higher and higher. Everyone seemed to be blind drunk. Louise was having the time of her life.

It was after midnight when they piled into the carriage to go home. First they dropped Edgar at his house and then headed to the Morisot home. Louise took off her top hat and shook her hair loose.

'I'm so hot!'

'I had a wonderful time tonight,' Gene said.

'Me too.'

Gene took her face in his hands and kissed her. She kissed him back, deeply.

It was a good distance to Passy.

At the house, Louise got down from the carriage and wove her way to the door. Giselle met her as she came in.

'What on earth are you wearing, Mademoiselle Louise?'

'Oh, shh, doesn't matter,' Louise whispered. 'Is everyone asleep?'

'Yes, they have all retired,' Giselle said, staring at Louise's clothes and messy hair.

'Don't tell anyone,' Louise giggled. She stumbled up the stairs and into the bedroom. She felt for the non-existent light switch. 'Oh, wrong century,' she said to the dark room, pulling off her suit jacket and conking out on the bed, still wearing her man's white shirt.

CHAPTER 24

SYNCHRONICITY

Louise woke in the middle of the night, desperate for some water, her head thumping. She got up and poured a tepid glass from the jug. If only she had a paracetamol.

Her mind was woozy, but one thing swam into focus. *Berthe can't marry Pierre Puvis. He's got a mistress, at least one.* Berthe could not give up painting for him – that was impossible.

She climbed back between the heavy crisp sheets. In her sleepy hungover blur, the signature she'd seen in the Impressionist book in her mum's cottage loomed into her consciousness: *"Berthe Manet"* it had said. *Berthe Manet.* Berthe married Édouard! That must be what happened! She had read it in the book in the future so it must be true. Édouard would have to divorce Suzanne. Louise didn't know anything about divorce in Paris in the 1870s, but Berthe and Édouard *had* to get married. It would be really sad for Suzanne, of course, but the future of art depended on it. Édouard and Berthe were perfect together. They were in love. And Édouard of all people would make sure Berthe kept painting. Not Pierre, twenty years older, boring. He'd imprison her. She couldn't marry him.

So it must be up to me!

That must be why she was here. She'd been sent for this reason, to make sure that Berthe married Édouard. Fate had dispatched her here, for this very purpose. The synchronicity of seeing that letter in the book, coming through the painting to arrive just at this crucial time in Berthe's life. It was all connected. She had to make sure Berthe and Édouard married.

Her head thudded as she lay back on the pillows. She would go and see Édouard tomorrow. Go to his studio. What would she say? She had no idea. But Berthe's life depended on it, on *her*. Berthe's *art* depended on it! Art history, the future, depended on it, on her.

She tossed and turned, tried to plump up the solid pillows, and fell into a deep sleep.

She had a strong belief in synchronicity.

CHAPTER 25

MY FURIOUS BEAUTY

Louise woke up at lunchtime. Berthe and Cornélie had gone out and the house was quiet. Now she couldn't tell Berthe about Pierre Puvis de Chavannes. That would have to wait. For now, she had a mission. She asked Giselle to help her get dressed. She put the shirt, suit, top hat and shoes into a basket, covered it with a cloth, and took a carriage through the grey day to Édouard's studio. She was still a bit drunk from last night and her head was thumping. She opened the door to the studio.

Amazingly, Édouard was alone, working on *The Absinthe Drinker*. He was painting in a dark empty bottle on the ground beside the man's feet.

'Ah, Louise, how nice to see you,' he said. 'I was getting lonely. No one has been in all morning. Shall we have a glass of wine? This painting is making me thirsty.'

Wine – the last thing Louise needed, but she agreed. She had to talk to Édouard. He went to get a bottle of red, and a warning light flickered in the back of her brain: *me, Édouard and a bottle of wine – dangerous.* He was so attractive, so charming. And a genius – the founder of modern art! This was the first time they had been alone together.

Édouard offered her a chair at the table and poured them each a large glass. Through her throbbing headache and fuzzy brain, she searched for the right words to begin. What to say? She fidgeted with her gloves. Only one phrase was going round in her head: "One more drink and I'll be under the host."

'So, mysterious Louise,' Édouard said. 'You're not really from Brittany, are you? What is your secret? I've been wondering.'

'Have you?' she said. How did he know? How had she let him initiate the conversation? 'Wouldn't you like to know.'

'Yes, I would. I have a feeling that you are a stray, but I'm not sure what you are straying from. Are you escaping something, or looking for something?' He raised an eyebrow at her as he raised his glass of wine.

'I'm here to talk to you about Berthe,' she said. 'You love her, don't you?'

'Ah, Berthe, my black raven, my furious beauty,' Édouard said. 'Yes, of course I love her.'

'But do you know Pierre Puvis de Chavannes wants to marry her? It's impossible! She can't!'

'Yes, I do know. In fact, I suggested him to Cornélie. I think he could be a good match for Berthe.'

'What? *You* suggested him?'

'Yes,' Édouard said coolly. 'He's an artist. He likes her work. She likes his work. They have a great deal in common.'

'But he's *ancient*! He'd swallow her up. She'd have to follow him around, be his wife. She might even stop painting.'

Édouard paused.

'She wants a child.'

'But *you* love her, you said so. And *she* loves *you*.'

'Yes, that's true, but I'm married to Suzanne.'

'You could get divorced.'

'Oh no, that would never do. And there's Léon.'

'What about Léon? Suzanne's brother?'

Édouard said nothing.

Louise gulped down her wine. This was all going horribly wrong.

'Berthe will get over me,' Édouard said. 'I think she could be happy with Pierre, although I admit he can be a bit of a bore.'

Édouard leaned back in his chair and took a long swig of wine.

Louise leaned forward over the table.

'But you and Berthe should be together. You *have* to be! *Have to be.*'

'Oh, don't be so dramatic, Louise. Maybe we'll still be able to see each other sometimes.'

Louise put her head in her hands.

'But what about *you*?' Édouard said. 'Why are you here in Paris? Maybe you are pregnant? Come to the city to have your baby?' He looked over her figure. 'No, I don't think so. Are you hiding from your lover then? Or perhaps looking for a new lover?'

'No, nowhere near.'

Édouard leaned forward over the table.

'But I have a feeling you have some experience. Perhaps you have had a few lovers?'

Louise said nothing.

'Maybe you'd like to sit for me one day, as my model?'

He stared into her eyes, and she couldn't help but feel a frisson. He was like a snake-charmer, luring her in. She pushed back her chair.

'I have to go.'

CHAPTER 26

CATASTROPHE

L ouise burst into the bedroom. Berthe was hunched over her desk, pen in hand.

'Berthe ...' Louise said, gasping for breath.

'Ah, Louise,' Berthe said, not looking up. 'I'm writing to Edma. I've just written "I think I will marry Pierre Puvis de Chavannes ..."' but I don't know if that's true. Is that what I should do? You're supposed to know the future. What should I do?'

'It was Édouard!'

'What was Édouard?'

'Bloody corsets ...' Louise gasped. 'Édouard! He suggested Pierre marry you. He suggested you to Pierre, and he suggested Pierre to your mother!'

'Do not be ridiculous,' Berthe said, putting down her fountain pen.

'It's true, he told me himself. Édouard wants you to marry Pierre.'

'You've been to see him? Édouard?'

'He thinks you'd be happy with Pierre.'

'He would *never* say that,' Berthe shouted. She stood up abruptly, toppling her chair over.

'He did. I swear.' Louise reached out to put her hand on her arm. 'I'm so sorry.'

Berthe pushed her arm away, strode out the room, down the stairs, and called for the carriage.

Louise rushed after her. 'Berthe, wait, where are you going? Don't go. I should come with you. I'm your chaperone …'

She stood on the doorstep and watched the carriage splashing away through the rain. *Oh God, what have I done? Should I have told Berthe? Have I made things worse? Has Berthe gone to confront Édouard?*

*

Louise paced around the bedroom, and waited, looking out the window, watching the clock on the mantlepiece tick, slowly, so slowly … Minutes, an hour passed.

The doorbell rang. Someone was coming up the stairs.

Giselle showed Suzanne into the room. Louise stared at her. What was Suzanne doing here?

'Madame and Mademoiselle Morisot are not at home, Mademoiselle Louise,' Giselle said. 'And Madame Manet would like to see you.'

'Me? Oh, er, do come in, Suzanne,' Louise said.

Suzanne had never come to call on her own before. Why was she here?

'Em, Giselle would you get us tea please?' Louise said.

Suzanne sat down on the chaise longue and twisted her gloves in her hands.

Louise's mind raced. Did Suzanne know that Berthe and Cornélie would be out? What if Berthe comes back and finds her here?

'Actually, I was hoping to catch you alone, Louise,' Suzanne said. 'I want to talk to you. She took a deep breath. 'Oh, this is so difficult. I know people say we're an unlikely couple. He's so handsome, talented, charming, and I'm, well …'

Suzanne seemed to be struggling not to cry.

'You see I know I'm not clever or beautiful, I know that, but I *do* love Édouard,' Suzanne gulped. 'I don't want him to leave me.'

'No, no, of course not,' Louise said. Did she know about Édouard and Berthe?

'Berthe is so clever, beautiful,' Suzanne said. 'I know they have feelings for each other. Anyway, I thought, well, I hoped maybe you could say something to her, to Berthe, I mean.'

'Oh.' Louise couldn't say anything, admit anything. Perhaps Suzanne didn't know. 'I don't know,' she said.

Suzanne gave her a half smile. Louise could see that she did know.

'And then there's Léon,' Suzanne said.

'Your brother?'

'Yes, but, well, he's not. You see ...' Suzanne said. 'Oh, promise me, swear to me that you won't tell anyone. No one must know. You see, Léon is not my brother. I know some people think I had an affair with Édouard's father and that he's *his* child ...'

'What?' Suzanne slept with Édouard's father? Léon is Édouard's father's child?

'But he's not. He is our son, mine and Édouard's.'

'Your son? Édouard's?'

'You know I was Édouard and Gene's piano teacher when they were teenagers? Well, later, when Édouard started painting, his school was near my apartment. He used to visit me and I, em, well, I got pregnant.'

'Oh.' Louise stared at Suzanne.

'Édouard couldn't tell his father, the judge, of course – an illegitimate child, what a scandal. He told his mother. And Madame Manet helped me. She helped me go home, to Holland, and have the baby there. And when the baby was born she had him registered as Léon Édouard Koëlla-Leenhoff. Leenhoff is my maiden name, you see, so it would be like he was my brother, like he was my mother's baby. But Léon has Édouard's name, his middle name.'

'What?' Louise said. 'Léon is your son, yours and Édouard's? And you have to pretend he's not? But that's awful!'

'But the Manets were so kind! They've been so kind. Of course, I had to stop tutoring the boys. They couldn't be seen to have a teacher with doubtful morals. But Édouard moved me and Léon into an apartment on Rue de Batignolles and visited us, while at the same time pretending to be the most eligible bachelor in the city.' Suzanne grimaced. 'And then when his father died, about ten years ago, we got married.'

'So, can't you tell people now? I mean, why didn't you say *then*, when Édouard's father died?'

'Oh, Édouard didn't want to. He still tells people that he's Léon's godfather. But the point is, you see, without Édouard, Léon and I would have nothing. We, Léon and I, are indebted to the Manets, completely dependent on them. They could have thrown me out, but they didn't. They looked after me, both of us.'

Louise said nothing. It was appalling. Women had no money, no independence, no power. They were the victims of this bourgeois society.

'I understand he has affairs, every man does,' Suzanne went on. 'I do mind, of course I do, but this time, it seems more serious with Berthe. I don't want him to leave us, me. You're Berthe's friend. Can you help me? Talk to her, please, make her understand?'

Louse couldn't think what to say. She couldn't admit that she knew Berthe was having an affair with Édouard, tell Berthe's secret, even if Suzanne had guessed. That would betray Berthe. She opened and closed her mouth like a goldfish, but her silence said it all.

'Is she with him now?' Suzanne said in a whisper.

Louise looked down.

'Well, I've told you. I hope you understand.' Suzanne reached over and squeezed Louise's hand. 'Promise you won't tell anyone about Léon.'

'I promise.'

Giselle brought in the tea, just as Suzanne left.

Louise sat frozen in place. She had helped Berthe betray Suzanne, poor kind Suzanne, the innocent wife. What was she thinking? When she'd been betrayed by her own husband?

She sat and gazed out the window, watching the sun go down over Paris. The light faded from the room.

*

Berthe burst through the door. She was dishevelled. Her jacket buttons were done up wrong, her hair was undone, hanging wet from the rain.

'You told Suzanne about me and Édouard, didn't you?' Berthe said. 'She said she had been here. You told her where I was. She came to the studio, found us. How could you? I trusted you! You betrayed me!'

'No, no … I …' Louise said.

Cornélie came in.

'Berthe, where have you been? Look at you! The state of you. I thought you were with Louise. You've been to see Édouard, haven't you?'

Cornélie turned to Louise.

'You're supposed to be chaperone! Why weren't you with her? Why else are you here? Her reputation will be ruined if anyone saw them, saw her like this. Look at her!'

Berthe strode out the room, into Edma's old bedroom, slamming two doors as she went.

Cornélie rushed after her and knocked on the locked bedroom door.

'Berthe. Did anyone see you? Berthe!'

Louise stood in the gloom of the empty room, tears falling.

CHAPTER 27

THE OLD CITY

In the morning, Cornélie told Louise that Berthe was not feeling well. She would not be down for breakfast.

'I'm extremely disappointed in you, Louise,' Cornélie said, frowning at her over her coffee cup. 'You should not have left Berthe alone yesterday, and with *Édouard*! You were supposed to be her chaperone. It was a condition of you staying here. I thought you understood that.'

Louise stared at the tablecloth in silence. She felt five years old, being told off by her mother. This new family she'd so desperately wanted to belong to, Berthe and Cornélie, she'd failed them. But they had both been using her as Berthe's chaperone, each for their own purpose: Berthe to cover her tracks with Édouard, Cornélie to protect her daughter, and her family's reputation. They didn't like her at all. She had just been useful to them.

Cornélie put down her coffee cup.

'But no harm done I expect. It's exciting – Berthe has agreed to marry Pierre! As long as no one hears about her and Édouard, her reputation will be saved. We need to plan a wedding, quickly.'

Louise glared at her. Whatever happened, Berthe couldn't marry that old man! But she realised: she still hadn't told Berthe about Pierre's mistress. She rushed up to the bedroom.

'Berthe, please let me in. Please! Don't marry Pierre. You can't. Let me in. I'll explain!'

Berthe didn't answer.

'Please, Berthe!'

No answer.

She stood outside, pacing up and down, clenching her fists, on the verge of tears.

'Berthe, Berthe, let me in!' She banged on the door. 'Berthe!'

There was no response. Louise leant against the wall. She waited and waited, begged and begged, but Berthe ignored her.

Eventually Louise dragged herself up onto her feet. She went downstairs and walked out of the house, out of the garden, onto the street. She kept walking. A mile of blurred streets went by. People were staring at her. Why were they staring? She looked down, she was wearing her tea dress.

Who cares!

She was fed up being smothered and suffocated by their corsets, their stupid rules. What was she doing here? She had ruined everything. Going to see Édouard, thinking she knew what was going on. She was an idiot.

In a daze, she walked away from the boulevards and into a maze of alleys. Now she'd lost Berthe, her only friend. But she had been using her; she wasn't her friend at all.

How stupid she had been! What had she been doing, helping Berthe and Édouard have an affair? She had been so angry at Paul and yet here she was, helping wreck someone else's marriage.

Mum would be ashamed of me.

The alleys became narrow and twisted. She trudged on and on into the dark labyrinth of the old city. Now Berthe would marry Pierre and Berthe wouldn't become a famous artist, her paintings wouldn't be in any books.

The painting of me won't be in that book.

She stopped and put her hand to her mouth.

Oh God, she wouldn't be able to get back! If Berthe didn't become famous, the painting wouldn't exist in that book in the future, and she'd be stuck here forever.

Louise stood in the middle of the dark alley, unable to move. A cart and horse lurched past; the back was full of human faeces which men were shovelling up from the pavement. She turned away, trying not to throw up.

The tall medieval houses loomed over her. She was somewhere in the maze of the old city, far from the bright boulevards of Haussmann's new Paris. The radiance of the City of Light didn't penetrate these alleys. Deep in the shadows, she couldn't see any landmarks, any indication, of where she was. She was lost.

Her feet were wet and warm. She looked down at her sodden white slippers, now turning yellow. She was standing in a pool of urine. Was it horse or human? It was flowing down the centre of the cobbles. She stepped out of the puddle and stumbled into a muddy hole where the cobbles were missing. Looking along the alley, she saw that whole sections of cobbles had been removed and were piled up against the walls.

There was so much rubbish everywhere. She took a deep breath to try to calm herself and gagged on the stench. A rat scurried out from a heap of putrid vegetables in front of her and ran behind a mound of horse manure. It was all so disgusting. History books never told you how bad the past smelt.

She sighed and wiped her forehead with her sleeve. How far had she walked? She'd left the house in such a rush, walking, running blindly, desperate to get away. She should have left a trail of breadcrumbs, like Hansel and Gretel, but then she didn't want to go back, couldn't go back, not now. Her trail had been of tears instead.

She put her head in her hands. What was she going to do? She had nowhere to go, no one to go to. She closed her eyes.

Someone grabbed her arm. A burly man loomed out of a dark doorway behind her.

'You're a pretty one,' he slurred.

Oh, what now? She didn't have the energy to deal with this. She shrugged him off. But he grabbed her again, tightening his grip. He breathed, reeking alcohol fumes over her.

'Get lost!' She tried to pull away. He held her firmly and pushed her against a wall. She hit him as hard as she could with her fists. She tried to kick him in the balls.

'Oh, feisty girl, are you?' he said.

He leaned in and pinned her against the wall with his weight. He was a big man; she couldn't budge him. She couldn't move anything but her head, so she bit his thick, grubby neck.

He slapped her across her face, hard.

She struggled as much as she could but when the cold of the knife blade touched her throat she froze. She could only move her eyes. She looked around wildly but there was no one in the dark street to help her.

The man's hand reached under her dress, between her legs. He put his hand through the gap in her underwear, that bloody gap. The knife was cutting into the skin on her neck. A warm drip ran down. Blood.

So, this is how it ended. In a filthy street in Paris, in this alley, this city, this century. How surprising. She'd travelled so far, and it had come to this.

I'll die here, now.

In the wrong place, in the wrong time.

Well, who would care?

The weight of the man lifted off her and his knife clattered to the ground.

'Leave her, you drunk!' a man's voice said.

Louise staggered. Someone caught her. The man took her arm and helped her down the dark lane, towards the sunlit boulevards.

'What are you doing here, you idiot?' the man said.

She stumbled over the holes in the street, struggling not to fall. She saw a woman in a doorway curtsy to the man who was holding her up. The sewage collectors doffed their caps to him as they passed.

She was pulled out of the gloomy alleys onto a wide bright pavement on a boulevard and shoved onto a café chair.

'You fool! You were nearly raped,' the man said. 'You could've had your throat cut!'

Louise sat in a daze, her head spinning. She slowly focused on the man opposite her. He was elderly with white hair, a bushy beard and a moustache, elegantly dressed in a top hat, dress coat and cravat.

'I'm sorry. I got lost, I …' she said.

He shoved a glass of brandy at her.

She drank a large gulp.

'I just walked …' she spluttered. 'I was upset, wasn't thinking.'

'No, you weren't thinking. You can't walk into these streets, wearing that – a tea dress? These people are starving. A woman like you wandering in, after the siege, the massacre. There were barricades in that lane, you know, made of wardrobes, chests. The cobbles were ripped up from the street and piled on. So many were killed there that now they drink absinthe to forget.' He looked back to the alleyways. 'These people, they're desperate, broken, waiting for their homes to be knocked down.'

'I'm sorry,' she said. Her hands shook. She drank some more brandy.

'It's all right. It's all right,' he said. 'Try to calm down. It must have been awful for you.'

'Thank you for helping me.'

He had kind eyes. Why had those people curtsied and doffed their caps to him?

'What were you doing there?' she said.

'They know me. I try to help them a little.' He sipped his brandy. 'You're hurt. Here.'

He gently wiped the blood from her neck with his handkerchief.

'What's your name?' he said.

'Louise.'

'Ah, Louise, like Louise Michel? Do you know her, "The Red Virgin"?'

'No, tell me, please,' she said, grateful for the distraction.

'She lived in that alley. She's an amazing woman, a schoolteacher. She became a leader in the Commune, dressed as a soldier, like Joan of Arc, and led them in the fight. Louise means "famous warrior", did you know that?'

'No.' Famous warrior. If only she were. She gulped down some more brandy. 'How ... how do you help them, the people?'

'I do what I can, here and there. And try to tell their story.'

'You're a writer?'

'Yes.'

'What do you write?'

'Well, many things. I wrote a story about a poor man who stole a loaf of bread and was sent to prison for ten years. When he got out, he stole again, from a priest, but the priest forgave him and gave him a chance to be a good man. He helped the poor, took a young girl in off the streets. It's a long story but really it's about the oppression of the poor by the state.'

Louise racked her brain. That sounded remarkably familiar. Oh my God, it's *Les Misérables*! She'd watched it on Netflix recently.

'Er, what's your name?' she asked.

'Victor. It's nice to meet you, Louise,' he said with a little bow.

'Your second name?'

'Hugo. Victor Hugo.'

She put her hand to her forehead and stared at him. *Victor Hugo!* She'd been saved by Victor Hugo.

'We need to get you home,' Victor said. 'I think you're in shock. You need to be looked after.'

The bruise throbbed on her cheek. She touched her neck, the cut of the blade and the blood drying on it. It stung. Where could she go? She couldn't go back to Berthe's. She couldn't go back home, to her time, now, or ever. There was no one, nowhere to go.

'Gene,' she said, 'Do you know the Manets?'

'Yes, of course. Édouard and Gene, Madame Manet. You're staying with them?'

'Er, yes. Take me there, please. Thank you so much, Victor.'

CHAPTER 28

GENE

Victor hailed a carriage and took Louise to the Manets' house. She hoped, prayed, Édouard would be out. She couldn't face him, or Suzanne. Hopefully, Madame Manet wouldn't be in either, to see her in this state. Would Gene take her in? If he was there …

Marie answered the door. Gene was in. She hurried to fetch him.

He came to the door and gasped.

'Louise, oh my God, what happened? Victor, where did you find her?'

'She was attacked. I think she's in shock. Can you help her in?'

They helped her up the stairs to a bedroom. She was shaking; her legs were so weak. She was only dimly aware of the ornate furniture and decorations of the luxurious Manet home.

Marie helped her wash and gently cleaned the wound on her neck. She found some of Madame Manet's clothes for her and took the filthy tea dress away to wash.

Louise thanked Marie for her kindness. Her neck hurt and the bruises on her face throbbed badly, but she went downstairs. Gene had coffee ready for her in the lounge. She slumped onto an embroidered sofa and tried to steady herself with heavily sugared coffee.

She told him only a little about the attack. She didn't explain why she was out walking in the first place, why she had gone to the old city. She could no longer trust herself to say the right thing to anyone. Thankfully, Gene didn't press her.

'Have you seen Édouard?' she said.

'No, he left early this morning. I didn't talk to him. He was in a dark mood.'

She rubbed her forehead. She didn't know what to tell Gene. She couldn't tell him about Berthe and Édouard's affair. Perhaps he knew or suspected, but she couldn't put her foot in it again and she couldn't tell him what had happened with Suzanne.

'Berthe won't speak to me. I can't tell you why, but I can't go back there,' she said.

'What's happened to Berthe? Is she all right?' Gene said.

'Yes, she's fine, but I, I hurt her, failed her. God, I've ruined everything,' She couldn't stop the sobs now.

'Oh, but you've had a terrible shock. You must go and lie down. You can stay here as long as you want. And tell me about it later, if you want to.'

He went over to her and put his arm around her.

'You look terrible if you don't mind me saying.'

She gave him a weak smile.

'Thanks. Yes, I will lie down. I feel awful.'

CHAPTER 29

THE MASKED BALL

For the rest of the day, Louise tried to sleep in the beautiful guest bedroom in the Manets' house. Marie brought her meals, but she couldn't eat. Gene popped his head round the door occasionally to check on her. He told her that he still hadn't seen Édouard; he was still out. Suzanne wasn't there, either. She and Léon had gone back to Holland to visit her family. She'd left suddenly – it was most unlike her and he didn't know when she'd be back.

Louise lay in bed, tossing and turning under the heavy embroidered blankets. They were suffocating her. The air was static and stuffy. The window screens were jammed shut and she couldn't get them open. Her mind reeled round and round. Why had Suzanne gone home? Had she and Édouard fallen out? Would she come back? That would be her fault, too, if their marriage broke up. She should never have interfered! If she hadn't told Berthe that Édouard had suggested Pierre for her, Berthe wouldn't have gone to his studio, and Suzanne wouldn't have found them together ...

She'd broken the first rule of time travel and interfered. What would happen to the future now? And to her? She'd be stuck here forever, where no one wanted her. Louise put her head under the pillow. She was as fragile as an eggshell – one more crack and she would fall apart.

Gene had reminded her earlier that it was the day of the masked ball, the first ball of the season. As evening approached, Louise got up to get ready for the most eagerly awaited social event of the year. Gene had told her she wasn't well enough to go but she had insisted. Berthe would be there, and she had to speak to her, to tell her about

Pierre, to stop her marrying him. They may no longer be friends, but she could still try to save her from that.

Madame Manet had been told only that Louise and Berthe had argued. She gave Marie a dress for Louise, an enormous black thing with layers of fabric. It was hardly elegant. Louise tried to cover her bruises with makeup. She asked Marie for a black choker to cover the wound on her neck. It just about worked.

It was midnight when Louise hauled herself into the carriage with Madame Manet and Gene to go to the Salle Le Peletier. Édouard had gone ahead. No one had seen him all day.

The carriage struggled through the mêlée of people as they approached the front of the Opera House, the same place she'd seen the ballet dancers. They pushed their way through crowds, up the elaborate staircase and along the corridor to the *loge*, a box, on the balcony level. Louise's eyes grew wider at every step. So many people, such elaborate clothes! She'd never seen anything like this.

Inside the box were eight gold chairs, plush red velvet curtains and a view over the floor. The Manets and the Morisots had rented it together for the evening. Cornélie, Tiburce and Berthe were already seated at the front. Berthe was wearing a velvet black dress cut low on her bare shoulders with a nipped-in waist and three white flowers across the skirt. She had a ribbon tied round her neck in a bow and long white gloves. Her dark hair was piled on her head. She looked stunning, but her face was like thunder.

'Ah, Louise. What happened between you two?' Tiburce said. 'Come and sit next to Berthe.'

Louise sat down and put her hand on Berthe's arm.

'Berthe, please. I'm sorry. Let me explain.'

Berthe got up and left the loge.

'Where are you going, Berthe?' asked Cornélie. 'Don't go onto the floor.' She turned to Louise. 'The floor is not for respectable women.'

To Madame Manet, she said, 'Berthe didn't even want to come tonight, but Tiburce insisted. I don't know what's wrong with her.'

Cornélie was obviously hoping that Madame Manet knew nothing about what had happened.

'It's a shame Suzanne isn't here,' Madame Manet said. 'She was so looking forward to it. Marie made a marvellous job of her dress and then Suzanne suddenly said she had to go home. She didn't explain. She took Léon with her. Some family issue, I expect.'

Poor Suzanne. Louise sat and flapped her fan in front of her face, biting her lip, trying not to cry.

The floor of the hall was packed with a strange assortment of people. There were young women wearing black masks alongside scantily clad women in bright costumes. Some wore laced boots, their calves covered with striped blue and white stockings with coloured bows, and fringed trousers.

Gene explained that some of the women were actresses or dancers courting fashionable men. They were hoping for a job, money, a part in a play. Others were *cocettes,* looking for an affair with a gentleman. A few men wore colourful Turkish outfits with turbans, others jester outfits. It was a riot of colour. Any other night Louise would have been entranced.

In the middle of the floor, a sea of unmasked gentlemen in shiny black top hats, capes and shoes created a shimmer of cool black. They were like a conspiracy of ravens, picking off the women from those gathered around them. Édouard was amongst them.

Louise had to talk to him, to find out what was going on. She waited until the others were distracted and slipped out into the corridor. She found a discarded mask on the floor and held it in front of her face as she struggled through the crowds. People were crowded around vendors selling fruit, drinks, cigarettes, flowers, fans, gloves and masks. She tried to shove through onto the dance floor to get to Édouard, but there seemed to be endless groups of boisterous people. The laughter and shouting hurt her head.

Then the orchestra started – the throbbing music of Strauss – and the floor trembled beneath the rush of dancers. Men grabbed women and threw themselves into the mêlée. It was wilder than any party

Louise had ever been to – a mad whirlpool of sensuousness. She couldn't get anywhere near Édouard.

She gave up and dragged herself back to the loge. Berthe was there.

'I saw you on the floor,' Cornélie said to Louise. 'You really shouldn't, you know.'

'Were you trying to talk to Édouard?' Madame Manet said, gazing out at her son. 'He's impossible to get near; the centre of attention as always, very much the star.'

'Édouard, Édouard,' Louise heard Gene say under his breath. 'It's hard to believe he's a married man.'

Berthe stood up and left the loge again. She was trying to suppress tears. Tiburce went after her. A few moments later he came back and said he was taking Berthe home. She wasn't feeling well.

There was nothing Louise could do but sit and watch the increasing mayhem. Cornélie and Madame Manet gossiped about who was with whom and who might be having an affair. Tiburce and Gene talked about business. Louise sat with her bruise throbbing, her neck stinging and her headache crushing her. She looked over to a loge opposite. A beautiful young woman gazed out, alone. She was wearing a white muslin dress, cut low across her shoulders in the latest fashion, cream and purple dahlias pinned to her left shoulder. They matched the flowers in her black hair. Silk white gloves held a fan and around her throat was a black choker. It looked tight. Perhaps there a lead attached to it, a man holding the end, restraining her.

Another caged woman. Like Berthe. Like me, now.

Louise was hot. Her clothes were so heavy, her corset so tight. She waved her fan frantically; she was suffocating. Her heart thumped, sweat broke out on her brow. She wished she could just walk out and get a taxi home as she would have done in her own time. And now she really wanted to go home, back to that little cottage in Harris. She wanted out, out of here, out of this time. She wasn't helping anyone, and no one wanted her. But she couldn't go back to Berthe's. She couldn't get back through the painting. She couldn't go home now, ever.

Louise staggered to her feet and stumbled out into the corridor. She leant against the wall and slid down onto the floor into a heap of black fabric and frills. She closed her eyes. To darkness.

'Louise! What's the matter?' Gene said. 'I knew you shouldn't have come. You're not well.'

Gently, he pulled her up and helped her down the stairs into a waiting covered carriage. He opened the windows, and she gulped in the cool night air. As the carriage trundled slowly through the dark streets, she began to breathe more easily, and her panic subsided.

'Thank you,' she said, reaching for Gene's hand. He at least seemed to care about her.

Gene took her hand and held it tightly. She fell towards him and put her head on his shoulder. He felt so good, so safe.

She turned her face to his, pulled him to her and kissed him. When they reached the empty house, she took his hand and led him up the ornate stairs to her bedroom.

'Are you sure?' he said.

'Yes.' She pulled him into her bedroom. She desperately needed some closeness, some human warmth.

'Are you sure? Really?' he said.

Louise kissed him to shut him up. They fell on each other, onto the bed. She tugged at Gene's jacket, pulling it off. She unbuttoned his shirt and ran her hands over his smooth chest.

His hands were everywhere on her but couldn't penetrate the endless fabric.

'Get me out of all this,' she said, standing up.

Gene unbuttoned her dress at the back, nibbling and kissing her shoulders as he did. She struggled out of it, tore off her petticoats and stepped over them.

'Now the corset. You'll have to do it.'

Gene started unlacing her corset behind her. What was he doing? He was taking ages. What a passion-killer corsets were. Is that another reason they were invented? He seemed to be fumbling and fiddling. Has he never done this before? She didn't want to think about that.

Eventually, Gene released her. He kissed her breasts.

'But wait,' he rushed out the room.

What now? Had she scared him off? Was he going to come back?

She took off her unsexy pantaloons and chemise and lay naked on the bed. What was he doing?

Gene rushed back in.

'God, you're ...' He looked shocked.

Did they not have sex naked in the nineteenth century? *Well, they do now.*

'Ready, I'm ready,' she said.

'I can see that.'

He tore off the rest of his clothes and lay beside her, gently caressing and kissing her body.

'I got this,' he said, holding up a crumpled bit of yellowing stuff.

'What on earth is that?'

'It's called a condom. It's to protect you.'

'But it's enormous!' She took it from him and rubbed it between her fingers. It was solid, stiff, crinkly. It smelt weird. It was the least sexy thing she'd ever seen. 'What's it made of?'

'Sheep's gut.'

'Yuk, sheep's gut!'

'It was father's. I found it in his room.'

'Your father's! He used this?'

'I suppose so. But I didn't have time to soak it.'

'What?'

'To rehydrate it. It's a bit crunchy.'

She stared at the creaky sack.

'It's disgusting!' Would she get syphilis from it? No, it obviously hadn't been used for a long time.

'You put it on me,' Gene said.

'I know, but it looks like it'll be really uncomfortable – for both of us.'

'It'll soon loosen up.'

She put it on him.

'You have to tie the ribbon at the bottom, so it doesn't come off.'

'Good grief. So much for spontaneous passion.'

Gene looked away as she tied him in.

'I'm sorry. This all seems so new to you.'

Not for the reasons you think, she thought. Did he think she was a virgin? She'd show him. She pushed him back onto the bed and sat astride him.

'God!' he said.

She kissed him and moved onto him. Soon she forgot about the sheep's gut.

CHAPTER 30

REFUGE

Louise woke in the early afternoon, alone in a mess of sheets and blankets. Now she had been unfaithful to her unfaithful husband. What next? Things were screwed up enough without this.

But she still had to get to Berthe, to tell her about Pierre. She found a pencil and some paper in the bedside table and wrote a brief note, asking Berthe if she could come and see her. She gave it to Marie who gave it to a messenger boy to deliver.

She dozed off and on through the afternoon and evening, hiding out in her bedroom, pretending to be recovering from the ball.

Marie came in to say that Gene would like to see her. Louise sat up abruptly in bed and tried to pull her hair into some kind of shape. Would this be awkward? Would Gene regret last night? Perhaps he would think she had been shockingly forward ... Perhaps he'd want her to leave the house ...

But no, Gene came in and sat down beside her. He held her hand and smiled at her, asked her how she was feeling, told her that last night had been amazing.

Louise held his hand and lay back on the pillows.

'Rest now,' he said.

Still there was no reply from Berthe.

CHAPTER 31

VICTORINE

Two days passed. Louise had sent more messages to Berthe but there was no reply. Suzanne was still away: perhaps she would never come back. Édouard was out all the time; he seemed to be sleeping at his studio. Madame Manet was on an endless round of social visits.

Louise wandered around the house in a daze. She was alone this morning; Gene was out, attending to some business. She vaguely surveyed the elaborate living room, its ornate furniture, extravagant tapestries, mirrors, Édouard's paintings, all perfectly displayed. It was like a stage set waiting for the following act.

What would happen next?

The doorbell rang. Was it Berthe? She rushed into the hall where Marie opened the door to reveal Victorine.

'Édouard said he left some paints for me here, to pick up,' Victorine said, fidgeting. 'Ah, there they are.' She pointed to a bag by the door. 'I'll just take them. Thank you.'

'Victorine, come in, please,' Louise said, pulling her past Marie. 'Marie, can you bring us coffee, please?'

Louise took Victorine into the living room. Victorine perched herself on the edge of a seat, gazing around.

Oh, she's probably never been invited in here before, Louise thought. She had committed another horrendous *faux pas,* broken another rule. She didn't care, she needed someone to talk to.

Victorine took off her gloves and revealed her pink "little shrimp" hands. *I bet a man gave her that nickname*, Louise thought.

'Who called you "little shrimp"? Was it Edgar?' Louise said.

'How did you guess?'

Marie came in with coffee and pastries. Victorine thanked her effusively.

Victorine put her hand to Louise's cheek.

'What happened to you? Your face?'

'I was attacked, my own stupid fault,' Louise said. 'I seem to be doing a lot of stupid things lately.'

'You do seem a little out of place. Where are you from?'

'Nowhere near here.' Panic and fear started bubbling up inside her again. Quickly she asked, 'When did you first start modelling for Édouard?'

'He saw me in the street several years ago. I was coming out of a café with my guitar. I play in cafés for extra money, you know. He said he wanted to paint me.'

'Ah, *The Street Singer*. I saw that in his studio.'

The painting of the woman in the grey dress, her hem frayed, guitar over her shoulder, eating grapes – not the usual portrait of a respectable woman. Victorine was wearing the same dress and coat now. The hem had been repaired.

'I'm doing less modelling now,' Victorine said. 'I paint too, you know, that's why I asked him for some old paints. I don't have much money. My family is not wealthy, not like this.' She indicated around the room.

'Neither is mine.'

'Édouard promised me a share of the profits from *Olympia* if he ever sells it. I said no at the time, but maybe I'll remind him some day, if anyone ever buys it, that is.'

'What do you paint?'

'Oh, this and that. Portraits mostly. But no one takes me seriously.

After *Olympia* and *Le Déjeuner*, everyone thinks I'm a prostitute.'

'Do they? That's terrible …' Louise paused. 'Has Édouard ever tried, you know, have you …?'

'Has he? He wouldn't dare. And he hasn't, actually. I know everyone thinks models sleep with their painters but not me. Anyway, I like Suzanne too much,' Victorine said, helping herself to another pastry.

Louise winced.

'So, do some painters have sex with their models? What about Edgar? You modelled for him too, didn't you?'

'Edgar. What a man! He never touches women. I think he's afraid of us. That's why he says such ridiculous things.'

'Yes, he can be really rude, can't he? And, em, I've heard rumours about Pierre Puvis de Chavannes. Do you know him? Rumours about him with his model.'

'Yes, I know him. It's true. I heard he ends his sessions with his models by saying, "Would you like to see the *you know what* of a great man"! Pah, I can't believe Édouard suggested Pierre for Berthe,' Victorine said, sipping her coffee.

'I know! I can't believe it either,' Louise said.

'He thinks he'd be a good husband for her. Insane! Pierre is nowhere near good enough for Berthe. He's so dull. And his paintings! Passionless, cold. I wouldn't want that for a husband. Anyway, I hear he's got syphilis.'

'Oh, God, no!' Louise put her head in her hands.

CHAPTER 32

THE MANETS

The third day after the ball and Louise was having breakfast with Madame Manet and Gene. Marie came in with a letter. It was for Madame Manet, from Cornélie.

'What wonderful news!' Madame Manet said. 'It is an invitation to the wedding of Berthe and Pierre Puvis de Chavannes. Oh, and it's in six weeks. So soon!'

Louise dropped her croissant. *Oh no! Berthe has given up.*

The invitation was addressed to the Manets: Madame, Édouard, Suzanne and Gene. Louise was not mentioned.

'You will come with me,' Gene whispered.

Louise excused herself and ran up to her bedroom. She sat on her bed and stared blankly out in front of her. How could Berthe marry Pierre, that old duffer? He'd kill her, her art, her future. She should have tried harder to see her, to warn her about him. *But Berthe hates me. And now it is too late.*

It was the last straw for Louise. She climbed under the covers and put the pillows over her head. She stayed like that for hours. Marie came in to say lunch was ready, but Louise told her to say she was ill, suffering from "woman's problems". That would keep people – Gene – away.

She dug herself into a pit of despair and wallowed at the bottom of it, turning her mistakes over in her mind: she should never had interfered with Berthe and Édouard. Suzanne will never come back; her marriage to Édouard will be over. She, Louise, had destroyed it.

What would happen to Suzanne and Léon? Suzanne had been afraid that the Manets might cut her off, abandon her. And her family in Delft had no money – how would they survive?

She should never have slept with Gene. She was still married to Paul. Yes, he had had an affair, but now she was as bad as him. She'd broken her wedding vows.

And Berthe – she had ruined her life!

She could never go back through the painting. She'd be stuck here forever. It was embarrassing to be in the Manets' home. They were polite to her of course but they must be wondering who she was and what she was doing here.

Her relationship with Gene couldn't go anywhere. He was probably thinking of a way to get rid of her. But she had nowhere to go – she had nothing and nobody.

She missed her mother so much it physically hurt. Her head, her heart, her whole body ached for her. Her mother would know what to do. But she was dead; she would never see her mother again.

Louise lay in the bedroom in the dark and tortured herself with her failures. She could see no way out, no way to continue living.

And she stayed like that for days. Marie brought her meals and told her that Gene would like to see her; he was worried about her. But Louise refused both the food and Gene.

*

Suzanne returned. She knocked on Louise's bedroom door and came straight in. She went over to the window and opened the shutters. Louise held her breath: surely Suzanne would blame her for Édouard and Berthe's affair? But Suzanne came over, sat on the bed and took Louise's hand. She said that Édouard and Berthe's affair wasn't her fault. It was Berthe's.

'She's so selfish, she thinks can have anything she wants,' Suzanne said. 'I know she was only using you as her chaperone.'

Louise said nothing.

'And of course, it was Édouard's fault, too,' Suzanne said. 'But he has said sorry, and we are back together, happy again.' She smiled. 'And you are better off here with us. I will help you get better.'

Over the next few days, Suzanne came in and chatted with Louise regularly. She brought delicious cakes which Louise could not refuse. Gradually, Louise began to feel better. There were notes and messages from Gene: how was she? Did she feel well enough to see him yet?

One morning, Louise got out of bed and opened the window. She took a breath of fresh air and stretched. Yes, she could see Gene today. She had turned a corner.

*

Every day she felt better. She settled into another new life at the Manets' and began to enjoy the summer days. She often went out with Gene. They walked hand in hand through parks and gardens and visited the sites of Paris. One day, they went to the Louvre. It was mostly the same as when she'd seen it in her time, but without its glass pyramid. They looked at the *Mona Lisa*. The gallery was strangely uncrowded. Gene said it looked like the woman in the painting was thinking about what she would have for dinner.

Another day, they went on a tour of the new Paris sewer system. Haussmann was encouraging visitors to his shiny new underground galleries; he proclaimed they were a celebration of modernity and progress. Gene and Louise piled into a boat with other sightseers and rode through the large tunnels in a motorised wagon. It was the new fashionable thing to do.

Gene thought this was hilarious.

'What will they get us to pay for next?' he said.

The tunnels were just the same as Louise remembered from the *Les Misérables* movie. Chloe would have loved this. She knew every scene of that film. And Chloe would like Gene; he was great fun to be with. Kind, generous, and easy-going, he was always attentive and interested in her. He made her laugh, so different from uptight Paul. Her heart lightened in his company.

She went out shopping with Suzanne some days. Edgar (Degas!) came with them a couple of times. Despite all his disparaging of women, he was fascinated with their fashions.

Suzanne knew about Louise and Gene's relationship.

'Perhaps we could be sisters,' she whispered to Louise.

It was difficult for Louise and Gene to get the chance to sleep together. The house was always busy. But one day, Suzanne told Louise that she and Édouard were going to Delft to visit her family and she had asked Madame Manet to go with them. They'd be away for a few days, she winked.

Gene dismissed the maid and the cook so that he and Louise could have the house to themselves. They enjoyed each other's company completely. The sex was good; Gene was a generous lover, better than Paul.

The day before the rest of the family came back they were lying in their sumptuous four-poster together. Gene got out of bed and went over to the dressing table. He took something out of a drawer and came back over beside the bed. He knelt on one knee.

'My darling, I have something to ask you. I've been thinking this over a great deal. I know this is a bit soon, but, I have really thought about it, I promise. And, well, I hope you will agree. I want to ask you ...' he paused.

'What?' Louise said; she wasn't quite awake.

'Will you marry me?'

What? What was he saying? She turned to him.

Gene took her hand, 'Louise, will you marry me?'

She stared at him. 'Oh Gene, you don't have to. Really!'

'No, I want to marry you. I would like you to marry me! You said yourself, we are similar in so many ways. And you don't seem to have anyone to look after you so —'

'Gene, I don't need you to look after me.'

'No, but we are good together, you and me. And, I love you.'

'Love me?'

'Yes, I think we could be happy together.'

'I ...' Louise stared at him.

'I know, this is very sudden. You need time to think about it. I wanted to ask you before I left; I have to go away tomorrow on business. Please, consider it. You can tell me when I return. I'll be back in a week.'

He kissed her gently on the cheek.

'My darling. Please say yes.'

CHAPTER 33

PARDON

Gene went on his trip, and Louise was left to consider his proposal. Should she marry him? She paced around her bedroom. She did like him – a lot – but what about Paul? Did she still love him? But he was having an affair. Here in Paris wives seemed to put up with mistresses, but she wouldn't be able to, if she ever went back. But then she couldn't go back. So if she was going to be stuck here, in this time, marrying Gene seemed like her only option. But did she love him?

A knock. Marie brought a letter in for her. Could it be from Berthe?

She ripped it open. It was from Giselle. It was a bit of a scrawl, but she managed to make out: *Come now. M –* Giselle had tried to write "Mademoiselle", but it had just turned into a squiggle. *M … Berthe not well. Come now.*

Thank goodness she'd taught Giselle to write.

'Help me get dressed! Quickly!' Louise said to Marie.

Louise got a carriage to the Morisot house. It seemed to take forever to rattle over the cobbles to Passy but finally she got to the kitchen door. Giselle met her, wringing her hands on her apron.

'Ah, thank goodness you're here. Madame Morisot is out, wedding preparations. But Mademoiselle Berthe will not come out of her room. I'm so worried. She's not well, I don't know why …'

'Is her bedroom unlocked?'

'Yes.'

Louise ran upstairs and went into Berthe's bedroom. The curtains were closed. There was only a slight glimmer of light in the room. She could see Berthe in bed, her long dark hair spread across the pillow. There were dark circles under her eyes and in her hands, a bottle of laudanum. Louise knew from historical novels that laudanum was dangerous. It was a sedative, but too much and it could kill.

'Berthe. Please give me the bottle.'

Berthe stared at her.

'Louise ...'

'Give it to me, Berthe.' Gently she prised the bottle out of Berthe's hands and put it out of reach on the table.

'What's wrong, Berthe?' Louise said.

'There is no future for me,' Berthe said.

'There is, of course there is.'

'No, I have given up. I am a possession now.'

Louise sat on the bed beside Berthe.

'What do you mean – a possession?'

'A belonging. I belong to that man. I am nothing.'

A shiver of fear ran up Louise's back.

'What happened? Did something happen?'

Berthe said nothing.

Louise took her hand. 'Berthe, tell me, what happened?'

'He tried ...'

'Pierre?'

'He came yesterday. Mother was out, fussing about wedding arrangements.'

'What did he do?'

'He tried ...'

'What, Berthe?'

'He tried ... he pushed me down, forced himself on me.'

'No. Oh no, Berthe. Did he manage to –'

'No, very nearly. Giselle knocked on the door and came in, with some cake or something. I think she was worried about me. He quickly moved off me.'

'He tried to have sex with you?'

'I struggled. I said no. I told him no.'

'But you must report him, tell the police,' Louise said.

'Police?'

Louise stood up and paced about the room. 'That's attempted rape, assault. You've got to report him.'

Berthe looked at her with sad, empty eyes. 'I do not understand you.'

'He can't get away with that. I don't care *what* century it is!'

Berthe lay back in her bed, tears quietly rolling down her cheeks. 'It is my fault. I agreed to marry him.'

'No, it's not your fault. You said no. He can't ...'

But Berthe was sobbing. Louise sat on the bed beside her and took her hand. 'Oh Berthe, I'm so sorry.'

'I have not told anyone. Giselle, I think she saw.'

'But you should tell your parents, your mother.'

'What would be the point?'

'Berthe, it's all my fault. I'm so sorry, I ruined everything for you,' Louise said.

Berthe looked at her distraught face. 'Oh, Louise,' she said, touching Louise's cheek. 'I heard you were attacked.'

Louise put her hand up to Berthe's hand. 'It's nothing. I'm so sorry Berthe. I was only trying to help you, honestly. You can't marry Pierre. Definitely not. Not now.'

They sat silently until Berthe asked: 'Why did you tell Suzanne about our affair?'

'I didn't. I promise. She knew when she came here.'

'But you told her I was at the studio, with Édouard.'

'No, no, she must have guessed. I didn't tell her anything. I didn't betray you. Honestly. You must believe me.'

'I'm sorry too, then,' Berthe said.

'I never meant to hurt you. I wanted to help. What happened when you went to see Édouard that day?'

Berthe sighed. 'When I arrived at his studio, I was frantic, furious with him. He had visitors and had to usher them out. I shouted at him for saying I should marry Pierre. He did not deny it. He said he loved me, but he could not leave Suzanne. And he said I *should* marry Pierre, that "he would be good for me".'

'I'm so sorry.'

'I was so upset, so angry, I beat him with my fists. He held me until I calmed down, and then we kissed, and then, well, it got a bit heated. Then Suzanne burst in. She saw us, together. I rushed out. It was awful.'

Berthe paused. 'But why did *you* go to see Édouard. Do you like him? Do you want him for yourself?'

'No, no, I was trying to help you. I was trying to persuade him to marry you. It was for *you*.'

'To marry me? And you did not tell Suzanne where I was?'

'No. I didn't say anything. But I should have lied, made something up, said you were somewhere, I don't know. I'm sorry. I couldn't think what to say to her when she turned up like that.'

'Well, it is my fault too. I should not have accused you like that. And I too am sorry. I used you, as my chaperone. That was unfair.'

'But I should have lied to Suzanne. After all you've done for me. I'm so sorry.'

They sat in silence.

'I was not really angry with you,' Berthe said. 'More with myself, with *him*, with *everything*. I am so very tired.'

'I know.' Louise took a deep breath. 'But Berthe, there's another thing. I'll tell you if you promise *never* to tell anyone. Do you promise?' Surely it was OK to break her promise to Suzanne if it was to help her – to make Berthe understand?

'Yes, I promise.'

'Suzanne said Léon is her and Édouard's son.'

'What? *No!*'

'Suzanne was so sad, so desperate when she came here. She said she'd be destitute if Édouard left them for you, if he threw her and Léon out. She begged me to persuade you to stop seeing him. That's why she came, but I didn't tell her where you were, honestly.'

'I never thought about Suzanne, or Léon.' Berthe shook her head.

'You won't tell anyone about Léon? Promise? She made me promise.'

'Yes, of course. I mean no, I won't tell. Léon …?'

After a few moments, Louise said softly, 'Berthe, there's another thing, other reasons you can't marry Pierre.'

And she told Berthe about her suitor's affairs with his model and the Romanian princess.

'Well, I did not know *that*,' Berthe said, sighing. 'I suppose I am not surprised. The hypocrisy of men. It is endless.'

'And, er, there's a rumour that he has syphilis.'

'Oh God,' Berthe said, rubbing her eyes. 'I'm so very tired.' She lay back in her bed as her tears began to fall again.

Louise climbed up beside her and hugged her. They lay wrapped around each other until Berthe fell asleep.

Giselle tiptoed in.

'It's all right, Giselle. She's resting now,' Louise said.

'You had better stay here tonight,' Giselle said. 'I have made up the bed in your old room.'

CHAPTER 34

INDEPENDENCE

'Louise, Louise, wake up!'

Berthe was sitting on her bed, gently shaking her.

'What time is it?' Louise said, trying to surface from the depths of sleep. Light was just starting to filter through the curtains and the birds were singing softly.

'I don't know, about six. Louise, I have decided. I am not going to marry Pierre. I have already written to him. I have had enough of men, thinking they can control me. How dare Édouard hand me over to another man, like some kind of baggage! I refuse to be treated like that. I am not going to marry Pierre, be his subordinate, his helpmate, his plaything.'

'Good for you!' Louise said, rubbing her eyes.

Berthe got up, opened the curtains and came back to pace up and down beside the bed.

'I am not going to marry anyone, be anyone's little wife. I'm going to stop my affair with Édouard, and I am going to devote myself to painting. I *will* be an artist. Why should I sacrifice my art for men! I shall wed art instead.'

Louise looked at Berthe, her black hair falling over her white nightdress, her eyes gleaming.

'Yes. And you will be magnificent,' she said.

Berthe talked on, striding around the room. 'I will achieve it only by perseverance, and by openly asserting my determination to emancipate myself. I will not be an idle wife, sitting around embroidering, having soirées. Work is the sole purpose of my existence. In fact, indefinitely prolonged idleness would be fatal to me from every point of view.'

'Yes, that's it Berthe. You're absolutely right.'

'I am going to be a "femist". Is that what you call it?'

'*Feminist*!' Louise laughed.

'You have helped me make up my mind. You have made me see that women can be independent, equal to men. I have watched you. You have no fear about going out, going to cafés, breaking the rules. You talk to men as equals. You have given me hope.'

Berthe rushed out the room in a flurry of white nightdress.

'I am going to burn Édouard's letters.'

Louise and Berthe went down to breakfast together to tell Cornélie the news.

'I am not going to marry Pierre Puvis de Chavannes,' Berthe announced. 'He has a mistress.'

'So? What do you expect?' Cornélie said, continuing to rip up her croissant.

'And he has syphilis! I will *not* marry him.'

'What? You have to. Don't be ridiculous. The wedding is next week. You cannot call it off. What would people say? It would be a disaster. I would die of embarrassment!'

'So, you would rather I die of syphilis than you be *embarrassed*?'

'Well, no, but …'

Louise nodded at Berthe. Surely she would tell her mother about Pierre's assault, his attempted rape, but Berthe shook her head.

'Tiburce!' yelled Cornélie.

Tiburce happened to be at home that morning.

'What?' he said from the study.

'Tiburce! You must come here. Now!'

Tiburce ambled in from his study, reading a document. 'What is it, darling?' he said without looking up.

'It is Berthe. She is refusing to marry Pierre. Talk some sense into her.'

'What is the matter, Berthe?' he asked, and Berthe explained the situation.

'Well, of course you cannot marry him.'

'But Tiburce. It is next week,' Cornélie said. 'The arrangements? What will we say?'.

Tiburce shrugged. 'Tell them she changed her mind. No one will be that surprised. Let Berthe do as she pleases.' He went back to his study.

So the wedding was cancelled. After the initial flurry and stress, Cornélie seemed to calm down and the tension in the Morisot house eased. Cornélie forgave Berthe for not marrying Pierre Puvis de Chavannes and even admitted he was a bit old and boring. She forgave Louise for being a bad chaperone, now that it seemed no one had heard about Berthe's embarrassment with Édouard.

'Pierre was very angry about the cancellation of the wedding, of course,' Cornélie said. 'He was particularly rude about you, Louise, something about you being an imposter, not from Brittany. I don't know, he said a lot of things. I suppose he was embarrassed about it all, what people will say. He'll get over it, eventually.'

Life settled back into a gentle routine. So peaceful, usually, but Louise was having tumultuous nightmares. One morning she woke up in a sweat. She'd dreamt that she'd been in an old time machine, like the one in HG Wells' book, *The Time Machine*. Dates had been whizzing around on dials and she had reached out her hand to try to set the date to the day before her mother died, so she could take her to the doctor and get her heart checked, but her hand went right through the dials. The dates kept whirring, round and round, faster and faster until they became a blur.

She sat up, dizzy, and put her head in her hands. What was wrong with her? She felt like everything was out of control. What was she supposed to do? The letter in that book was signed *Berthe Manet*. Berthe was supposed to marry Édouard, but how could she? Did she marry him in the future maybe? Louise just didn't know. She sighed, shook her head and dragged herself down to breakfast with Tiburce.

'Are you all right?' he asked. 'Not sleep well?'

'I'm fine,' Louise said.

It was impossible to talk to him about any of this, so she tried to settle into their usual silent, companiable breakfast. She watched him reading his papers. Her own father must be about the same age as Tiburce. What was he doing now? Did he ever think about her, his lost daughter? Why had he never come to visit her? Maybe her father had fallen in love with another woman, and perhaps her mother had told him not to come back. If Louise had learned anything, it was that love could be complicated.

Her father's sons, they would be mid-twenties now, her half-brothers. What were they like? Maybe they were like Édouard and Gene.

'Well, I'd better be going,' Tiburce said.

Louise sat in the dining room alone, staring into her coffee cup. Gene would be here in a few days, and still she had not decided whether to accept his proposal. She missed him – but enough to marry him? Did she love him, or only think she did? Was she just confused about Paul? Did she love Paul or Gene, both, or neither?

The door was flung open and Berthe came in.

'What shall we do today?' she said, pacing up and down. 'I want to do something different.'

Louise wished she could talk to Berthe about Gene, but she was caught up in her new life and Louise didn't want to disturb her new-found confidence. She alone had to decide.

'I don't know,' Louise said. She shook herself out of her torpor. 'Ah, I *do* know – would you like to have some fun?'

'Of course! Fun is *exactly* what I need today,' Berthe said.

'Do you think your father, or your brother maybe, have some old clothes we could borrow?'

'What?'

'Let's go up and look around. Maybe in your brother's old room?'

'Why?'

'To dress up!'

They rummaged around in Berthe's brother's wardrobe and drawers until they found white shirts, black ties, trousers, topcoats and shiny black shoes. They dressed in the uniform of gentlemen, as *flâneurs*. Louise piled Berthe's hair up and tied it tightly under her shiny top hat.

'You know,' she said, looking Berthe over, 'Bert is a man's name in Britain, and Bertha is the woman's version. I guess they both mean bright. I'll call you Bert.'

'Bertrand would be more French,' Berthe said, admiring herself in the mirror. She was radiant in her new outfit, freed from her petticoat prison.

'Astonishing!' Louise said. 'You look amazing. Let's go.'

'Go? Go where?'

'Out.'

'No. I cannot go *out*!'

'Yes you can. I've done it. It's easy.'

'No, impossible! What if someone recognises us ... me?'

'Don't take off your hat. Or speak! All we have to do is walk out the door and down the street,' she said, pulling Berthe to the door.

On the threshold, Berthe hesitated. 'But it is illegal for women to wear trousers.'

'Is it? Well, that's stupid. Come on.'

'I am not sure about this ...'

'Don't be silly. No time like the present,' she said, taking Berthe's arm.

On the pavement, Berthe took tentative little steps, like an old man walking on ice.

'Take bigger strides. Hold your head up,' Louise said.

They walked down the hill to the boulevards and Berthe started to enjoy herself. No one gave them a second glance.

'I am invisible,' Berthe said. 'I can go anywhere, do anything!'

'Yes! Let's run,' Louise grabbed Berthe's hand, and they ran, laughing, Berthe struggling to keep her feet and stop her hat toppling off. She got out of breath very quickly.

The smell of fresh bread and coffee lured them onto some outdoor seats at a café. Louise ordered coffee and croissants in her lowest possible voice. They tried not to giggle.

'This is wonderful,' Berthe said. 'Is this what it is like to be a woman in *your* time, in one hundred and fifty years?'

'Yes, a little.'

'What is different? There must be a lot of things that are different. Tell me.'

Louise looked around at the busy street. Where to begin? She looked at the people, couples walking arm in arm chatting.

'Everyone would be looking at their phones.'

'Phones?'

'They're these amazing little devices.' She folded up her napkin to the size of a mobile phone. 'About this size. You can speak to your friends, family, anyone, anywhere in the world. And you can take photos, selfies.'

She held up the napkin and pretended to take a selfie of herself and Berthe, smiling at her napkin. Berthe stared at her.

'You can send photos to people over the world. And videos, they're like moving photos. You can send them, too.'

'That is surely not possible. It sounds like a form of magic.' Berthe took a sip of coffee. 'Maybe it is not so surprising you came through a painting after all.'

Mobile phones and time travel must seem equally implausible to someone in 1871, Louise thought.

'They discovered these little silicon chips,' she said, putting her napkin down and ripping into her croissant. 'I don't really know how phones work, the signals travel through the air, bounce off satellites, which are machines in space, up there, that orbit the earth.'

'What? I do not believe you. Surely they would fall down?' Berthe said, looking up into the sky.

'And there's the internet. You can find out anything on your phone through the internet. Like I could ask it "How does a mobile phone work?" And it would tell me.'

'And then you could tell me.'

'I could ask it what happens to you. I wish I could do that. What happens to Berthe Morisot? I know you become a successful painter, but that's all. If only I could Google it.'

'Google?'

'It's like looking something up in a book, a book which knows everything.'

'Gosh. Everyone must be so smart,' Berthe said, looking around her. 'It must be a much better world.'

'Well, yes and no. There are still wars.' Louise stopped. She couldn't bear to tell Berthe about World Wars One and Two. 'I mean, in the future, we have lots of problems, like pollution and climate change because we've messed up the planet, consuming everything with all our bright ideas and progress.'

'Oh no, really? We do that? What is this "climate change"?'

'The climate, the weather, gets warmer all round the world because we burn fossil fuels, coal, oil. The sea levels rise, people lose their homes, all kinds of species, animals, die.'

'What? But that is truly awful! Why do we do that?'

'We don't mean to. We're greedy, careless.'

'But you must do something now. You could tell people to stop it.'

'*Me*? But who would listen to *me*?' Louise imagined trying to tell people about climate change, her little voice drowned out by a steam train thundering down the tracks to progress. 'I'd be like that hare in Turner's painting, running terrified in front of the train barrelling down on top of me. Have you seen that painting?'

'No,' Berthe said.

'Well, anyway, I'm not supposed to interfere.'

'What do you mean, interfere?'

'Well, if I remember right, it's called the "Grandfather Paradox". Why not "Grandmother's Paradox"? Let's call it the "Grandmother's Paradox". So, if you go back and kill your grandmother, that means you won't exist.'

'Why would you kill your grandmother?' asked Berthe.

'Well, not intentionally, say by accident. It's logic. If you kill your grandmother, or father, or your mother, it wouldn't be possible for you to be born, to exist.'

'But if you killed your grandmother, you would not exist in the first place, so you could not travel back in time and kill her.'

'Oh yes. Well, I don't know,' Louise said. 'But the point is that the smallest thing I do here could change the future, could have unintended consequences. So, I have to be careful.'

'I do not understand.'

'Well, say I order another coffee from the waitress here. It could make her late and maybe she's going home for lunch. So, she'd have to rush and she could get hit by a carriage crossing the road and die. And then she wouldn't be able to marry her sweetheart and have kids. And one of her daughters might have invented a new medicine or something. And people would die because she didn't manage to do this. All because I ordered another coffee.'

'Oh!' Berthe put down her coffee cup and looked at the waitress. 'Maybe we should not have any more coffee then.'

'Yes, I think we'd better go.'

They paid the waitress and strolled off down the wide pavement.

'Actually, I am unsure that the future is good now,' Berthe said.

'But many things are better: medicine, antibiotics, vaccines. We can cure many diseases, a lot of them.'

'So are people happier, in your time, with medicine, and all their machines?'

'That's a good question ... No, actually, I don't think so. We're more disconnected from each other. It's strange when we have all this power to connect. Everyone is so busy all the time, rushing about. Doing *what*? Actually, I think *your* lives, or at least rich people's lives here, are better.'

'Really? That is very depressing.'

'Well, maybe not for women. I think *you* would be happier in my time. But you have such important things to do here, now.'

'Like what?'

'Your art of course! You have to change art, with Edgar, Édouard, Claude, Auguste, Paul, all of you. You will revolutionise art. People will love what you do, you have no idea.'

'No, I do not. I have no idea. I think you are mad,' smiled Berthe, 'more than ever now.'

They laughed.

'What shall we do now?' asked Berthe.

'I know.' Louise took Berthe to Café Guerbois. Auguste and Claude were there, and Berthe greeted them enthusiastically.

'Berthe?' Auguste said.

'Bertrand?' Claude said.

The proprietress came over.

'Welcome, gentlemen. I don't think I've seen you in before.' She looked more closely at Louise. 'Or perhaps *you've* been in?'

'Yes, I have,' Louise said. And her voice gave her away.

The proprietress looked at Berthe.

'Ah I see. I have a brand-new clientele. What can I get you *gentlemen?*'

Auguste, Claude and Berthe launched straight into a conversation about painting. They talked about light, colour, brush strokes, new techniques, and subjects, the new art they were creating, the risks they wanted to take. Louise sat back and watched, delighted to see Berthe engaged and animated. Berthe let loose was a wondrous sight.

Two hours passed and it was time to go. Auguste and Claude thanked Berthe for her jewellery. It had saved them, their families, their painting, they said. But as Berthe was saying goodbye to Auguste, Claude took Louise aside and told her that his money was gone. He had so many debts. He was back in the same situation as before, looking for work. Auguste was also struggling. But he thanked them for trying to help; they really appreciated it.

How had the money been spent so soon? Louise looked at Berthe and was about to tell her, but she was so happy, so radiant, she couldn't bear to burst her bubble. Another secret to keep from her.

Berthe strode confidently down the boulevards; her manly gait had improved no end. She even tipped her hat at a pretty young woman.

'That was fun, so interesting,' she said.

Louise laughed. *Berthe would be great in my time*, she thought. *So clever and talented.* With the opportunities available, she'd shine even more brightly. What a waste for her to be stuck here, in this society. How many other women like her were excluded, unable to fulfil their potential?

'Do you think your mother would enjoy this?' asked Louise. Her own mother would have loved this day, dressing up, talking about art.

'Mother? She would be appalled.'

'I don't know. She's obviously smart. And *she's* stuck, too. Her only role in life seems to be to control your family's position in society.'

'And she takes that very seriously.'

'But she seems conflicted about you. On one hand she's encouraged your painting, but on the other she wants you to fit in with society's expectations. Perhaps she's so tense all the time because she's confused, frustrated, bitter maybe, that her own life is so restricted.'

'Do you think so? She has never said anything like that.'

'You know it's like this for decades, a century or more,' Louise said. 'Women will be stuck like this for years, except for the wars when all of a sudden they become important.' Oops, don't mention the war. 'Then in the 1950s, they're firmly put back in their box, stuck in their kitchens with new time-saving toys to play with, to distract them.'

'Toys?'

'Yes, machines for washing clothes, drying clothes, sucking up dust ...'

'Sucking up dust?'

'Yes, and food mixers, processors, freezers, microwaves ...'

'Stop! You are making my head hurt.'

'Women can only watch from the side lines as men screw things up, with their wars, their arrogant posturing across the globe.'

'Not all men. They are not all like that.'

'No, Tiburce, Gene, Édouard – they're different.'

'I wonder why women put up with all this.'

'I suppose we're trapped by our biology, by childbirth. Until the sixties, that's the 1960s, when a knight on a white charger releases us from bondage with a tiny pill, the contraceptive. I told you about that. Then we can control when or if, we get pregnant. That makes an enormous difference, frees us from our bodies. But we're still trying to catch up with men in my time. The patriarchy is hard to shift.'

Berthe smiled and took her arm.

'Well, at least you have given me a taste of what it must be like. Free at last, if only for one day.'

The two handsome young men strode down the boulevard arm in arm and agreed they would like to wear the trousers all the time.

CHAPTER 35

AN EXHIBITION

Berthe was looking through her paintings, searching for inspiration for what to paint next. Louise sat on the chaise, pretending to read *The Hunchback of Notre Dame*. But she was too excited. Gene would be back tomorrow. She had decided she would accept him. She would marry him. It would be a great surprise for Berthe when she told her.

'I do not know what to paint for the next Salon exhibition,' Berthe said. 'I want to make sure they accept it, but I want to do my own style.'

'You should do what you want,' Louise said, only half listening.

'To capture moments, that is what I want. After all, moments are all we have. It is so difficult, though, to grasp the light of an instant and put it down in paint. I think I am beginning to find my own way, but I do not know. Am I crazy?'

'Absolutely not, no,' Louise put her book down. 'What you are doing is new, it's brilliant.'

'But the Salon. They will never allow this style.'

'Well, why not have your own exhibition then? That's what artists do in my day.'

'What, *me*? On my own? I could not do that.'

'Ask someone else to join you then. Édouard or Edgar.'

'What, our own exhibition?'

'Yes, do it yourselves. Escape from the Salon you all hate so much.'

Berthe sat down. 'But it is the Salon, the tradition ...'

'You could invite the others too – Claude, Auguste, Paul Cézanne.' Louise stood up. This was a brilliant idea, the solution for Claude and Auguste, too. They could sell at their own exhibition, make money and get back to painting full time.

'Do you really think so?' Berthe said.

'Yes, why not? Why don't you ask them at least?'

'Do you think so? I suppose I could at least talk to them about it. That would not do any harm. Our own exhibition! But I cannot invite them here. Mother would hate the idea.'

'Meet at Édouard's studio then.'

'Édouard's?'

'Oh, but you probably shouldn't see him.'

'No, it will be all right for me to see him. We have exchanged letters. He has apologised to me for suggesting Pierre as a husband. He said he *had* thought he'd be a good match for me, but he was sorry if he was wrong. He was very sorry he upset me. We have agreed that this affair is over. I feel that I am over him now.'

'Good, if you're sure. But maybe don't tell Édouard about the idea for an exhibition. He'd take over, wouldn't he?'

'Yes, that is true. Do you really think it would be possible, our own exhibition? It would be a revolution, such a challenge to tradition. People would be outraged.'

'It's about time.'

After further persuasion, Berthe gathered up courage and sent messages to the other painters, asking them to meet at Édouard's studio the following afternoon. She told Édouard only that there would be a meeting.

CHAPTER 36

RENDEZ-VOUS

Next day, Louise and Berthe climbed into the carriage to go to Édouard's studio. How would Berthe and Édouard act together? Would they be able to resist each other? Or would there be a tension between them?

Édouard greeted them both warmly, and they sat together at the table to have coffee. Louise could see that Berthe was nervous, glancing over at Édouard occasionally, smiling a little awkwardly as he talked about his latest painting. At one point she bit her lip and turned away to hide her brimming eyes. *Not over him yet, then*, Louise thought.

A clatter of footsteps and Claude arrived, closely followed by Auguste and Edgar. While Berthe talked to Auguste, Louise asked Claude how his painting was going.

'Are you still working on getting the water right?' she said.

'Yes but I've been painting a sunrise at Le Havre harbour. It's a bit different. It doesn't really look like Le Havre, or anywhere really. I don't think the Salon will accept it.'

'Why? What's it like?'

'Well, it's very loose, hazy; it's more about light and atmosphere. It's the *feeling* of a sunrise, I suppose.'

'An impression?'

'Yes, that's right, an impression of a sunrise …' Claude drifted off into his sunrise.

Louise turned to Edgar. 'And what are you painting, Edgar?'

'I've become fascinated by the racecourse, the horses. You know the new photographs of the racecourse, how they sometimes cut the horses off, and they go half out of the frame?'

'Cropping?'

'Yes. I like that, cropping, it gives you the feeling of movement and energy. I'm working on a carriage at the racecourse which is on its way out of the painting. It's difficult to get right. You know I like to craft my paintings in the studio. No art is less spontaneous than mine. But this one is so unconventional. I don't think the Salon will accept it.'

'Good.'

'Good? Why could that possibly be good?' Edgar said.

'Is everyone here now?' Louise said to Berthe. 'Shall we get started?'

'Paul is not coming,' Berthe said.

'He sends his apologies,' Auguste said. 'Well, he didn't actually, just said he wasn't coming.'

'Let's take a seat,' Louise said, moving to the table.

'This is intriguing,' Edgar said.

'It is indeed,' Édouard added. 'I have no idea what's going on.'

Adèle poured the wine and silence fell over the group. Louise nodded to Berthe to begin.

Berthe took a deep breath. 'Well Louise has an idea, hmm, *we* have an idea ...' She hesitated and Louise gave her an encouraging nod.

'We think we should have our *own* exhibition,' Berthe said and stopped. She looked at Louise.

'Yes,' Louise said. 'You're all always complaining about the Salon, about not getting your paintings accepted, and how they're displayed. You have a new art, it's a new era, so why not have an exhibition of your own?'

'We could find our own space,' Berthe said, 'and put our paintings on show how we like, without anyone judging them.'

'Hmm,' Claude said. 'I could put in my sunrise.'

'And Edgar, you could show your new carriage painting,' Louise said, 'the one you think the Salon would reject.'

'I might even make some money,' Claude said.

'It would be difficult,' Auguste said, 'but if we could sell some paintings ... I have several I could put in. I think Paul might join us.'

'Yes. He was annoyed with the Salon rejecting his paintings,' Claude said.

'Berthe,' Edgar said. 'You have many good paintings you can show.'

Louise raised her eyebrows. 'Yes Edgar, she does,' she said. Despite all his insults about women, Edgar was supportive of Berthe. What a strange contradictory man he was.

'Yes,' Auguste said. 'It would be a challenge to the Salon, a defiance of tradition, a revolution, in fact!'

Édouard sighed loudly. 'I tried this before, you know, about four years ago. I used my inheritance to set up a pavilion at the Exposition Universelle. I had fifty paintings in there, but it was not successful, despite Émile's complimentary reviews.'

'Why not try again?' Edgar said. 'We have nothing to lose.'

'It won't work,' Édouard said.

'But so many of our paintings get rejected,' Berthe said.

'"Yes, the Salon is stuck in the past. Let's do it!' Auguste said, rubbing his hands together. 'What would we call it, call ourselves?'

'The Impressionists!' Louise said. 'The French Impressionists.'

'What?' They all turned to look at her.

'What does that mean?' Auguste said. '*Impressionist?*'

'What's an Impressionist?' Claude said. 'Impression of what?'

'Like your sunrise,' Louise said, 'An impression of –'

'That sounds ridiculous!' Edgar said. 'We will have enough trouble trying to get people to take us seriously.'

'Yes,' the others murmured.

Louise sat back quietly, confused. When did the name "Impressionist" come in? Hadn't they always called themselves that?

'How about the Independents?' Edgar said.

'Or The Society of Artists and Painters,' Berthe said.

'And Sculptors and Engravers,' Claude said. 'That would bring more artists in and help bring in some more money.'

'It should be a proper society with a charter,' Auguste said. 'Like my local baker – he has a bakers' union.'

'Yes,' Claude said, 'like that, a cooperative.'

Édouard sat back and folded his arms.

'Do you really not think it would work, Édouard?' asked Berthe.

'No. It's not for me,' Édouard said.

'Why not?' Edgar said. 'The way the Salon treats you is humiliating.'

'I will stay loyal to the Salon,' Édouard said. 'If you want to receive recognition, it's best to remain with them. They are the only ones with the medals and commendations. The best thing to do is to confront the situation, not run away.'

'I do not understand you,' Berthe said. 'You were the first to say we have to paint our own time, what we see around us. You want only to break convention.'

'I will make them acknowledge me,' Édouard said. 'They will give me the Légion d'honneur one day, like my father. I am not looking to cause any further trouble. Berthe, you will just offend them. I don't think you realise the danger you are in, the harm it could do to your name. My advice? Don't do it.'

Édouard left the table. Berthe looked devastated.

'But I'm sure it will be successful,' Louise said. 'You're all such wonderful painters. People are going to love you. I just know it!'

The famous artists looked at her, indulgently, like she was a little touched in the head. They turned back to the discussion: who else they could invite, where could they have it, who had the space. They forgot about Édouard.

Louise sat back. Surely Édouard was part of the Impressionist exhibition, one of the founder members? Louise watched Berthe and the others talk increasingly enthusiastically. She was no longer needed, no longer a part of it. She was ignored, even by Berthe. She had become invisible again.

But Gene would be back tomorrow. She would be Gene's wife, part of the Manet family, with Suzanne, Édouard, and Madame Manet. She would help the artists set up the exhibition, and she would be close to Berthe to help her. She would be comfortable and safe here.

CHAPTER 37

BERTHE MANET

I *t was Gene!*

Louise sat up in bed, wide awake. Gene. That was why Berthe signed herself "Berthe Manet" in the letter in the book in her mother's cottage. She married *Gene*! Not Édouard!

Louise's heart sank to the bottom of the ocean. She couldn't marry Gene – Berthe had to marry him. She would have to give him up. Her chance at love, happiness – she'd have to give it all up.

She got out of bed and paced around the bedroom, racking her brain for a way out. But it was clear – if she married Gene, she would destroy the future, Berthe's future, everything. And she was certain that this time she'd got it right.

She called Giselle and gave her a letter for Gene, asking him to meet her at a nearby café; not Café Guerbois, but somewhere quiet, where they wouldn't be known. There was a little one just off the main street in Passy. She could walk there.

*

Passy was quiet in the afternoon. The tiny café was empty after the lunchtime rush. The fat owner raised an eyebrow when Louise entered alone but said nothing. He probably thought she was a prostitute.

She found a table in a dusty shaft of sunlight next to the window. The owner shuffled over, in a less than clean apron, and wiped the stained table half-heartedly with his grey cloth. She asked for coffee and fidgeted with the spoon. It was breaking her heart to refuse Gene and it would probably break his too. But Berthe, her art, the future of art, depended on this. If Louise married Gene, she would totally screw up the future.

Gene rushed in minutes later and embraced her. He sat down opposite, leaning over the grubby table. He said he was sorry not to find her at home, at his house, when he returned, but was pleased she and Berthe had made up.

'Berthe is not marrying Pierre Puvis de Chavannes,' Louise said.

'Yes, I heard,' Gene said, 'and thank goodness! But Louise, I have missed you. Don't keep me in suspense. Have you made your decision? What do you say?' He reached across the table and took her hands. 'I have been desperate to see you, to know your answer. Please say it is "yes"!'

She took a deep breath. 'Gene, I want to but –'

'Please, Louise. Marry me!'

She looked around at the drab empty café. Why not marry Gene? But she took her hand away. She was twisting her left hand, her empty ring finger, hard under the table.

'I can't,' she heard herself say quietly.

'*Can't?* But why?'

'There are things you don't know about me.'

'What is it?' Gene looked at her tormented face. 'Are you in trouble? I can help you.' He reached for her hands again.

'No, it's –'

'Is it Édouard? It's him, isn't it?' Gene said, sitting back in his chair. 'Everyone's always in love with Édouard.'

'No, no, it's nothing to do with him,' Louise looked directly at Gene. 'It's been wonderful, *you* are wonderful. We are … but I'm … I'm not in a fit state to be involved with anyone right now. I'm sorry if I led you on, gave you the wrong idea. I like you a lot, a whole lot, I do, but I can't marry you. I can't.'

She said she was too confused about what she was doing with her life just now. She didn't know if she would be staying in Paris at all. It was all rather vague and feeble, but it was the best she could manage. She looked into his eyes. He looked so sad, so desperately disappointed.

She got up quickly, scraping the chair. 'I'm so sorry.'

She rushed out of the café and walked as fast as she could along the cobbled pavement back to the house.

What am I doing? Gene – kind, gentle, loving Gene. I could love him, have a life here with him, with Berthe.

*

She climbed up the stairs to Berthe's bedroom and found her drawing up a list of potential artists and engravers for the new exhibition.

'There are so many people we can approach,' Berthe said, 'and we will have to find premises of course. I must talk to Father. Maybe he has some ideas …' She raced on with details of her plans and ideas.

'And what have *you* been doing?' Berthe asked her eventually.

'Gene asked me to marry him.'

'What?' Berthe said stopping in her tracks. '*Gene?* But how? What? Have you been seeing him?'

'Yes.'

'You never said …'

'No. I know.'

'And have you …?'

'Yes, the night of the masked ball, and while I was staying there …'

'Oh, I did not know. You have kept so very quiet about this. But this is wonderful news! You said "yes" of course? How exciting!'

'No.'

'No?'

'I said "no."'

'But why? Marry him and you can stay, be with me. We could have great fun together! It would be wonderful. And Gene is such a lovely man.'

'Berthe, you don't know anything about him. You barely ever talk to him. And anyway, I'm already married.'

'But he is not here, is he? I thought you had left him behind? I thought you wanted to stay?'

'No, he's not here. Anyway I'm not sure marriage is the solution to anything.'

Louise went to her bedroom and closed the door. If she was to make any sense of this, she had to find a way to get Gene and Berthe together. Could she get Berthe to think of Gene as a husband? To her he was just a friend, the brother of her lover, ex-lover. She barely even acknowledged him.

She lay down on the bed. She was so tired.

CHAPTER 38

THE BAD FEMINIST

There was someone in her bedroom; she could feel it. Tentatively, Louise opened her eyes.

A woman was standing at the window, her back to her, caught in the early morning light. The woman turned slowly to face her.

'There you are,' she said, smiling.

'Mum,' Louise whispered. She sat up slowly in bed, carefully, so as not to create the slightest ripple of air.

'I've been looking all over for you,' her mother said.

'Mum …'

'It's time now,' her mother said, 'time to come back.'

She turned away and gently, gradually, started fading away into the light.

'No, no, stay,' Louise said, reaching out for her. 'Please …'

But she was gone.

Louise wrapped her arms tightly around her stomach, and tears rolled down her face. She missed her so much. Her beautiful mum …

Time to come back, she had said. And Louise knew that her mother didn't only mean it was time to come back to her own time, she meant it was time to come back to herself, to who she really was.

She slipped out of bed and wrapped herself in a warm wool blanket. She sat huddled on a chair by the window and watched the dawn break. She could smell the first sweet scents of autumn's decay.

What had happened to her, her own life? How had she got so

lost? It had started with little comments.

'Are you wearing *that*?' So she'd change her outfit. 'I don't like that restaurant.' So they went to another. He decided where they would go on holiday, told her which of her friends he didn't like, didn't want to see. At first she'd argued but Paul only became more forceful. It was easier to give in. What did it matter, really? But each small forfeit had eaten away at her confidence until she couldn't even decide what to wear by herself.

She'd moved to London for Paul, given up her job, her friends, failed even to visit her mother. Gradually, imperceptibly, she'd shrunk, become invisible. She'd become a ghost of herself, flowing through life without ruffling the air. If quantum physics said she was not a solid thing, that she was a process, an event, then she was an event that was falling apart. The marquee had blown away, the band had left, the bar had run out of drink and the food had dried up. Everyone was leaving. Only empty bottles on the floor and the smell of stale beer were left. Not a very good event.

She had been so desperate for security that she'd put up with anything to hang onto Paul. Maybe it was because her father left that she couldn't bear to lose anyone else. But she had let Paul take over her. She had relinquished control of her life to him, like some sort of surrendered wife.

Just the kind of wife that Berthe feared becoming, that Berthe rejected. How had Louise let that happen? One hundred and fifty years in the future and she had fallen into that same trap.

And she almost did it again, gave up her life, became dependent on Gene. What would her mum have thought of that?

She shivered and pulled the blanket tighter around her.

Berthe is a better feminist than I am.

CHAPTER 39

ENTANGLEMENT

Berthe had stopped nagging Louise to marry Gene.

'Who needs men?' Berthe said. 'Who needs Manets? You will stay here, with me.'

'But Berthe,' said Louise. 'I can't stay forever. I have no money. And you've all been so kind already.'

'Of course you can stay! Father likes you. You are my companion.'

'And Cornélie?'

'You are my chaperone,' Berthe said with a laugh. 'And I do need someone to go out with, for appearances. She is happy with you now.'

At lunch, Cornélie did seem content, and she had a suggestion.

'Let's have a soirée on Thursday, Berthe,' she said. 'And goodness, it's autumn now, so we'll have to start planning for your birthday. Where *does* the time go?'

Round in circles, maybe? Louise stirred her coffee. Other cultures, Buddhists, some Eastern cultures, believed in rebirth, reincarnation. For them, life went round in circles, as the earth moved round the sun, as the seasons cycled through the year. Or maybe time hopped around like a rambunctious rabbit.

'We will have to plan a big party for Berthe's thirtieth birthday in January,' Cornélie continued.

'What?' Louise said, crashing back to the nineteenth century breakfast table. '*When*'s your thirtieth birthday?'

'January.'

'Yes, but what day?'

'The 14th,' Berthe said.

'What?' Louise said, almost dropping her cup. 'Your birthday is on the 14th of January?'

'Yes,' Berthe said.

'But that's my birthday too! I'll be thirty as well.'

She and Berthe looked at each other in amazement.

'Good, it will be a party for both of you,' Cornélie said. 'Maybe I can find some eligible bachelors for you. But first, the soirée.'

Louise sat in a stupor, staring at Berthe as Cornélie talked on about plans for Thursday evening. Then she went off to discuss the menu with Nanette.

Louise and Berthe went out into the garden and sat on one of the ornate iron benches in a sheltered spot by the wall. The sweet smell of honeysuckle wafted over them. Louise looked up at the stems climbing and twisting around each other as they wound towards the sky. She traced some of the entwining strands with her fingers. Berthe's birthday was the same day as hers. They were exactly the same age in different centuries. What a weird coincidence! They were both at turning points in their lives. They both wanted a baby but didn't know how that would ever happen. They'd both just ended relationships with a Manet brother. They'd both been attacked, nearly raped. How similar their lives were. She stared at the interwoven honeysuckle stems and breathed in the perfume.

'We're entangled!' she said.

'What?' Berthe said.

'You and me. We're entangled! Entanglement. It's from quantum physics. Of course, that's it!'

Berthe looked at her blankly.

'Shall I explain? Louise said. 'It's a bit complicated.'

'Yes, I will try to understand. I enjoy your little lessons.'

'They've found that pairs of particles, remember they're the smallest things in the world, well, they can become entangled with each other. That means that any change to one instantly affects the other. The behaviour of one is linked to the other, no matter how far apart they are. It's really weird. If one particle changes its spin direction, the other changes its as well. And the particles communicate instantly, across quite big distances.'

'I do not understand any of that,' said Berthe.

'It's amazing!' Louise said. 'Some scientists think entanglement explains how photosynthesis works – that's how plants work. And it might explain how birds navigate using magnetic fields.'

'I did not know birds did that.'

'And some scientists think it can even explain consciousness, how the mind emerges from a lump of flesh, our brains. They think neurons might possess molecular machinery which behaves like a quantum computer.'

'What? What is a *computer*?'

'A very clever machine,' Louise said. She couldn't explain everything. 'Entanglement: Einstein called it "spooky action from a distance". Two particles are interdependent, regardless of the distance separating them.'

She looked at Berthe in expectation. Berthe gazed back at her, open mouthed.

'But don't you see? Maybe it also works across time! And people! Maybe it ties two people together, like you and me. We have the same birthday. Everything about us is the same. It's like we're synchronised.'

Berthe just stared at her.

'There are so many similarities between us,' Louise said. 'Look, we're like these two strands of honeysuckle, entwined with each other. You and I – we're entangled.'

She wound her arm through Berthe's, beaming with excitement.

'Whatever you say, my dear,' Berthe said, laughing.

They remained on the bench together — two young women synchronised across time.

'You know, I have been thinking about time,' Berthe said, 'and your trick with the pack of cards. We can only see one way time is ordered. Is that what you said before?'

'Yes. There might be other ways of organising time that we don't know about,' Louise said.

'But how do we know if we do not know about it?'

'What? Well, em, I don't know.'

'But we only see time going one way, forward, into the future. Is that right?' Berthe said.

'Yes. There's this thing called "the arrow of time". It's to do with entropy.'

'Entropy?'

Entropy. *How to explain that to Berthe?*

'Do you have any watercolour paint?'

They went up to Berthe's bedroom.

'And a glass of water,' Louise said.

Berthe poured a glass from the jug.

Louise picked up a brush, dipped it in the water and took up some dark blue paint. She put the brush into the glass of water.

'Now watch how the paint spreads out.'

They watched it bloom, swirl and diffuse through the water.

'Very beautiful,' Berthe said.

'Yes, it is, isn't it? That's entropy. The paint starts organised, in a tightly organised small ball, and then it spreads out through the water. That's how the universe works. It started with the Big Bang and spread out from there.'

'Big Bang?'

'The universe exploded from a tiny thing, from nothing actually. All matter, everything, was created then.'

'What? You're making *my* head explode.'

'We're all made of matter created at that moment, at the Big Bang. Everything was made then – the stars, planets. Actually, we're made of stardust, matter from the stars.'

'Made of stars ...'

'Yes. Stars. So "the arrow of time" – are you still listening?'

Berthe's head was up in the stars. 'Yes. What?' she said. 'What were you saying?'

'The universe is spreading out,' Louise said. 'It started small and organised, like the paint, and it's spreading out and becoming more and more disorganised through time. That's what creates the arrow of time, the expansion of the universe going forwards. Entropy is like ... You remember when you threw all the cards up into the air and they fell down, all disorganised? It's like that. Everything tends towards chaos. Or like scrambling eggs – you can't put them back in their shells. You can never go backwards. Eventually, the universe will spread out so much everything will disappear.'

'Disappear? Everything? Even people? But that's really sad.'

'Yes, I suppose it is. But it'll take a really, really long time. Anyway, we exist in this universe. We're just like a small dot of paint on an ever-expanding canvas. It's the growth of entropy that distinguishes the past from the present, that's the arrow of time.'

'You say this arrow of time always points forwards,' Berthe said.

'Yes.'

'But how did you come backwards then?' Berthe said.

'Oh. Good point. I did, didn't I?' Louise said. 'Hmm, I have no idea. That shouldn't happen. It shouldn't be possible. I don't know. But they do say that time might work differently in other places, that we can only see one way it works, like the cards thing. Or maybe time doesn't exist at all.'

'So have they tested any of this?'

'No, I don't think so. I think it's just theories. It's quite confusing, isn't it?'

'So, it is all just ideas people have had? Stories?'

'Well. No, er, yes …'

'Oh, well. Never mind about all that then,' Berthe said, getting up. 'The sun is shining. Shall we go to the Bois de Boulogne?'

Louise sat quietly in the carriage on the way to the park. How *had* she come backwards? That definitely shouldn't happen. Her arrow of time seemed to be flying all over the place, like a weathervane in a hurricane. Berthe had found *her* sense of direction but where was *hers*? What was she going to do? She wasn't going to marry Gene. She couldn't stay here forever teaching Berthe about quantum physics.

As they entered the park, Berthe was in a chatty mood. She explained that the Bois de Boulogne used to be a forest where the royal family hunted, then it became a hiding place for brigands and vagabonds. It was hard to imagine now. It was tamed into a beautiful park with lakes, a racecourse, a zoo, botanic gardens, restaurants. It was a playground for the bourgeoisie.

Three in the afternoon and the promenade was in full swing. The upper and middle classes paraded in carriages or on horseback, fashionably seeing and being seen. Elegant horsemen rode alongside women in carriages. The women lay back in their furs and muslins, vaguely listening to the gallantries bestowed upon them by their suitors. Servants, perpendicular and stiff, pretended not to listen.

'Let's go on a boat,' Berthe said.

They found a man to row them over the lake to a little island with a café. As the boatman rowed, Berthe sketched Louise. She was dressed in white, sitting next to a woman in a blue coat. They were a nice contrast, blue and white, wearing straw hats: Louise's had a big blue ribbon.

Louise watched Berthe sketching her. She was drawing and painting all the time now, inspired by everything, fired up by her art and the idea of the exhibition, their *own* exhibition.

I'm so glad she's happy. I wish I had her energy, her sense of purpose. We may be entangled, but we're not the same at all now.

She dragged her hand through the cool lake water.

CHAPTER 40

MEMORY

An autumn morning, and Louise stepped into the garden. The leaves were beginning to glow: reds, golds and yellows. A leaf fluttered down from a tree; she reached out and caught it.

'If you catch a leaf, you can make a wish,' her mother had said.

Louise looked at the beech leaf in her hand, its green now turning yellow, its edges becoming brown. She stroked its smooth, silky surface, tracing its tiny veins with her fingertip. *Is it a memory if it happened in the future?* We are only our memories, she'd read. The self is made up of memories, but a memory is an unreliable thing, a wavy distorted image, almost there, but not quite, like an impression of a moment in the past.

She breathed in the musty smell of autumn and closed her eyes. Sweet memories, parcels of time wrapped up in string and given as a gift, a present from the past to the present. Little packages locked up in our brains and opened by the smallest, most unexpected thing, like a smell, a song or a sound.

She heard the crunching of leaves. Berthe appeared with a cup of coffee and a shawl.

'Here, you must keep warm. I do not want you getting ill like I did last winter.' Berthe sat beside her. A slight breeze sent more beech leaves flying into the air. They stretched out their hands to catch them.

'Did you do this as a child?' Louise said.

'Yes, with Edma and Yves. We used to run around catching leaves for hours.'

'Me too. I was alone, though. It must have been nice to have brothers and sisters.'

'You do not have any?'

'No, I'm an only child.' A lonely child. Louise stroked the delicate leaf she'd caught. But she did have brothers, at least half-brothers. She had seen them when they were little boys in Pizza Express. What were they like now? Were they like her? If she went back, maybe could she find out.

'That must have been sad for you,' Berthe said, 'to have no brothers or sisters.'

Louise gazed at her leaf. 'Do you know in the brain there are cells called neurones. They're like little trees. There are millions, billions of them. They reach out to each other with their branches, like these veins in a leaf, and send messages, chemical messages, to each other. That's how the brain works.'

'Really?' Berthe stroked the veins of her leaf in her hand.

'Yes. Memories, too. You know if you put all your memories together, all the little pathways that makes up a person, you get a whole self, all your dreams, hopes and feelings. Memories make you who you are, from a child to a grown up.'

'When do you ever grow up? I often wonder,' Berthe said.

'Yes. Me too.'

Louise and her best friend, Catriona, had always joked about getting "grown-up points". They got points when they passed their driving test, when they graduated, when they got their first jobs, as if when you got enough points you were invited up to a podium and given the "Grown-Up" badge.

'Do you think you're "grown up"?' Louise said.

'Not according to mother,' Berthe said, and laughed. 'If I'm not married, I must forever be a child. That is what she would say. But I must go in now. It is chilly. Do not stay out too long.'

Louise watched Berthe crunch back into the house. Berthe still had some self-doubt, even if she did feel surer of her purpose. Édouard was still desperate to be recognised, approved of, by the grown-ups at the Salon. Seen from afar, from the future, you'd think these famous artists had always known what they were doing, that they had a plan, a clear path to success. But no, they struggled as much as anyone. Did anyone ever really grow up?

She put down her coffee cup on the gravel beside the bench and crushed the leaf in her hand. No one knew what they were doing. Everyone was pretending they knew what was going on, including her. She thought she was doing the right thing by going along with everything Paul wanted, but she had given herself up when she became a wife. In the process she had lost her self, disappeared.

She got up and paced around the garden. She had created a story about herself as a nice person who always did the right thing. She'd chosen her memories to make up that self, her self-selected self. But that wasn't her at all. She was someone who betrayed a friend: Suzanne. She was not a trusting, loyal, nice person; she got things wrong, badly wrong. She had slept with Gene. And she hadn't saved her mother.

She had created a story about herself, and it was a fake. Who was she now? How could she come back to herself, as her mum wanted, if she didn't know who she was? Surely it was about time she knew. She threw away the fragments of the broken leaf.

CHAPTER 41

BURIED

Louise went into the house and found Berthe in her room, preparing a canvas, a new painting for the exhibition. Louise sat on the chaise longue and watched her.

'I'm so happy you have decided to be a painter,' she said.

'Well, it is easy for me. I have my family to support me.'

'Yes but it's unusual for a woman at this time. You're brave.'

'Well, we will see.'

After a pause, Louise said, 'I've not been very brave.'

'What do you mean?'

'Before I came –' she stopped. How could she speak about this?

'You have not told me much about your life before,' Berthe said, putting down her brush. 'You always avoid talking about it. It seems to make you uncomfortable.'

'Yes, I know. I've been a bit confused. I used to feel I could do anything, but recently, well, before I came, I felt so bad, sort of shrunk.'

'Why? What happened?'

'I don't know. I used to be this confident woman. But it all changed. In the last few years, since I've been with Paul –'

'Paul? Is he your husband? Is it to do with him then?' Berthe came over to sit with her.

'Yes, I think so.' Louise took a deep breath.

'You have not told me anything about him.'

'I seemed to let him take control of me. Everything, little things. I'd hear him saying things to people that I had said to him, impressing them with *my* thoughts. Everything in the house was his, his choice, his style. I was trying to please *him* all the time, doing what *he* wanted. I lost my confidence. I'd sit in meetings at work and say nothing, let people steal my ideas, let these smart young men blag their way into jobs I should have got when I knew I was smarter than them.'

She sighed. 'I moved to London with Paul, left my job, struggled to get a new one. I felt I was invisible, that people didn't see me at all. Sometimes I wondered if I *was* really there.'

She looked hard at the painting propped against the wall, the painting she'd travelled through.

'It's like in your painting of me; I'm only half there. I'm disappearing.' She took a deep breath. 'Paul, my husband, he's having an affair. Maybe it's not so surprising. I'm not the same person he married.'

'But is that *your* fault? It does not sound like he is nice to you. I do not think he is a very nice person.'

'I know. When I talk about this, say it out loud, I can't believe I put up with it. The way he treated me, it *is* terrible, isn't it? I just pretended it wasn't happening. Buried it. All of it ... I've buried so much.'

She couldn't stop herself any longer. She burst into tears.

'What is it? Tell me,' Berthe said gently.

'My mother ...'

'Your mother?'

'Yes. She died. And I wasn't there. She died. Alone, not long before I came here.'

'Oh, I am so sorry,' Berthe took her hand. 'What happened?'

'She was walking on the beach. Had a heart attack,' Louise gulped. 'I was supposed to be there that weekend. Mum had asked me to come. It was so unusual for her to ask, she knew I was very busy. Maybe she knew something was wrong with her. She asked me to go and I didn't. Paul was free that weekend, for once, and I insisted we went away to a nice hotel. I was trying to make things work between us, to sort out our marriage. But it was awful; he struggled to talk to me at all. I should have been with my mum. I *wanted* to be with her.'

She turned to Berthe.

'And if I had been with her, I could have saved her. I wasn't there when she needed me most. I feel like, like, I killed her ...'

After a few moments, Berthe said, 'Tell me about your mother. What was she like?'

'She was wonderful. She worked so hard, brought me up all by herself. My father left when I was little. I always thought that was my fault, that there was something wrong with me. My mother tried so hard to make up for him. She wanted everything for me, taught me about art, how to paint, to be independent. She gave me everything and then I ... I failed her, completely.'

Louise sobbed harder, gulping for air.

'But do you really think you could have saved her?' Berthe said.

'Maybe. Oh, I don't know. But I should have been there. I've been carrying this massive grief and this guilt around inside me. It's like a huge iceberg weighing me down. I feel so guilty."

'No, you do not know,' Berthe said. 'You will never know. You probably could not have saved her. You cannot keep thinking that, tormenting yourself. And would she want you to feel like this? She would not want you to blame yourself, would she?'

'No. I suppose not. Maybe I couldn't have saved her, you're right. She would want me to be happy. She always told me that. But I've failed her in that, too. I let people, Paul, walk all over me. I don't know what's happened to me. And I did that stupid thing with Édouard. And I hurt you. I don't know who I am anymore.'

Louise put her head in her hands.

'It is very hard to know who you are,' Berthe said, putting her arm around her.

'You see, I believed in marriage,' Louise said. 'I was so angry at Paul for having an affair. But it's more complicated than I thought. Édouard loves you but he also loves Suzanne. Maybe you *can* love two people? And I've slept with Gene. I'm no better than Paul.'

'It is complicated. Love and life – both are extremely complicated.'

'Maybe I should go back and give Paul another chance, but I'm afraid I might just become the weak wife again. I don't understand how I could have let all that happen to me. *A weak wife!* It's exactly what my mother *didn't* want to me to be, exactly what *you've* decided not to be.'

'But I do not see you as weak in any way,' Berthe said. 'I see someone who is a little lost perhaps. But you are so clever, so interested and so curious. You have such confidence talking to people. You have much more strength than you know. You just have to find a way back to yourself. We both do. I do not know if I have made the right decision, but I have hope now. It was you who encouraged me, helped me decide. You gave me hope.'

'Did I?' Louise said. 'That's wonderful. It's crazy. I'm nearly thirty and I am still waiting for other people to see me, to validate me somehow.'

'But I cannot understand why it is so difficult for you. You told me that you can have your own job, your own money, your own house even. What is the problem? I cannot begin to imagine having that freedom.'

Louise stood up.

'You're right. It *is* ridiculous. Compared to you, I have every opportunity. I need to get a grip. Really. You know I have begun to feel a lot better here, with you. I feel like something is beginning to shift inside me now.'

'What do you mean?'

'It's you. You see me. I feel like you've made me real again. I feel more like myself, my normal self.'

'*Me? Have* I? Well, I am pleased to help,' Berthe said, getting up and giving her a hug. 'We have helped each other, then. You saved me from loneliness and boredom – and marriage!'

CHAPTER 42

HUMAN BECOMING

It was Thursday morning, the day of the soirée. Louise was lighter than air. Dragging her worries into the open had shrunk them, the light had shrivelled them away. They were no longer the dark, all-consuming monsters they had been. Telling Berthe had been such a relief.

She had coffee with Berthe in her bedroom. They were discussing who might be coming that evening, but Louise was distracted. She kept looking at the painting of herself stacked against the wall. Something was niggling her about it. What was it?

'I'm an event!' she said. 'Berthe, you've painted me as an event!'

'What are you talking about?'

'Look, I'm not really there am I, in the painting? I'm disappearing, or appearing, I'm not solid. You see, scientists say that there are no *things*, just *events*. You've captured that exactly.'

'What do you mean, things, events?' Berthe said. 'Is this one of your science things? You will have to explain, slowly.'

'Well, *things*,' Louise picked up a paintbrush, 'like this brush, don't exist. *We* don't really exist. Every *thing* is just a process in time. Some things, like rocks, last longer than others, but nothing is permanent. It's the same for people. Our bodies will disintegrate, our atoms will become something else. We are *becoming*, not being. And that's exactly how you've painted me.'

'Buddhists – do they not say that? That life is a perpetual becoming, like a flowing river you step in and out of. Is it like that?'

'Yes, that's right. Buddhism,' Louise said. 'That's brilliant.' Why had she never thought of that?

'But are we really that insubstantial?' Berthe reached out and touched Louise's arm. 'You feel solid, but I suppose that does make sense. Moments are fleeting. In fact, yes, that is what I try to capture when I paint.'

'And you got that perfectly with me. Look, I'm not a human *being*. I'm a human *becoming*!' Louise laughed.

They looked at the painting for a while.

'You know, I think it's time for me to be a human becoming again,' Louise said. 'I've been stuck for too long, not changing.'

'What do you mean?'

'I used to think I could do anything, be anyone. I had the world at my feet. I stopped feeling like that. But you've helped me become that person again. I really want to be a woman *becoming* again ...'

'Yes, and what will you become?' Berthe said.

'I don't know, I have so many ideas.'

'What ideas?'

'I've been thinking about making a TV series about women artists.'

'What is TV?'

'Oh, it's just another way of telling stories. I want to tell the stories of women like you.'

'Me?'

'Yes, women artists, feminist artists, women who changed the world. Women who are so often ignored. Women who struggled, like you. Mary Cassatt. Have you heard of her?'

'No.'

'You might meet her soon. I'm sure she's around about now. Frida Kahlo, Georgia O'Keefe, Louise Bourgeois. There are so many.'

'I wish I could see their art.'

'They are all wonderful, but you will be the first in my series.'

'Well, thank you, but do not tell all my secrets to everyone, please,' Berthe said.

'No, I won't. Don't worry.'

'Can you tell me about them, these women artists?'

Louise sat down at Berthe's table and picked up a pencil.

'Frida Kahlo is, was, will be – these tenses are so difficult – Mexican. She did a lot of self-portraits, about her own life, her experiences. She had these really dark eyebrows.'

She started trying to draw Frida Kahlo.

'She had a bit of a moustache. She loved colourful Mexican things, folk art, flamboyant traditional clothes.'

She used Berthe's watercolours to add some flowers in Frida's hair, some big jewellery, bright clothes, and then she drew in a monkey.

'She had a difficult life. She had polio when she was a child and then she was badly hurt in an accident. But she kept painting herself, her own trauma, her pain, her feelings. You would have loved her use of colour.'

'Yes, I think I would like her, Frida Kahlo.'

'And Louise Bourgeois. She's a sculptress, in my time.'

'Bourgeois. Is she French?'

'I think so. I think she was born here, in Paris,' Louise said. She drew a giant spider with a tiny person underneath. 'She made these enormous spiders and called them *Maman*. They represent the difficult relationship she had with her mother. She saw her mother as protective, but also controlling, a bit menacing, I think.'

'Like my mother?'

'Yes, like Cornélie,' Louise laughed. 'But I can't do justice to their work. You'll just have to imagine. And there's the Guerrilla Girls. They made posters saying, "Do women have to be naked to get into the Met Museum", protesting that there aren't enough women artists' paintings in art galleries.'

'Yes, that is very good. I should make a poster like that. "Do women have to be naked to get into the Salon?"'

'And Tracy Emin. She made art out of her own unmade bed.'

'Her own bed?'

'Yes, her own actual bed. She put it in an art gallery.'

'She put her bed in an art gallery? That's disgusting. Why would she do that? How is that art?'

'Well, I suppose art has changed quite a lot since now, since this time. I could tell you what happens next, after this, if I can remember my art history.'

'Art history?'

'After you, the Impressionists –'

'We're really called that?'

'Yes, I don't know how that happens, but you become known as the Impressionists.'

'Oh. I like that – The Impressionists!'

'Then there's the Post-Impressionists, like Van Gogh. You'd love him, his colours, very intense, the expression in his paintings. And there's George Seurat with his dots, of course, and Gauguin, Cézanne. Paul becomes quite important, you know.'

'Paul? Important? Why?'

'It's to do with, let me think, how he strips away the surface detail of objects and landscapes to show the geometry beneath, the shapes, cylinders, spheres, cones.'

'Really? *Paul?*'

'And then Cubism – Picasso. Oh, I have to draw you a Picasso.' She got a pencil and paper and drew a Picasso head with its eyes, nose and ears all in the wrong place and at different angles.

'Ooh, why did he do that?' Berthe said with some disgust.

'It was a new way of seeing, I suppose. It's like relativity, seeing things from several different angles at the same time. Groundbreaking, he did this before Einstein even came up with relativity. Then there's Surrealism. Surrealists painted dreams, the subconscious, artists like Salvador Dali.' She drew a watch melting down over the side of a table. 'Look, it's time melting. He was influenced by Einstein and relativity – that gravity affects time.'

'That is very strange. I do not understand.'

Louise drew a pipe and wrote "*Ceci n'est pas une pipe*".

'What's that?'

'It's Magritte. "This is not a pipe".'

'But it *is* a pipe.'

'No, it's a *picture* of a pipe. See?'

'No … What?' Berthe rubbed her forehead.

'Anyway, then there's Abstract Expressionism. Rothko and Jackson Pollock, who threw paint at enormous canvases.'

'Why did he do that?'

'I suppose he liked the patterns. He was expressing himself.'

'Oh.'

'Pop Art, Andy Warhol, soup cans. That's all about mass production, consumerism. In the future there are huge factories making tons of identical things for us to buy. And contemporary art, that just means art of today which doesn't really make any sense. Art is always art of today. Performance art, minimalism, installation art, Earth art, street art like Banksy …'

She stopped. 'I've missed loads out.'

'Goodness,' Berthe said. 'Art is certainly different. I do not think I like it at all.'

They stared at her drawings.

'Maybe my series should just be about painters,' Louise said.

'Yes. The story of women painters,' Berthe said. 'What about Rosa Bonheur?'

'Who? I don't know her.'

'She does these beautiful realistic paintings of horses and animals. *The Horse Fair* is a great painting. She said, "As far as males go, I only like the bulls I paint"! Is that not excellent? She has short hair and likes to wear trousers, like us, but she got police permission to wear them. She claimed it was for practical reasons, so she could go to horse fairs. She was the first female artist to get the Légion d'honneur. That was just a few years ago.'

'How have I never heard of her? I'll look her up.' Louise made a mental note. 'Or I could do a programme about the Impressionists, I mean, about all of you, Édouard, Auguste, Claude, Paul … I know so much about you all now, your struggles with the Salon and everything.'

'Too much, perhaps.'

Louise rushed on. 'And I have other ideas too. I want to do a TV series about science, the stuff I've talked to you about, when I can figure out how to do it. It's quite hard to explain, as I've discovered.' She stopped. 'But I can't do any of it here, now.'

She took a deep breath. 'Berthe, I think I have to go home. I can't keep hiding out here. It's not my time. I have to go back to my own life and become whatever I'm meant to be.'

'But I would miss you so much.'

'I know, I don't want to go, but what would I do here? The rules would drive me mad eventually.'

'I understand. It is true, you should not hide away here.'

'Do you think you will be all right? It might be difficult for you, to establish yourself.'

'Do not spend a minute worrying about me. I feel much better now.'

'What about Édouard?'

'I think we will be good friends. Honestly, all that was like a madness. I am glad you brought it to a head. It is over now. And you have taught me so much, especially about, what do you call it, your tiny world?'

'Quantum physics,' Louise said. 'And you've taught me how to paint. I'm so much better now. You, your family, everyone has been so kind to me.'

She got up and paced around the room. 'But it's time I faced things. I'm stronger now. I will follow your example and be brave, be independent, become my old self. You know I was interfering with your life when I should have been sorting out my own.'

'What will you do?'

'Maybe I'll go travelling. Paul never wanted to go anywhere. I don't know what will happen with our marriage, but I want to move back to Scotland. Maybe my old boss will give me a job, now that I have all these brilliant ideas! I'll definitely keep painting, see my old friends, get a new flat.'

Perhaps persuade Chloe to come with her to Scotland; she could get in touch with her father and her brothers; hopefully they would want to see her.

'When are you thinking of leaving?' asked Berthe.

'Soon; tomorrow.'

'Tomorrow?'

'It's exciting,' Louise said. 'A new life! You and me, both. We'll be independent women; we'll take on the world. We can do *anything*!'

She pulled Berthe to her feet and danced around the room, singing:

Who runs the world – girls!

Who runs the world – girls!'

'It's hard to dance to this wearing all this stuff,' she said puffing, and sat down to draw Beyoncé's outfits to an astonished Berthe.

CHAPTER 43

THE CLAIRVOYANT

Louise and Berthe were ready, dressed and powdered. Louise enjoyed the palaver of preparing for the soirée this time, knowing it would be the last time she'd get to wear such a fancy dress. Berthe had a new black dress cut low across her shoulders and looked stunning, as usual.

As they waited for the guests to arrive, Louise stood next to Tiburce, watching as Berthe organised the flowers with Giselle. They were laughing together.

'Berthe seems happier now, don't you think?' Louise said.

'Yes, she does,' Tiburce said. 'But I worry how long it will last. It's not in her nature to be content.'

They were interrupted by the arrival of the first guests. Cornélie introduced Louise to an elegant man, Jacques Offenbach.

'Jacques writes anti-establishment operettas. You love poking fun at the establishment, don't you, Jacques?' Cornélie said.

'Yes and I have two new ones for next year,' Jacques said, handing a servant his coat and hat. 'I hope they will be even more scandalous than the last.'

Then there was Stéphane Mallarmé. He arrived at the same time as Edgar. Mallarmé was a poet. Edgar was telling him about his own attempts to write poems.

'It isn't ideas I'm short of. I've actually got too many,' Edgar said.

'But Degas,' Mallarmé said, 'you can't make a poem with ideas. You make it with words.' He continued talking at length.

When Suzanne arrived, Louise rushed over to her. 'I'm sorry I haven't seen you,' she said. 'There's been a lot going on. And Gene –'

'Yes, I heard,' Suzanne said. 'I'm sad we're not to be sisters, but I'm sure you have your reasons.'

'You're so kind, Suzanne.' Louise gave her a hug.

'I hope we'll still be friends. Shall we go shopping soon?' Suzanne said.

"Eh … yes, that would be nice, but excuse me for a minute.'

Over Suzanne's shoulder, Louise had spotted Victor Hugo. She had discovered that he was an important politician in Paris, a revolutionary and a campaigner fighting against poverty, for free education and against the death penalty. Many regarded him a national hero. He was certainly her hero.

'Victor, how good to see you. I want to thank you properly for rescuing me that day.'

'It is nothing, Mademoiselle,' Victor said with a little bow.

'No. You saved me. I could have died. Thank you.'

'You're very sweet, my dear.' He patted her hand.

'But how are *you*?' she asked. He looked tired.

'Well, I'm nearly seventy. My son died and after losing my wife a few years ago, I feel bereft. And politics … Ahh.'

'I'm so sorry,' Louise said. 'But you are a wonderful writer. You will be recognised around the world. People will enjoy your work for decades, centuries to come. *The Hunchback of Notre Dame, Les Misérables*. There'll be plays and musicals …'

'Thank you, my dear, you are exceedingly kind, but what are you talking about? How could you possibly know that? Are you clairvoyant?' he laughed.

'Yes, that's it. I am clairvoyant,' Louise said. She looked around the room. There were so many incredible people there, but they had no idea how famous they would become. There was Claude Monet talking to Paul Cézanne, both poor, depressed, struggling. She went over to them.

Paul was saying to Claude, 'I don't see why we should be limited to one perspective in a painting. You could have many angles on a subject at the same time. And why not paint different moments at the same time, have multiple perspectives?'

'What? On the same canvas? Ah, Louise,' Claude said, with some relief. 'Paul is thinking of going home to Aix. He's run out of money. Can you dissuade him?'

'You should go back,' she said to Paul. 'You should paint your mountain.'

Paul stared at her, open-mouthed. How did she know about his mountain, Mont Sainte-Victoire?

'But Paul, make sure you're back for the exhibition. Oh, and don't forget card players, they're a brilliant subject for a painting.'

She turned to Claude. 'Have you been to Rouen, Claude? There's a beautiful cathedral there. And Giverny, a wonderful place for water lilies. They'd be lovely to paint – the colours, the water.'

'Really?' Claude said.

'And haystacks ...' she said over her shoulder as she went over to Édouard. Berthe was still trying to persuade him to join them in the exhibition.

Louise interrupted. 'Édouard, you're right. I do have a secret and I'm ready to tell you. I'm a time traveller. I came from a hundred and fifty years in the future. I travelled through one of Berthe's paintings.'

Berthe looked at her, appalled, but Édouard said, 'Hah, that's a good one!'

'And that's how I know that you will be famous. You will become known as "The Father of Modern Art". So, don't give up hope.'

Édouard laughed.

'I'm serious. 'You are very important to art.'

'Yes, Louise, I'm sure. You can tell me your *real* secret one day,' Édouard said, patting her on the arm.

At the other end of the room, Victor had gathered an audience around him. He was talking about the ruthless straight lines of Haussmann's Paris.

'We have lost the anarchic atmosphere of old Paris,' he said. 'Haussmann is "the Attila of the straight line". Now our city is pierced from side to side, our streets are aligned like soldiers, all roads usefully leading out from the barracks. It's much easier now for the military to suppress riots. We're controlled by our autocratic government. Thank you, Mr Haussmann.'

'At least he's been sacked now,' one man said.

'Yes, but his work continues,' another said. 'The construction, the devastation ...'

'How much debt is the city in now, Tiburce?'

Tiburce, the astute politician, just smiled.

'We've lost the freedom of discovery on a stroll through Paris,' Victor said, 'but I believe in progress. In the next century, man will live. There will be no more war, poverty or hatred.'

Louise sighed. *If only that were true.*

She saw Gene arriving and dragged him out into the garden with her. It was a beautiful autumn evening, dusk was falling and the sweet scent of the roses hung in the air around them.

Louise took his arm and apologised again. 'Another time, maybe it could have worked out with us,' she said.

Gene squeezed her hand, too upset to talk.

She told him she was thinking of going home.

'I'll miss you,' she said, choking up. 'I probably won't see you again. I've really enjoyed our time together.'

'I could come and visit you in Brittany?' he said. 'You might change your mind?'

'No. I'm sorry, I don't think that will work. But I want to thank you. You helped me so much. You really have no idea. You've restored my faith in men, actually.'

'I'll miss you so much, my love,' Gene said. 'Although to be honest, I've been confused since you arrived. You seem so … different. Maybe we'll meet again sometime. It might work out for us then.'

They walked together in the darkening garden, reluctant to part.

Eventually they went back into the house. Louise looked around the candle-lit room. It was full of brilliant young men and one brilliant young woman. Geniuses, but they didn't know it. Would they find out in their own lifetimes? She had no idea.

CHAPTER 44

AU REVOIR

It was Louise's last morning. They had not told Cornélie or Tiburce about her plan to leave. Berthe would say later that a letter had arrived saying that her sister was sick, and she had to return home immediately. Louise had written an effusive thank you letter to Cornélie and Tiburce for their warm, extended hospitality. She'd written a letter for Suzanne as well.

She was nervous through breakfast and barely spoke. What if the painting didn't work and she couldn't go home? Or if she got stuck in it? If she did return, what would she find in the cottage? Another Louise? A parallel life? A dead Louise?

What time would it be there? She'd been here for over three months now. It would be autumn in the Outer Hebrides, too. What would have happened there? Probably the car hire people would be the first to notice she hadn't returned the car. They would have told the police. They'd contact Paul, her next of kin. Next of kin – the kind of kin who betrays you.

There would have been a search, on the beach, looking for a body. Maybe they'd investigate Paul, find out about his affair. He'd be the prime suspect.

How would she explain where she'd been when she got back?

So many questions ... Louise would have to face Paul, and deal with him, all of that upset. It would be so much easier to stay. She could still accept Gene.

She went down to the kitchen to find Giselle. She was alone, washing pots. Louise gave her a handkerchief.

'Oh, thank you, Madem– I mean, Louise,' Giselle said.

'No, look inside.'

Giselle gasped.

'But, Louise, you can't give me this!' She held up Louise's gold wedding ring.

'It's for you and your family. I don't need it.'

Giselle hugged her tightly, sobbing. 'Oh thank you, Louise!'

What would happen with her and Paul? Louise had no idea, but Giselle and her family needed her ring much more than she did. She didn't care if she was interfering in the future.

'Giselle, I have to go now,' she said.

Giselle stepped back, wrapped the ring in a kitchen cloth and pushed it deep into a pocket in her uniform. 'Take this back,' she said, handing Louise her handkerchief. It was the lace one, with the *L* on it, the one Suzanne had given her.

'Thank you, Louise,' Giselle said, wiping her nose on her sleeve.

With hesitant steps Louise climbed the stairs to Berthe's bedroom; her left hand on the warm ornate wooden banister pulled her up, her right hand clenched the handkerchief. It wasn't too late. She didn't have to go. She could stay here with Giselle, Gene and Berthe.

She went into the bedroom. Berthe was wearing the same painting dress she'd worn the day she arrived. Her hair was tied tightly back. Louise had on the same white tea dress. She positioned the chair in exactly the right spot by the window and sat down.

'I'm ready,' Louise said, feeling far from ready.

Berthe frowned, silently pulled out the painting and put it on the easel. She selected her paints.

'Remember, don't do the hands,' Louise said.

'Are you sure you want to go?' Berthe said, picking up her brush.

'Yes, I'm sure,' Louise said, completely unsure. 'But I'll miss you so much.'

'I will miss you, too.'

And Berthe, with tears in her eyes, began painting.

A few moments passed. Nothing happened. Then, the tips of her fingers, her hands, started to tingle. The room began to go out of focus. It was working. She was leaving.

'Gene would make a great father,' Louise said as she disappeared.

Her last sight was the look of astonishment on Berthe's face.

*

Louise opened her eyes. There was her painting, her attempt at copying Berthe's painting of her. She was sitting on the chair in front of it, in her mother's cottage in Luskentyre, wearing her mother's dungarees again.

The grandfather clock started to chime. One, two. She waited. It stopped.

It was two o'clock – the same time as she'd left. But what was the date? She grabbed her phone. It was still charged. It was the same day. It was exactly the same moment that she'd gone through the painting.

Time had stood still.

It seemed that painting really did pause time.

CHAPTER 45

ART TRIUMPHS OVER THE DESTRUCTIVE POWER OF TIME

Louise wandered through the rooms, unable to believe she was back in her mother's cottage. It still felt so empty without her mum, and now she had lost Berthe and Gene too – she'd given them up to come back here, to nothing. But she felt different, lighter. The guilt over her mother's death had lifted a little. A whisper at the back of her mind said that perhaps she would be all right.

What had happened to Berthe after she left? Did she marry Gene? Louise opened her laptop and started Googling.

Berthe married Gene in 1873, two years after she'd left. 'Yes!' Louise said to the kitchen. She looked for the letter she'd seen in the book and read it carefully: "Berthe Manet". It was clear; Berthe was *Gene's* wife. If only she'd read it more closely the first time, it would have saved a lot of grief and distress.

Berthe had continued to paint. She signed her work "Berthe Morisot". That was very unusual for a married woman in that time. Édouard had stopped painting Berthe after she married Gene. No letters between Berthe and Édouard existed – Édouard must have burnt his too. No one knew how close their relationship had been, although there was a lot of speculation by art historians. How strange: Berthe and Édouard would have seen each other all the time as brother and sister-in-law. They must have found a way to co-exist.

Berthe was happy with Gene: "I have found an honest and excellent man who, I believe, sincerely loves me. I have entered into the positive life after having lived for a long time by chimeras" she wrote in 1874.

She Googled *chimera* and assumed Berthe meant *illusions, unrealisable dreams,* not *a fire-breathing she-monster in Greek mythology with a lion's head, a goat's body, and a serpent's tail.*

Louise clapped her hands in delight. Berthe was happy!

Gene devoted himself to helping Berthe. He promised to make her "the most adored and pampered woman on earth." They had a daughter, Julie, the child Berthe had longed for. Julie was the subject of many of Berthe's paintings.

Did Berthe tell Gene where she was from, that she was a time traveller? What would he have thought? Maybe he wouldn't have been surprised; it would have explained a lot to him.

Édouard never acknowledged Léon as his son. That must have been very sad for Suzanne.

How long did it take for the Impressionists to become famous? Louise tapped away at her laptop.

In 1873, only Édouard had a painting accepted at the Salon. It was *Repose,* his painting of Berthe slouched across the sofa. But it was not a success. Critics said she looked like a woman resting after sweeping the chimney, or as if she was suffering from seasickness. One called her the goddess of slovenliness. Not quite the portrait of melancholia Édouard had been aiming for.

The others were all rejected by the Salon that year. So, had they gone ahead with their own exhibition, or had their nerve failed them? Yes! Berthe, Claude, Edgar, Auguste, Paul and others held their own exhibition the following year. Édouard was not part of it. He continued to try to stop Berthe being involved. And Pierre Puvis de Chavannes tried to dissuade Berthe, too. He said he accepted that the Salon had rejected her work, but she should avoid the risk of being anti-establishment; she should be careful not to draw attention to herself. That would have infuriated Berthe enough to get her to abandon the Salon.

Edgar had written to Cornélie to persuade her that Berthe was too important for them to do without in the exhibition. He was Berthe's surprise supporter.

But, oh dear, Édouard was right: their work was not well received. The public had flocked in to the exhibition, but people had been shocked and appalled. Why would they want to look at laundresses, dancers, or unfinished landscapes? People laughed at the artists and called them lazy anti-establishment rebels who had obviously gone mad.

Louise got up in disgust and made a cup of tea. How could they think that? Were they blind? She read on. Claude had showed his painting of the sunrise at Le Havre and called it *Impression, Sunrise*. But one critic said, "a wallpaper pattern in its most embryonic state is more finished than this seascape." He used the term "Impressionism" to describe the painting. He meant it as an insult but the painters, after some argument, decided to call themselves "The Impressionists". Ah, so that was where the name originated.

The painters got no more commissions for the portraits which were so important for their income. Everyone assumed Édouard was the leader of the group despite the fact he wasn't even in the exhibition. Their second exhibition in 1876 fared no better. One critic said that the artists took a canvas, some paint and some brushes, threw a few colours around randomly, signed it and called it a painting. Another said it was like a cat walking across the keys of a piano, or a monkey with a box of paints.

One critic said that Berthe was interesting; she had a little feminine artistry among her bursts of madness.

Crowds mocked them. When one of Berthe's paintings came up at an auction, a man shouted 'whore' and Pissarro punched him. Meanwhile, Claude was still completely broke. Louise rubbed her forehead. Maybe she should have given her wedding ring to Claude. It was worse than she could have imagined.

The third exhibition was in 1877, the fourth in 1878; Edgar's *Petite danseuse de quatorze ans* took Paris by storm. The sculpture of a young dancer aged fourteen, strangely midway between a large doll and a small child, hips thrust forward, head back, a real tutu and ribbon in real hair. She shocked the critics who compared her to a monkey.

How strange. Everyone loves the little dancer now. That afternoon at the ballet rehearsal – would Edgar have painted and sculpted ballet dancers if she hadn't suggested it?

After the first shock of the "little dancer", people began to love Degas, but they never quite understood him. Edgar said later in his life: 'People call me the painter of dancing girls. It has never occurred to them that my chief interest in dancers lies in rendering movement and painting pretty clothes.'

Then about his later images of women bathing he said: 'The women of mine are simple, honest folk.' But unfortunately he went on: 'There is another; she is washing her feet. It is as if you looked through the keyhole … Oh! Women can never forgive me; they hate me, they can feel that I am disarming them. I show them without their coquetry, in the state of animals cleaning themselves.'

And: 'I have perhaps too often considered woman as an animal.'

Louise put her head in her hands. Why could Edgar not keep his mouth shut? But she could not hate him; he had supported Berthe more than any of the other artists, even Édouard.

Paul Cézanne went back to Aix-en-Provence and painted Mount Victoire many times, from many angles often on the same canvas. He was the founder of Cubism.

Auguste stayed in Montmartre and painted his cheerful women and windmills.

Claude struggled for decades and only started to become successful with his paintings of Argenteuil, Rouen Cathedral, and the water lilies of Givenchy.

Édouard finally got the Légion d'honneur towards the end of his life. He was finally recognised as a renowned artist.

Berthe had been a founder member of The Impressionists and exhibited in seven of their eight exhibitions, but she was the least well known of the painters. She'd been written out of art history.

*

Louise looked out the window and watched a gathering storm. They had all struggled so much, for so long. How much were their paintings worth now? She looked up the latest amounts their paintings had sold for:

Berthe Morisot *After Lunch* – $11m

Edgar Degas *Little Dancer* – $41m

Édouard Manet *Spring* – $65m

Claude Monet *Haystacks* – $110.7m

Auguste Renoir *Bal du Moulin De la Galette* – $188m

Paul Cézanne *Card Player* – $340m

They would never have believed it! Their paintings were on prints on walls across the world, on postcards, mugs, scarves, bags, keyrings, fridge magnets. If only they'd known that they would become so loved. She sighed. She wished she could have helped them more, given them hope, made them see their brilliance. But they wouldn't have listened. They wouldn't have understood how she knew.

Louise sat and watched the waves, one after the other, proceeding up the beach. The tide was coming in.

Time and tide wait for no man, the proverb went. But what about a woman? How had she got through the painting? Was time travel possible? After all, it happened to her.

She went back to her laptop and started Googling scientific theories on time travel. Einstein discovered space-time: time is relative. That's proven. So far so good. But there were so many different theories on time travel. You'd have to go faster than the speed of light, fold space-time over to create a wormhole, or two parallel strings could bend space-time. Theories, stories, as Berthe would say. There was no evidence, no agreement. But most scientists did agree that, while it might be possible to time-travel to the future, going back in time was impossible because of causality, the

Grandfather's (or Grandmother's) Paradox that she'd explained to Berthe. You can't kill your granny. You can't interfere with cause and effect.

Had she interfered with cause and effect? She had tried not to, but she *had* suggested the dancers to Degas, Mount Victoire to Cézanne, Rouen and Giverny to Monet. And the idea of the exhibition, that was hers. She interfered with Berthe and Édouard and Berthe and Pierre, so Berthe had become a painter. But all those things *could* have happened anyway; Louise probably had nothing to do with them.

She rubbed her forehead. The science was clear: time-travel to the past was impossible in the world of space-time. It goes against the arrow of time, against entropy, the continuing disorder of the universe.

But what about in the other world, the *Alice in Wonderland* world of quantum physics? There, everything is different. Time isn't real at all in the quantum world. There, the difference between past and future vanishes. In the quantum world there is no time. Time is not __ but ... And events can bounce around in time. They can be both before and after.

Like me. I am both before and after.

She read on and discovered that entanglement was crucially important. In fact, it could be the explanation for everything: space-time itself might be created by entangled quantum particles. And our 3D reality could be a projection of entanglement, our reality could just be an illusion created in our minds.

Oh, *what*? So this laptop, this mug is an *illusion*? She picked up her mug of tea, looked at it closely and tapped it. Really? She went back to her reading.

In entanglement, a change in one particle affects the other, as she had explained to Berthe. A signal can travel instantaneously between entangled particles – or entangled people, like her and Berthe. That's why she was able to bounce through time. She had travelled instantly – she'd come back at exactly the same time as she'd left.

Louise rubbed her eyes. She couldn't believe this. It was like she and Berthe had been in superposition across centuries, like entangled particles in a wave state, both living in an uncertain wavy way, not knowing what to do. When Berthe decided to be an artist, she stopped being a wave and became a particle with a certain, determined position. And because she, Louise, was entangled with Berthe her wavefunction collapsed too and she was forced to decide her future. When Berthe was down, she helped her up, by giving her the strength to be independent. When *she* was down, Berthe helped her up, encouraging her to take control of her life. They had needed each other at exactly the same time.

And we were entangled through a painting: by me copying Berthe's painting which turned out to be a painting of me.

Berthe would love this theory. 'I do not understand this story of yours,' she would say.

Louise stood up and stretched. 'Well,' she said to the tiny cottage kitchen, 'I've just come up with a new theory: time travel through a painting.'

Why not? she thought. Science doesn't know everything. It changes all the time. We used to think the earth was flat, that the sun went round us. Science is always growing, developing, disproving what it had assured us was true. So, entanglement explains time travel. Entanglement between people, through a painting. Maybe art knows more than science. After all, artists predicted many scientific discoveries, even if they did so unknowingly. Édouard Manet and Paul Cézanne used multiple perspectives to show relative views well before Einstein came up with his theory of relativity.

Louise gazed out. The waves continued their rhythm as they had through centuries.

"Art triumphs over the destructive power of time," Marcel Proust, he of the famous madeleines, had written. Art is stronger than time. For sure, the art of the Impressionists had triumphed over time. It was more loved now than when it was created.

Why couldn't a painting be a portal through time? That, she

decided, solved the question of time travel.

The answer is art.

She clapped her hands in delight.

CHAPTER 46

THE QUEEN OF QUANTUM THEORY

Louise found the book and looked closely at Berthe's painting of her. It was almost exactly the same as when she had left Berthe's bedroom, areas scraped off, no hands visible, zig zag brush strokes. Berthe had called it *Summer*. She'd not exhibited it until 1879.

What had Berthe painted after that? Louise started Googling again.

Summer's Day, 1879: two women in a rowing boat in the Bois de Boulogne. One of the women was Louise, as Berthe had sketched her that day. She was in the centre of the frame, her dress a mass of wiggles and scribbles of white with brown and grey shadows. She was looking at Berthe, wearing that ridiculous straw hat with the big blue bow, and a blue parasol across her lap. The other woman on the boat was cut off at the left of the canvas. The water was dashes of white, green blue and lilac, and an orange flash – a duck's beak. The figures were just suggestions of figures. Louise was barely there, just a flicker of brush strokes. She looked slightly surprised, bewildered at being caught in these light strokes of paint on this rowing boat. She had been so confused at that moment, wondering what to do with her life.

Louise scanned through more paintings, beautiful, but nothing surprising until she came to Berthe's paintings from the Isle of Wight. She gasped. *Harbour Scene.* Boats, insubstantial boats, only suggestions of boats. Long loose brushstrokes, rapid, sketchy, bold, energetic flew across the canvas. Boats and figures came in and out of focus, in the foreground and the background, emerging, disappearing.

Then another – *Young Girl with Greyhound* – and a chair that was barely there. *In the Country After Lunch* – a woman is vanishing into a glorious tapestry of colour.

The critics said Berthe left her paintings unfinished, "just like a woman". The loose brush strokes were a typical sign of female timidity and indecision.

One critic wrote that Berthe didn't care to put in any pointless details. For a hand she'd made five strokes of paint for the fingers and that was it done.

Another called Berthe, "The Angel of Incompleteness".

They didn't know Berthe. There was something magical about her paintings, like she could see beneath the surface of things to the energy, the life beneath.

Louise stared at the paintings. They were like reality swimming in a field of waves, dissolving in light. People, boats, chairs, insubstantial, not solid. They were not painted as things, not solid things. Not *things*. No. They were painted as events. Events in time, processes, that existed only for a brief time. Not things being, but events *becoming*.

Chills ran over her skin, and she froze. Berthe had listened to her! She'd taken it all in. Louise could see it clearly in her paintings. Berthe had understood everything she had told her. Berthe Morisot had preceded science by about a hundred years.

Berthe, the Queen of Painting, had painted quantum theory.

CHAPTER 47

THE ANGEL OF INCOMPLETENESS

Ahead of their time, time caught up with the Impressionists too soon.

Édouard died of syphilis in 1883 at age fifty-one. Berthe was furious at him for being so careless as to get syphilis, throwing away his life. Gene died in 1892.

After the death of both brothers, Berthe wrote: "I have sinned, I have suffered, I have atoned for it." And that was all she said about it. Was she referring to her affair with Édouard? No one would ever know – except Louise.

Berthe died of pneumonia in 1895, aged only fifty-four. Just before she died she wrote:

"With what resignation we arrive at the end of life, resigned to all its failures on one hand, all its uncertainties on the other. For so long I have hoped for nothing, and the desire for glorification after death seems to me an overblown ambition. My desire is limited to capturing something of the passing moment, oh, just something! The slightest thing and yet this ambition is still unreasonable."

Oh Berthe! You *did* capture the passing moments, so well, so wonderfully. But Louise was pleased to read the next quote:

"I don't think there has ever been a man who treated a woman as an equal, and that's all I would have asked for – I know I am worth as much as they are."

Louise smiled. Berthe had been an amazing painter, and in the end she had known that she was as good as any man.

She was buried with Gene, Édouard and Suzanne in the Manet family crypt in the Passy cemetery in Paris. Together as ever.

And I did make a difference to Berthe. It's there in her paintings.

The front door squeaked. Louise jumped up and stumbled over her chair. She went into the little hallway. Paul was stepping over the parrot lying on the floor.

'Paul!' she said.

'Louise. I came straight here. I thought you must be here. I had to leave work ...'

'What?'

'I left the shoot. Flew to Stornoway. Louise, you didn't answer my calls, my messages. I was so worried.' He took her hand. Louise removed her hand and stepped back into the kitchen.

'Ah, you're painting,' Paul said, following her. 'That looks just like you. But have you changed your hair? There's something different about you.'

'What are you doing here?' Louise said.

'I had to come. You were gone when I got home yesterday and ...'

'Yesterday?'

'I came straight up this morning.'

'Why?'

'Why? Because I love you, Louise.' He reached for her hand again. Louise turned away.

'I'm so glad you're OK,' Paul said. 'I'm sorry. Forgive me.'

'What about *her*?'

'I love you. I'll give her up.'

'Will you now?'

'Yes, I love *you*.'

'Well, you don't have to.'

'What?'

'Give her up. I don't want you to.'

'But Louise!'

'I don't know why you're here. You've treated me terribly. Stealing my idea. But it's not only that, it's everything. All of it. Anyway, I've met someone else.'

'Someone else? *Who?*'

'You should leave.'

'I just got here.'

'Oh dear. What a shame. I'm sure there's another flight. You can get back to your shoot.'

'What do you mean, *someone else?*'

Louise ushered Paul to the door and slammed it behind him. She watched him sitting outside in the car for a while. He looked stunned. Then he drove off.

Louise looked up to the sky. A storm was blowing in, rain hurling in on a westerly wind. She stepped outside into it. She found herself walking, then running to the beach. The wind tugged at her clothes and whipped her hair around her face.

She ran through the wet sand down to the sea and put her face up to the dark grey sky.

'Thank you, Berthe,' she said. 'You are my angel – my Angel of Incompleteness!'

Berthe had helped her become complete. She had been stuck, disappearing in her own life, until Berthe made her see that she could become someone – herself. Now she would use the freedom of her time to make something of her life, for Berthe's sake. And for her mum. She would carry both of them in her heart and become her best self for them.

I'll become a great event — one with champagne, balloons, party poppers, and a band. An event people will talk about for years.

The cottage could be rented out, it might pay for itself. She would keep painting. It would be impossible to stop now; it was her connection to her mother, and to Berthe, the best teacher possible.

The sky and the sea merged into a wash of grey and blue-black inkiness, blurring far out on the horizon. Louise stood and watched the clouds scudding low over the water, the wind whipping up white horses. Gannets plunged like spitfires into the raging waters. She licked her lips – that sweet salt taste. Sheets of rain streaked down and swept across the waves all the way out to the horizon.

The wildness at the edge. Beautiful! Exhilarating!

Suddenly a streak of brilliant silver light broke through the dark clouds far out to sea. It struck the water, glittering and shimmering. She watched the intense bright beam sweep over the waves like a searchlight. It seemed it was looking for something.

It was coming towards her.

Closer and closer.

Suddenly the light struck her, and she stood in a pool of brightness in the midst of the stormy darkness.

She gasped, looked up into the sunlight, and smiled.

'Berthe. Yes, Berthe, I know. Light is everything.'

THE END

Our revels now are ended. These our actors,
As I foretold you, were all spirits and
Are melted into air, into thin air:
And, like the baseless fabric of this vision,
The cloud-capp'd towers, the gorgeous palaces,
The solemn temples, the great globe itself,
Yea, all which it inherit, shall dissolve
And, like this insubstantial pageant faded,
Leave not a rack behind. We are such stuff
As dreams are made on, and our little life
Is rounded with a sleep.

William Shakespeare
From The Tempest, Act 4 Scene 1.

ABOUT THE AUTHOR

This is Dorothy M. Parker's first novel. She is an ex-BBC journalist. She lives in Aberfoyle in the Loch Lomond and Trossachs National Park in Scotland with her husband Neil and dog Finn. She enjoys painting the wild landscapes of the west of Scotland, reading about Art History and trying to understand quantum physics.

She became fascinated by Berthe Morisot when studying Art History. Berthe was a founder member of the Impressionists but is less well known than her male contemporaries. In her beautiful paintings the solidity of the world melts into the air. As Dorothy studied them she saw that they have a strange similarity to the world described by quantum physics, and she wondered – what if Berthe was inspired by a time traveller who told her about today's scientific discoveries?

Instagram: The_Angel_of_Incompleteness

I WISH TO THANK:

Helene Witcher for inspiring me to start writing
Chris Cleave for his encouragement when I attended an Arvon
Foundation writing course.
Karen McKellar for her insightful editing of my chaotic first
drafts. She's a brilliant editor. She understood what I was trying to do
and helped me achieve it.
My husband, Neil McDonald, for his supportive love throughout
My wonderful children.
And Joseph and Freya whose imminent arrival encouraged me to
finish this novel. How can writing a book take longer than making a
human being?

Printed in Great Britain
by Amazon

30471057R00163